Keeper of Slaves

Book Two of Antebellum Struggles

A Story of Love, Lust, Pain & Freedom in the Deep South

Dickie Erman

ANTEBELLUM STRUGGLES – Book Two (Keeper of Slaves).

ISBN: 9781981051458

First Edition: February 2019

Author: DICKIE ERMAN

PREFACE

Amazon reader reviews of "Antebellum Struggles" (Book One in the series), "Keeper of Slaves" (Book Two), and "Slaves of Fools" (Book Three) have, gratefully, been overwhelmingly positive. The few negative reviews have been based primarily on perceptions that "grammatical errors" or "misspelled words" have gone uncorrected.

Exhaustive proof-reading efforts are made to avoid any errors. I believe the misperception lies in the dialect spoken by the slaves depicted throughout.

The historical settings are in the 1850s – 1860s. Slaves did not speak the "King's English".

For example:

Instead of saying: "We thought a lot about that", the slave's dialogue would read: "We's' thought 'lots' 'bout 'dat".

Instead of saying: "It's just that the Colonel is never sick", the slave's dialogue would read: "It's 'jus' 'dat' 'da' Colonel ain't never sick", and so on.

'Apostrophes' are also included to mark the omission of one or more letters.

Are there any spelling errors? Possibly. Human beings are involved.

I hope this serves to dispel the misconception that such spellings were the result of sloppy proof-reading, rather than intentional usage.

— Dickie Erman

1

WHERE WERE WE?

Oh yes ... It was the summer of 1852.

Colonel Trent Winters had ordered his men to tie the field slave, Tabari, to the 'tree', awaiting his punishment for trying to escape from the plantation.

Trent's wife, Collette, had suffered a nervous breakdown after she surmised that her beloved husband had a torrid affair with the beautiful slave, or 'house servant', Amana, and was guilt ridden from her own infidelity with her dear friend, Caroline, the wife of Senator Jeb Harrison.

Incensed over Amana's and Trent's triste, Collette ordered the plantation overseer, Mr. Tolivar, to see to it that Amana was not just 'gone', 'whipped' or 'sold' ... no ... Collette wanted Amana 'dead'!

And what about the Doctor? That conniving charlatan had duped the Colonel into believing that Tabari was responsible for the Doctor's house having been burned to the ground, and had fleeced Trent into paying thousands of dollars to make the Doctor 'whole' again.

Poor Tom Wilkins and Melba. They were about to lose their Underground Railroad newspaper, the 'Herald Beacon', because Deputy Harley and the two hapless saddle tramps, Randy and Seth, had captured Tabari by piecing together the fact that Tom and Melba had assisted in Tabari's escape.

And then there's the humble and God-fearing Jeffersons, Frank and Freda. Harley was also after this aged couple for aiding and abetting Tabari in his escape. Violating the Fugitive Slave Law. To punish them, he was hell-bent on taking the Jefferson's farm, 'lock, stock and barrel'.

And let's not forget the Reverend Baxter and Pastor Jessie, whose 'Chapel Cross Church' was also facing the wrath of Deputy Harley. He'd threated to punish the Church as well, for aiding and abetting Tabari's escape.

2

"**I** HAVE BUSINESS IN N'AWLINS late this afternoon" Trent had said to his beloved Collette as she lie in bed recuperating from her nervous breakdown. "That is, of course, if you're feeling well enough. Sadie will be here. If you need me, I can postpone my meetings. I'd never leave unless you're feeling well enough".

He was on one knee, their cheeks almost touching. Trent truly loved his wife, and would have adjourned all of his business duties if necessary to insure her recovery.

"Oh, I'll be just fine. I'll miss you something terribly" she whispered lovingly. "I'm getting my strength back now. Yes, I'm feeling much better and, like you said, Sadie will be here. Now you go do what you must. I'll be just fine".

* * *

BEFORE Collette had walked to Tolivar's cottage to deliver Amana's death sentence, the Colonel had a brief discussion with him.

About Tabari.

Trent had asked the Doctor and his two sidekicks to tie Tabari to the 'tree'. This was forty-eight hours ago.

Fortunately for Tabari, the Colonel hadn't told them *how* to tie him up. Seth and Randy had simply stood Tabari up straight, wrapped his arms around the trunk, and then tied each wrist.

Still, no water, no food, no relief from the scorching sun.

After an hour, Tabari had moved his wrists back and forth in a 'sawing' motion, which slightly stretched the length of the rope, enough to lower it on the tree trunk so, in time, he was able to kneel on the ground. His wrists still remained above his head. Extremely painful, but still much more preferable than being forced to stand and be 'hung by the wrists'.

Try as he might, he couldn't loosen either knot.

By dusk on the first day, the rope had burned through both wrists nearly to their bones. By nightfall, he had no choice but to empty his bladder and bowel. For a brief moment, he almost chuckled at this otherwise horrific experience - how the pain in all of his muscles and wrists made this degrading act seem pale in comparison.

Now, he was near death.

And Trent was conflicted. He believed Tabari had caused the Doctor's house to be burned to the ground, a cowardly act that was costing the Colonel thousands of dollars in damages to a quack doctor that he couldn't stomach. He'd already whipped Tabari for that unforgivable transgression.

It was obvious to him why Tabari tried to escape. A person's natural inclination is to avoid further pain. The same must be true of negroes, even if they're only three-fifths human.

But what most conflicted Trent was fear of a possible uprising among his nearly one hundred slaves. He knew well the publicized slave revolt that took place in Virginia some twenty years earlier. About seventy blacks, both slaves and freemen, rose up and killed nearly sixty white folk, before the militia stepped in and stopped the carnage. Nearly half were hung or sold to owners in other states. But the damage was done.

Trent remembered how he just recently stopped Mr. Tolivar from whipping an innocent young slave woman, who was about to be used as a sacrificial lamb if no slave would reveal where Tabari had planned to escape to. Trent sensed that Tolivar thought he was getting 'soft'. A statement needed to be made: "Protecting a runaway slave would be severely punished".

The Colonel knew the threat of punishment was necessary, but he also had to consider the havoc that a revolt would have on his sugar cane plantation. He generally employed five 'overseers', including Tolivar, and each carried a shotgun, rifle or pistol. This threat had always proven effective, since it was nearly inconceivable that only one or two slaves would attack a white man or woman, knowing that their death would be quick and certain.

But mob mentality could overcome that fear. Trent couldn't allow a large number of his slaves to become angry and assemble. One physical confrontation could whip the others into a fury and fuel a battle that he could quickly lose. Slaves' quarters could be burned, animals let loose, perhaps his own mansion set on fire. There were many 'militia' in New Orleans that would certainly gather and restore the status quo, but repairing the damage would set him back for months and severely damage his pocketbook. New slaves could be purchased, but the setback would take an ugly toll.

He knocked on Tolivar's door.

"Mr. Tolivar, I'd like to have a word with you".

Tolivar was buttoning his shirt as he answered the door.

"I'm sure you've seen Tabari tied to that tree" as he looked and pointed.

Tolivar's expression acknowledged the obvious.

"Of course" Tolivar replied. "I didn't say anything because I figured that was between you and the two men the Doctor brought by two days' ago".

He started to sweat. "Please don't ask me to kill Tabari" Tolivar thought to himself. "I done told that nigger that no harm would come to him if we lied about who caused the fire to the Doctor's house. I know he tried to escape, but damn!"

"I'm on my way to N'awlins for a day or two" Trent continued. "I haven't decided what to do with him. I have a lot on my mind, especially with Mrs. Winters. The Doctor feels she was overwhelmed with exhaustion, and wants her to have complete rest. You're aware of that?"

"Well, I knew the Doctor had stayed last night to tend to her. My condolences. But she's a strong woman and I'm sure she'll get better right away".

"Yes, yes. I'm sure she'll be just fine" Trent replied.

"About Tabari. Untie him and take him to his quarters. Hell, he may be dead already. His kind can tend to him. Let him rest today and tomorrow. But the following day I want him back in the fields, hard at work. Is that understood?"

"Yes sir. Let me finish dressing and I'll see to it right away".

Tolivar went back inside and watched the Colonel mount his horse and ride off.

"Hank! Hank! Come help me with Tabari" he yelled to one of the overseers.

The two walked up to the tree. Tabari was unconscious, his head bowed and forehead resting against the trunk.

"Jesus" Hank stammered. "Look at his wrists!"

"Never mind" Tolivar barked. "Cut the rope".

Hank took his knife and cut the rope off Tabari's left wrist. He swayed to the right and slumped lifeless to the ground. His skin was pale, his lips grotesquely chapped as he lay motionless.

"Is he alive?" Hank asked. "He don't look alive".

Tolivar went to squeeze Tabari's left wrist to feel if he had a pulse, but instantly rejected that idea when he saw how ugly a wound he had. They both just continued to stare at his lifeless body.

"I don't think so" Tolivar replied. "Poor bastard" he thought. "He sure got the short end of the stick".

"Naw, he ain't dead!" Hank stammered. "I see his chest movin'. He's breathin'".

"Quick! Grab a cart and we'll haul him to his quarters. And tell one of the women to fetch some water. Quick!"

3

AFTER THE COLONEL HAD LEFT, Collette spoke with Mr. Tolivar and ordered Tabari's death sentence. She now sat on the side of her bed, face in hands, sobbing uncontrollably.

"My God, what have I done?" she screamed silently to herself. She felt powerless to control the two voices in her head. One filled with venomous hatred to carry out revenge over her belief that Amana and her husband carried out a lustful romp, the other ashamed at her un-Christian need to avenge the despicable act.

"Hell hath no fury like a woman scorned" the first voice repeated.

"Vengeance is mine, sayeth the Lord" spoke the other.

Her mind was trapped. Unrelenting, incessant chatter flooded her thoughts. "That harlot Amana … poor Trent … my sinful lust with Caroline … Trent's infidelity". Try as she might, her mind refused to divert from these destructive judgments.

"I've got to stop this before it's too late. What if it's already too late? What if Mr. Tolivar is going for her now? What will Trent do?

"I must tell him! I must tell Trent what's happened! But I must tell him everything. No, no, I can't tell him everything. Oh my God! What am I to do?"

And then, she laid down and fell deep asleep. Her caustic thoughts finally took their toll, exhausted her mind, and forced her to rest. At least through the rest of the day and most of the night.

* * *

COLLETTE woke the next morning with a terrible headache.

"Sadie! Sadie! Where are ..."

"I's right here Misses Winters. Been right here next to you all night. My, you tossed and turned 'da whole night. Kept mumblin' in yer' sleep. You musta' had some awful nightmares".

Collette was horrified at the thought that she might have unconsciously disclosed her demons for Sadie to hear.

"What did I say" she pleaded, hoping the answer didn't confirm her worst fears.

"I don't know" Sadie replied honestly. "'Deh weren't so much words, just a lotta grunts and groans, you know? Like your mind was scared and you was tryin' to get aways from somethin'.

"I's made your favorite tea" as she handed Collette her cup.

Collette took a sip. "Ah ... thank you Sadie" as she smiled gratefully. "This helps".

"Now you knows what da' Doctor and da' Colonel said. Stay put and gets some rest. Me an' Amana's gots everthang' under control".

"Good God!" Collette exploded inwardly. "Will this nightmare ever end?"

Each time she was ready to tell Tolivar to call off the 'hanging', Amana's name would pop up and the lethal thoughts would start all over again. "Kill her ... don't kill her ..."

She fell into another deep sleep.

4

THE DOCTOR HAD SLOWLY made his way from the plantation to the outskirts of New Orleans, still wearing a slight grin at the thought of all the fresh cash he carried in his wallet.

Six hundred dollars. Five hundred for returning Tabari to the Colonel and another hundred for taking care of Mrs. Winters. Jackpot!

"The hundred is for myself, period. Seth and Randy don't need to know nothin' 'bout that money" he told himself.

"Those two rubes only know about 'three hundred' dollars", as he reminded himself of how he lied about the full amount the Colonel paid for Tabari's return.

"That's four hundred bucks in my pocket. Hmm … what else can I do to reduce the amount of their 're-ward'?" the materialistic weasel chuckled to himself.

His grin got even bigger as he passed the Mad Dog saloon and approached the Cloverdale Hotel.

Seth and Randy practically camped out there last night, waiting for the Doctor to return and keep his promise.

"Gentlemen" the exasperated desk clerk cleared his throat for the umpteenth time. He was clearly intimidated by the size and imposing girth of these two disheveled saddle tramps.

He slid his round spectacles to their proper position on his nose and, just above a whisper, pleaded: "I've told you again and again you can't stay in the Hotel lobby. This area is for payin' guests and it's unfair for them to …" his skinny upper body leaned backward as Randy leaned over the Hotel desk to get as close to his face as possible.

"Unfair for *who*? Is someone complainin'? Randy yelled, spraying spittle in the clerk's face. He then scanned the room and stared each guest in the eye. Everyone diverted their eyes and silently prayed that this uncomfortable situation wouldn't escalate.

"Are *you* complainin'?" he hollered at a well-dressed middle aged man, obviously shaken by this dirty ruffian and afraid that he might get his nose broken if forced to defend his wife, visibly traumatized and cowering at his side.

"How 'bout *you*?" Randy shouted and pointed, calling out a young man who much resembled Ichabod Crane, pretending to read his book – inches from his nose. The scarecrow pretended he didn't hear.

Randy turned back toward the hotel clerk.

"Well? I don't see nobody complainin'. Not a peep from nobody".

Seth now moved next to Randy and placed his right hand on his holstered gun's handle for added effect. Reacting to Randy's machismo, and not wanting to be outdone, Seth kicked a lavish wooded stand over, causing the crystal glass vase to fall to the floor and shatter.

The clerk's knees were trembling. He now expected one of them to pick him up, turn him upside down, and pile drive him into the wooden floor.

Just then, the front door opened and all eyes were riveted in the hopes that whoever was entering would calm the violence that was about to occur.

Enter, the Doctor.

You could hear a pin drop. The Doctor didn't know what was prompting all eyes to be cast upon him, but he relished the attention in any event. Genuinely surprised and pleased that his presence was recognized by this unexpected gathering of hotel guests, his gaze acknowledged them one by one with a smile, and then the hotel clerk. He was caught by surprise when he saw Seth and Randy.

"Well, I'll be" he stated, starting to grasp what all the tension was about. "Randy and Seth … Seth and Randy" he greeted them, feeling emboldened by his continued superiority over these two minions.

"Damn, Doctor" Randy gushed. "You finally made it!"

"Of course I made it". He sensed the palpable discomfort the guests were feeling and quickly worked to deescalate the situation.

"My dear Beauregard" he addressed the Hotel clerk by name. "It looks like you've met my friends, Randy and Seth".

The four of them looked toward the front door as all of the patrons scurried out, one by one.

"Err, yes. Yes I have" he replied, his shaking beginning to subside. He managed a nervous smile in an effort to imply he felt a liking toward the two bullies.

"Well my friends, why don't we go over to the saloon for a bit" the Doctor offered. "I'm sure you'll want to talk business, and maybe join me for a drink or two".

Seth and Randy could've peed themselves. Somehow, the Doctor always made them feel somewhat important, gave them a little self-esteem.

As they stepped out onto the wooden boardwalk, the Doctor turned to them.

"Gentlemen, let me have a moment with Beauregard. I'll meet you at the Mad Dog. Order me a shot of whiskey, if you please".

"Sure thing, Doc" replied Seth. The two put their arms over each other's shoulders, as they nearly skipped their way to the bar, giggling like school boys.

"Beauregard" the Doctor said as he stared at the stand and broken vase. "I'm guessing those two did this?"

"Well, yes Dr. Wesley. I didn't want no trouble. I was very polite to them. Didn't want no trouble. But they just wouldn't leave. Some of the other guests were complainin', you know. They felt uncomfortable. Before you walked in here, I was afraid they were gonna' start a fight. Look at me! I'm not even half their size".

"I know, I know. Calm down. You see, they're not bad boys, just down on their luck. You might say they're sort of my 'employees'. Every now and then I try to find 'em some work to do. Keep them busy and out of trouble".

"Gee, Doc. Like I said, I don't want no trouble. But I've got my job to do, and I don't want the owner to fire me. I'll be honest with you. I don't want to, but if I have to, I'll call the Sheriff. I've got to protect the guests, and myself".

They both looked at the shattered crystal.

"I'll see to it that you're reimbursed for that" the Doctor promised. "Put the damages on my bill". "The Colonel's bill", he chuckled to himself.

"Well, that'll be fine. I know you're good for it. You've been here 'near four weeks now, and you pay right on time. You're one of my best paying guests, and I appreciate that".

"Not a problem, my dear Beauregard". With that, the Doctor turned toward the door to square things with his two 'employees'.

* * *

"FELLAS, we've got a problem" the Doctor stated, as he sipped his whiskey from the shot glass. The two simpletons stared with their mouths open.

"Yup, a real problem. Several problems, actually" as his mind began to stitch together a plan to keep more of the Colonel's reward money for himself.

"That hotel clerk, Beauregard, knows the Colonel real well. Yes sir, real well. Turns out the Colonel regularly stays at the Cloverdale when he's in N'awlins on business".

"What's that got to do with us?" Seth asked, feeling his slight beer buzz being sucked out of him.

"What's that got to do with *you*? You broke an expensive crystal vase and wooden stand, that's what! Who'd you think is gonna' pay for that? You?" he shouted. He then looked at Randy. "You?"

The two looked at each other in disbelief.

"Now you both know, I've got three hundred dollars of the Colonel's money, right here in my pocket. One hundred for each of you. And like I said before, there's more where that came from. The Colonel's got a runaway nigger every month. Sometimes two. There's always work in that regard. Yes sir.

"But what I can't do, what *we* can't do, is jeopardize our relationship with the Colonel. No sir. We mess that up, and we mess everything up. You understand?"

The dumbbells nodded.

"And another thing. Beauregard also knows Deputy Harley" he lied. "Knows him real good also. If Harley found out that you two busted up the Cloverdale, how'd you think he'd react? You think he'd have any interest in helpin' you find and capture another runaway slave? I don't think so. What he'd probably do, what he'd *have* to do, is arrest both of you for … vagrancy and vandalism. Now, wouldn't that put you in a fine spot?"

Seth and Randy just stared at each other, dumbfounded that all of this was unfolding.

"So, here's what we're gonna' do. First, we're gonna use *your* reward money to pay for the damage you caused to the Hotel. Probably fifty bucks".

"Fifty bucks?" Randy stammered. "Are you kidding? Fifty bucks for a lousy wooden stand and vase?"

"Crystal, Randy, crystal. Crystal glass vase. Very expensive. You think a fancy hotel like the Cloverdale has cheap furniture? That's maybe the most expensive hotel to stay at in all of N'awlins".

"Fifty bucks" Seth sighed. He took three large swigs of his beer.

"Next, we're gonna' pay another fifty bucks to the hotel clerk so he keeps his mouth shut and doesn't tell Harley what happened".

Seth was about to explode. "Fifty bucks! It probably takes him, hell I don't know, two months to make that much".

"Shhh!" the Doctor mouthed as he slowly shook his index finger back and forth in front of Seth's face.

"This isn't about egos, fellas. It's about maintaining what you've built so far. You might call it a sort of 'investment'. An investment in your future careers. You both know that slave capturin' is a much easier profession than workin' side by side with those darkies in a cane field. Right? Am I right?"

"Well, shit" Seth admitted.

"'Shit' is right" Randy agreed. "Goddamn. We went from a hundred dollars each to … how much now?"

"Fifty …" Seth was calculating.

"That's right, Seth. Fifty dollars each. Look, I don't like it any more than you".

The Doctor slowly retrieved an envelope from his vest pocket and leisurely removed two fifty dollar bills, then gently placed them on the table in front of him for Randy and Seth to savor and ogle for a moment. He then softly slid one in front of each saddle tramp.

The more they stared at the money, the more gratifying it became.

"Ah, what the hell" Randy giggled, as he picked up his fifty and snapped the ends back and forth a few times.

Seth brought his to his nostrils, and exaggerated a deep breath to smell his new money. The both looked at the Doctor.

"Say Doc" Seth started. "Do you think …?"

"Say no more" as he motioned the bartender to pour three fresh shots. "Gentlemen, tonight's on me".

5

SADIE HAD TOLD AMANA that the Misses had suffered some kind of nervous breakdown and that she'd stayed up all night with her.

"Oh my. Oh my!" Amana cried as she paced back and forth in her room in a near panic, almost falling over as her right hip banged into her dresser drawer.

"What did I do?" she asked herself over and over again.

"I don't knows" Amana remembered Sadie telling her. "All I knows is she's had a terrible las' couple a days. Sleeps most 'da time and always has a headache. A real bad one".

"Did she say my name?" Amana pleaded. "Did she tell 'ya that I did somethin' wrong".

Sadie thought. "No, no. I don't 'member her sayin' nothin' 'bout you. But I does know that somethin' real bad is botherin' her. I jus' don't knows what. But I thinks she's doin' better now. 'Dat Doctor man, 'da Colonel let him go back to N'awlins. I don't think he'd let him go if she wasn't doin' good".

* * *

AMANA continued to pace back and forth in her room.

"She couldn't know … she jus' couldn't. I knows 'da Colonel didn't tell. No ways. I knows 'dat for sure.

20

"Maybe she *don't* know. Maybe it ain't got nothin' to do wid' me. Maybe she's jus' havin' one of those 'spells' that white womens get ever once in a while.

"Alright girl, there ain't nothin' I cans do right now, 'cept to get to work and stay clear of the Misses".

But no matter how much she delved into her work, how much she tried to keep herself occupied, the recurring worrisome thoughts wouldn't leave. Collette hadn't openly accused her of anything. Amana never once had to defend herself.

At least not yet.

What was that saying? 'A coward dies a thousand deaths, a brave man dies but one'.

Or maybe it was 'Death by a thousand cuts'?

No matter.

Either way, it was guilt.

But guilt means you did something wrong. Amana hadn't done anything wrong. She was forced by her master to have sex with him.

'Have sex with me or else!' 'Or else I'll have you whipped, beaten, sold … or worse'.

Those weren't Trent's words to her, but the implied consequences of her refusal to submit equaled the same.

Why should she feel guilt because of that? Defending herself was nothing to feel guilty about. Avoidance of pain is a natural human act of survival.

She'd suppressed the answer for as long as she could. Pacing back and forth in her room, sometimes deep into the night, the unacknowledged fact finally emerged.

"Because I enjoyed it!" she heaved the words out, the retched truth almost causing her to gag.

She sat down on her bed, struggling to breathe. The bottled-up emotion having fully surfaced, Amana was both surprised and grateful for the sudden feeling of relief the realization had given her.

A calm descended upon her. Was she wrong to have delighted in the delirious sensations the Colonel had given her? As long as she was ordered to perform, what's the fault with enjoying the experience?

Obviously, because it involved another woman's husband. The wife of her master. A woman who'd done her no harm. Who'd rescued her from the hot field work and putrid conditions. Who'd provided her with clean clothes, nutritious food, and a wonderful mansion to enjoy.

"Oh, Lordie, Lordie" she softly sobbed.

There was no resolution. No closure. The fear of the Misses' retribution would remain.

Again …

"There ain't nothin' I cans do right now, 'cept to get to work and stay clear of the Misses".

She hurried off to the kitchen.

6

TABARI was recovering from nearly being hung by his wrists at the tree. He laid on his cot, still exhausted but fully hydrated and with a belly full of gruel and bread.

Two women had attended to his wounds, loosely wrapping both wrists with clean linen smeared with, of course, slippery elm salve.

Their looks of concern seeped into his own mind, now causing him depression, on top of the physical pain from his exposed nerves.

As he stared at the ceiling, his thoughts returned to the slave ships that eventually brought him to the plantation. Like Amana, he too remembered the horrendous ordeals he endured.

The odds of his safe arrival? Slim at best. Amana's trip had been short, indeed, compared to Tabari's. Martinique to New Orleans, not counting the various ports of call, was a mere couple thousand miles, give or take. For Tabari, the many ships he was stuffed into took him more than seven thousand miles.

His lengthiest leg of the journey was from Liberia (Africa) to French Guiana (South America), across the vast Atlantic Ocean, about two thousand miles. A six week voyage in the best of weather. Unlike Amana's skipper, Tabari's captain at least brought enough food and water to last this leg of the sojourn, although barely.

About one-third through the trip, the early morning brought on an eerie thick fog and drizzle. Tabari was led up to the deck for a 'bath', along with two other male and three female slaves. The bath ritual was universal. Bucket after bucket of salt water was hauled up the ship's side, then unceremoniously dumped over the heads and bodies of the naked prisoners.

Tabari had long ago gotten over the humiliation of standing naked in front of the crew and his fellow slaves. The survival instinct far outweighed that degradation.

Spooky it was, the mist, the cold, the limited visibility. It then became sinister and frightening, as the outline of another ship appeared through the cloak-like fog.

"Sound the bells" Captain Frederick hollered. "Sound the warning". The ship's young cabin mate clanged the bell five times in rapid succession, then repeated the act while all of the crew rushed to the bow to see what was appearing. The quiet was deafening.

Momentarily, no one paid attention to Tabari and the others. They stood together, shivering, peering toward what seemed like a ghost ship, floating motionless in a grey shroud.

They all spoke different languages, except Tabari's Swahili was a bit similar to another slave's Bantu language.

"What is it" Tabari asked?

"Looks like a ship".

"Yes. But there's no sound, no movement".

"I know. It looks ... dead".

Tabari's shivering ceased. The sails had been taken in to stop forward progress. Captain Frederick ordered five of his crew to lower a row boat and approach the vessel. All watched in silence as the wooden dinghy was tied to the mother ship. The five sailors then scampered up the rope ladder in crab-like fashion.

A few minutes passed.

"It's empty" the First Mate cried back to the ship. "Nobody. There's not a soul on board".

Captain Frederick looked at his Bosun (third mate). "Did he just say there's nobody on board? Impossible. How can that be?"

"You've checked below deck?" Frederick yelled back.

"Aye! Nothin'". One of his crew had shimmied up the mast and was looking down from the Crow's Nest. He shook his head.

"Come back and tow us over" the Captain yelled. "I've got to see this for myself".

Tabari and the others didn't understand what was being said, but it was clear nonetheless. It *was* a ghost ship. Everyone was dumbfounded. Complete disbelief. Seven hundred miles from land, a ship bobs aimlessly with no soul aboard.

"Captain on deck" yelled the First Mate.

Frederick stood straight, hands on hips, and surveyed the ship. Everything was intact. No sign of a fire. No evidence to suggest a mutiny. The decks were cleared.

No blood, no swords, no pistols. No cargo was askew. The sails were furled and neatly secured.

"Check the barrels for food and water" he ordered. "I'm gonna' look down below".

"Aye, sir".

Incredulous. All of the bunks were tidy, no signs of any foul play. Captain Frederick returned to the top deck.

"Well ... I'm speechless" he announced to the other five, all thinking the same thought. "In 'near twenty two years at sea, I've never seen such a thing".

"The water's fine, sir, and there's plenty of good food. Whoever they were, they left everything intact" the First Mate reported.

"It's hard to believe they were all taken by another ship" Frederick pondered out loud. "They wouldn't have left their food and supplies behind".

"Maybe they weren't taken by another crew. Maybe space aliens took 'em" chuckled one of the men, a crusty sea farer for most of his life.

Frederick's scowl and grunt let the sailor know his humor wasn't to be tolerated.

A younger sailor then added his theory.

"Maybe they left in a smaller boat. A lifeboat?"

"Maybe" Captain Frederick replied. "Maybe they had one. One big enough to carry their entire crew. Maybe they didn't" as he looked each crew member in the eyes, acknowledging an important point but choosing not to speak it out loud.

The sailors all looked at each other. They knew what the Captain obviously meant, without saying it. Their own ship had no lifeboat. If they had to abandon ship, intentionally or not, there would be three possibilities. Grab hold of something that floats, swim, or drown.

"It's cursed".

"What?"

"It's cursed" the crusty sailor stated again. "No matter what happened, this 'ere ship's cursed!"

A fearful silence descended on them all. Even Captain Frederick, who'd fought in several sea battles, felt the eerie pall.

"Humbug!" he nearly shouted, trying his best to give authoritative assurance that 'jinxes' were the imaginations of simpletons. He inwardly wondered whether his confident rejection of the idea was enough to calm the men because, truth be told, he wasn't so convinced himself that the ship wasn't cursed.

"Well then, let's get busy" Frederick ordered. "Bring all the food and water to our ship and take everything that's not bolted down. Saw up some of the planks and boards that might be of use to us. If you can manage the anchor, bring it. And whatever else we can use".

The Bosun shook his head incredulously as he watched the crew on the ghost ship. He started to speak to the sailor next to him when he then caught glimpse of Tabari and the others standing by themselves.

"Get back down there" he hollered. "Get those blacks back down there!" as Tabari and the other slaves made a beeline for the hatch entry.

The good news was that they now had no worries about having enough food and water for the next thirteen hundred miles or so before they reached French Guiana.

For Tabari, the bad news was that his ship would reach French Guiana a tad too soon.

* * *

TABARI had no idea. No idea that a year ago, the French had abolished slavery and freed the ex-slaves. This new law obviously applied to France and, by implication, should have applied to French Guiana. But French Guiana was a long way from France and, communication being what it was, it took a long time to inform the population and an even longer time to enforce the new law.

The ship docked off the port near Cayenne, and Captain Frederick and five of his crew rowed to the dock.

"Mr. Thomas, get a room for you and the men at the best hotel this shithole has to offer. One room. And rent another for me. We'll meet back here, at the dock, at sunrise tomorrow".

"Aye, Captain".

With his ship safely moored, a clean room awaiting, and food and whiskey enough to satisfy a most gluttonous palate, Frederick's mind now focused on opportunities to make some quick money.

He was now looking to see when, and if, a slave auction was scheduled. A printed flyer, nailed to a pier piling, gave him the answer in both French and English:

"SLAVE AUCTION

Held Every Third Saturday

In Front of the *Hotel de Luxueux*

10:00 in the morning

Auctioneer is Monsieur Martin"

"Monsieur Martin" the Captain pondered. "Now, where can I find this slave auctioneer?" he asked himself.

* * *

"WHY, he's the owner of this Hotel" the clerk answered Frederick's question as he was checking in. "He always has dinner here, every evening, at seven o'clock sharp".

"Why thank you, sir" the Captain replied. "If you see him before then, please tell him I'd like to speak with him about some business".

"Will do, Captain".

* * *

"MONSIEUR Martin?" Frederick asked of the middle aged man nicely dressed in a three-piece suit despite the early evening humidity.

"Yes? Ah, you must be Captain … Captain?"

"Frederick".

"Ah, yes. My hotel clerk said you might meet me here this evening. Please join me, and pull up a chair".

28

The Captain was relieved that Monsieur Martin spoke fluent English.

"Will you be dining tonight?" Martin asked.

"No, no. Well, I think most of my dining will be done at the saloon, next door" he joked.

"Ah, I understand. That's also one of the establishments I own in this beautiful port of call. Captain Frederick, how can I be of service to you?"

"Well, as you might know, my ship's docked here. Our eventual destination is New Orleans. Have you been there?"

"No, I haven't yet had the pleasure. The closest I've been would be the Biscayne Bay Country."

"Ah, yes. Tip of Florida. Not too far away". They both chuckled.

"Actually, I'm looking to purchase a few slaves. Females".

"Shhh!" Monsieur Martin mouthed. "Not so loud" as he scanned the room to make sure they weren't overheard.

"Technically, slavery's not allowed here anymore" he informed the Captain, barely above a whisper. "Or at least it won't be soon. France just recently abolished it. I half expected the Country to revolt, but apparently it's now well received. What a change of conditions. Many owners lost much of their property as a result. And I fear the same will happen here."

"Monsieur, I don't understand. I just read a flyer, announcin' slave auctions were happenin' every third Saturday, right here in Cayenne. That's two days from now!"

"I know, I know. Trust me. It's changing. It's quite likely no one shows up. The government police, well, they haven't taken any aggressive action yet. But they're watching. They'll be two or three of them outside the Hotel the morning of the auction. It's all but done".

"Damn!" the Captain pondered.

"Well, what I'm lookin' for is three females. I don't *need* them, mind you. I'm already loaded with some seventy five on board right now. But

I've got a long way to go, and I know my crew would appreciate some additional companionship during the voyage. Ya' know what I mean?" Frederick smirked.

"Of course, Captain. I understand" he replied.

"And I have just what you want. Young girls. Well, one's probably in her early twenties. Quite attractive, actually. But they're all strong and ready to produce. Lots of babies.

"You can have them for five hundred dollars each".

Frederick thought to himself, then spoke: "Monsieur, I'm guessin' you don't play poker?" Martin's perplexed expression gave him away.

"If slavery were still legal, I'd certainly consider your offer" he whispered. "But as you say, the government's about to crack down. There might not even be any buyers showin' up at the sale. That said, I can offer you two hundred dollars apiece. Providin', of course, they're as healthy and strong as you say they are".

Martin thought. "Captain Frederick, it seems you've got me over the proverbial barrel. Six hundred dollars total, it is. When do you leave?"

"There's nothing keeping me here, now. I've already got all the provisions we'll need. Weather looks good. We'll up anchor at ten o'clock tomorrow morn'.

"And, ah, perhaps you can see to it that the two younger ones are escorted tonight to the room where my men are stayin', in your hotel here. And, ah, maybe have the attractive one cleaned up and brought to my room?"

"Captain, you drive a hard bargain" Martin snickered. "Consider it done".

* * *

AND so, fate being fickle, Tabari had arrived a little too soon. The government hadn't yet been properly informed, and its law enforcement, such as it was, was under no compunction to interrupt Captain Frederick or confiscate and then free Tabari and his fellow prisoners for what should have been illegal contraband.

And so, Frederick was allowed his additional slaves and to sail on, unfettered. Next stop: Barbados.

7

WHEN COLLETTE HAD FINALLY STIRRED from her deep sleep, she felt compelled to get out of her room and enjoy some fresh air.

Far from the mansion was one of her most cherished spots to relax and enjoy the beauty of the plantation.

A small dock protruded ten feet or so out, and over, the twenty acre natural 'pond' that was spring fed year round. She sat on the wooden swing that Trent ordered custom made from a well-known New Orleans' craftsman. Light but sturdy, the seat swiveled back and forth from two iron posts anchored to the dock. Collette particularly loved to read one of her romance novels and enjoy a bit of inebriation from one of her 'fruit juices'.

The pond was mostly shallow, with some deep pockets here and there, and some bald cypress tree trunks that turtles and snakes used to sun themselves during the day. The water was usually murky, the flow from the small spring that fed the pond usually wasn't strong enough to carry away much of the algae and bottom weeds.

Even with a full moon rising, dusk was beginning to cast its shadows as Collette took another sip and turned the next page. Sadie was right there, keeping company and ready to tend to anything Collette might need. A few slaves walked by, mostly finishing up with their day's chores and preparing to retire for the night.

Finally, she was beginning to relax. Her ugly thoughts about Amana hadn't appeared for the last several hours.

* * *

SHE was there. And watching. She'd been there for most of the day. Motionless. Quiet. Watching. Always watching.

Collette was oblivious. So was Sadie, daydreaming of how wonderful it would be to own such a magnificent plantation. She'd always heard rumors of free blacks, some right in New Orleans, who owned their own plantation. "Ah …"

* * *

TRENT returned from New Orleans, after trying to recruit a young physician to make a house call to the plantation twice or so a month. No luck, as this new doctor was glued to his residency at the Charity Hospital. He did promise that he would ask around and would let Trent know the next time he visited the City.

Trent was now with Tolivar on the other side of the mansion, inspecting the health of one of his huge tall oak trees.

"Tomorrow, have some of the workers re-dig the trench around this tree" he told Tolivar.

"And add some more manure. You know, there's no fertilizer like a farmer's own shadow on his field".

He chuckled to himself. He'd stolen that line from a friend, and looked at Tolivar to see if he was impressed by the Colonel's philosophical waxing.

Tolivar was clueless. The words washed over his head, unnoticed.

"Yes sir. I'll see to it first thing tomorrow".

Trent looked up to see Amana on the front porch, sweeping. He motioned her over to him. She ran the fifty yards.

"Yes 'em?", a little out of breath.

"Amana, step and fetch me and Mr. Tolivar some ice water please. Mr. Tolivar?"

"Yes sir, Colonel. That would be nice".

"Hmm … I wonder if Collette could use another fruit juice" he pondered.

He knew that she and Sadie were down by the pond, and that Collette seemed to be doing much better now – at least today. He was also deeply concerned that her 'exhaustion' might not have been caused solely by her trip to Caroline's, as the Doctor had suggested. It could possibly have something to do with Amana. But why? How could Collette have any reason to suspect?

But he sensed real tension whenever Amana's name was now mentioned. Collette's eyes would close and her face would partially contort, as if she was in some pain.

But, at all costs, he needed to protect his investment in Amana. He needed to find a way to bring her back into Collette's good graces.

"Gradually" he thought to himself. "Gradually. One small step at a time.

"And Amana, bring a small glass of Mrs. Winters' fruit juice to her. With ice of course".

Amana froze. She wanted to keep as far a distance from the Misses as possible. Trent sensed it. He knew it. Words weren't necessary. But they needed to work together, 'gradually', to bring Amana safely back into Collette's acceptance.

"It's alright, Amana. Just give it to Sadie. She's sitting with the Misses right now, on the dock at the pond. Just hand it to Sadie. You don't need to say a word".

Amana stared at the red clay dirt. "Yes 'em". She turned and began walking toward the house.

"Damn! Damn! Bad idea" she stammered to herself. As a woman, she intuitively felt this was not the time to try to make amends. She wasn't even certain that Collette's 'headaches' had anything to do with her. But this gut feeling followed her like a dark cloud.

"Oh, jus' do it" she yelled to herself as she stirred the 'fruit juice' carafe and began pouring a small drink.

* * *

SHE was still watching. With endless patience. Only her eyes were visible. Black eyes. Intently focused. Collette was now her life blood.

* * *

AMANA was almost to the dock. She could see the Misses with book in hand, leisurely reading, and Sadie, sitting cross-legged, relaxed, almost regal, as the darkness began a quicker descent and the candle lights from the mansion began to cast a warm glow.

"I's wonders what it'd be like to read?" Amana asked herself. "What does 'da words tell you? My, my, I'd sure likes to know".

* * *

AMANA saw it. At least the last part. Sadie didn't see it. But she heard it. A blood curling scream. And then a 'splash'. And then … nothing but silence.

"Help! Help!" Amana yelled at the top of her lungs as she raced toward the dock. Two nearby slaves heard her screams and came running as fast as they could.

Amana stood at the dock's edge, staring into the murky water.

"Gimmie 'dat! Gimmie 'dat!" she screamed to the slave who'd just arrived. She snatched the shovel from his hands and jumped into the dark water, then stood straight up as the mucky bottom was only three feet deep.

None of them knew what she knew. But she'd just seen it.

The long mouth of an alligator lurched out of the water, grabbed Collette by her dress hem and pulled her into the pond.

At least an eight footer. You can tell the size of a 'gata by the length between the tip of its nose and its eyes. Eight inches is eight feet, give or take.

Collette couldn't comprehend what was happening. She knew she was about to go under, and sucked in as much air as possible before her mouth submerged, inhaling a good tablespoon of water into her windpipe.

She still didn't know it was a 'gata. She opened her eyes but saw only twigs and 'things' floating around, the water much too murky.

Then she saw the fuzzy silhouette of the 'gata's tail swish, at the same time she felt the bite to her left calf, the force trapping her from escaping to the surface.

Sadie and the two slaves stared at the water, desperately searching for Collette but too afraid to jump in. Amana held the shovel over her head, frantically scouring the surface for the opportunity to stick the creature and release Collette from its death grip.

Like a peaceful wave, Collette felt no more pain, as the lack of oxygen began her descent out of consciousness.

"So this is what it's like to drown?" she thought, as the peaceful wave expanded into a warm and inviting sense of serene pleasure, much more than she'd ever experienced in life. She was slowly surrendering to the beautiful invitation to leave the physical world for good.

Then she felt the 'gata's teeth unlock from her calf, leaving her floating motionless between the bottom and the surface. Unattached to any particular result, she felt her right toes touching the muddy bottom, and then gently push off, slowly and effortlessly propelling her mouth to the surface.

A sharp ripping pain then struck Amana's left ankle. She screamed as her eyes riveted upward toward the darkening sky, then to the water where the 'gata held her. Instantly, she stabbed downward, repeatedly, until she felt the monster's release. She looked to her right and saw Collette breach the surface, coughing out water as she tried to scream.

One of the slaves then jumped in, grabbed Collette by the front of her dress, and dragged her alongside the dock and onto shore. The other reached out toward Amana, who grabbed his wrist as he pulled her out of the water and onto the dock.

Collette laid on her back, coughing and spitting. Sadie thrust herself next to her, burying her knees into the soft sand as she cupped the back of Collette's head and raised it slightly.

"Colonel! Colonel!" she screamed. "Quick! Go gets 'da Colonel" she yelled to the frightened slave standing next to her. "He's at 'da udder' side of 'da house. Hurry!"

Trent had already heard the screams and was racing toward the pond.

"My Lord! What happened"? he pleaded to them all, dropping to his knees in front of Collette. "My dear, my dear! What in the world …?"

"A 'gata got her" Sadie cried softly as she wept, tears rolling down her cheeks.

"What?"

"We was jus' sittin' there, on 'da dock, when a 'alligata' musta' reached up and grabbed her".

"My God!" Trent moaned, as he looked around for more explanation. He saw only the frightened expressions of the other two slaves, and then saw Amana, lying on her back, chest heaving for air, and blood oozing from her ankle onto the dock.

Collette stared into Trent's eyes, too traumatized to speak. He saw blood seeping into the bottom of her dress. He slid his arms beneath her legs and underarms and gently scooped her up.

"Get Amana to the house" he yelled in between deep breaths, as he trotted toward the mansion. "Sadie, get lots of towels and boil some water. And hurry" he ordered.

"Yes 'em.

"Oh Lordie, Lordie" she cried to herself as she ran toward the mansion, following the Colonel and Misses.

"And Tolivar. Find Mr. Tolivar and bring him to the house!"

8

"JESUS!" TOLIVAR HOLLARED, as he entered the Winters' bedroom and saw Collette, drenched in water, lying on the bed in her blood soaked dress.

"What the hell happened?"

"Sadie, help me get her dress off!" Trent ordered.

Collette's whole body shivered as she began to go into shock. Her skin cold and clammy, her heart racing. The panicked expression on her face exposed fear and confusion.

"Sadie!" Trent hollered. Sadie's whole body was trembling as she stared at Collette's contorted face. She looked once more at the blood, then fainted and slumped to the floor.

"Mr. Tolivar! Get her out of here, then grab some ice and towels. Fetch a couple of women slaves to help. And send Hank and Cooter to N'awlins. Immediately. Tell them to find the Doctor and bring him here. Fast!"

"The Doctor?" Tolivar almost asked out loud. "Does he mean Doc Wesley?" he wondered incredulously.

"Yes sir!" he replied.

"The 'Doctor'! For Christ's sake" Trent anguished. "That useless quack". No time to torment himself over that dilemma. Collette was his only concern now. Hoping Tolivar's men would find a 'real' doctor to bring back would take … who knows how long? His beloved wife needed medical attention now. Even if it meant Doctor Jeremiah Wesley.

Tolivar scooped up Sadie and laid her on the bed in the next room, then ran to the kitchen for ice. Hank had already heard the commotion and was standing in the hallway.

"Hank!" Tolivar yelled. "Get Cooter and hightail it to N'awlins. Fetch Doc Wesley. He should be at the Cloverdale Hotel".

"Is she alright?" he hollered back. "Is the Misses alright?"

"I don't know. Right now, it don't look too good. She's lost a lot of blood. Now hurry! Git' goin'!"

"Damn. It's dark" Hank thought to himself, contemplating a hard ride to New Orleans. But he wasted no time. Within minutes, he and Cooter were at a full gallop headin' toward the City. The light from the full moon helped tremendously.

* * *

IT was after one in the morning when they arrived.

"He's at the Mad Dog" Beauregard, the Hotel clerk, told them.

"Probably half shitfaced" Hank said to Cooter as they jogged down the street toward the saloon.

The Doctor was there alright, but a little more than just half smashed. A middle aged red haired saloon gal, complete with her short black dress, corset, and garter belt, was sitting on his lap, being passed back and forth between Randy and Seth.

"Doc, I don't know if you remember me" Hank started. "But me and Cooter work for Toliver and the Colonel. You ain't gonna believe this, but Mrs. Winters done got bit by a 'gata. Bit real bad. She's lost a lot of blood. You gotta' come with us. Now!"

"Hey! Y'all just back off" Seth yelled as he stood up ready to fight. This was the most fun he'd had his entire life, and he wasn't going to let these two cowpokes ruin his buzz.

"The Doc ain't goin' nowhere he don't wanna go".

"Yea!" Randy jumped in. He grabbed the redhead's arm and pulled her close. "You're crashin' our little party, and y'all ain't welcome".

"Ah shit!" the Doctor moaned to himself. His brain slowly fought through the booze as he began to realize the seriousness of the situation.

"Fellas, calm down" he said to Seth and Randy. "These men are from Colonel Winters' plantation and, as you just heard, Mrs. Winters' needs my medical attention. Now!

"You wouldn't wanna' get on bad terms with the Colonel, now would you?" he whispered. "Not after the reward money you just received … and which is payin' for this entertainment?" he asked as he looked lecherously at the redhead.

This was a no-brainer, even for Seth and Randy.

"Aw shucks, Doc" Randy replied. "We was jus' havin' such a good time".

"Well, I see no reason you can't go on … without me" his eyes fixated on the 'entertainer's' voluptuous breasts. He reached into his pocket.

"The rest of the evenin's on me" he bragged, as he laid a five dollar bill on the table. "Carry on. I'll be back in a day or two".

"Gentlemen" he addressed Hank and Cooter as he struggled to stand without falling over. He pulled on the hem of his vest and adjusted his belt.

"Lead on. My buckboard's at the stable next door. I just need to go to my room and fetch my medical bag, and I'll meet you in front of the Hotel".

For the first time in his life, he now actually owned a real medical bag, compliments of the Colonel's generosity in replacing the Doctor's possessions that were lost in the fire.

The contents? Mostly useless.

A brass blood-letting instrument, thought by many doctors to cure various ailments by draining some blood from the patient.

One bottle of Moth & Freckle Lotion to smooth the skin and lessen scar tissue.

The always required gruesome looking set of amputation and surgical tools.

And, of course, the Doctor's favorite: two large flasks filled with whiskey, for medicinal purposes only, of course.

As he reached the front door of the saloon, he looked down the street toward the Hotel.

"Ah, shit" he mumbled, as he stepped toward the street and stumbled forward, nearly doing a 'face plant'. "Whoa. I'm more drunk than I thought".

He stopped, stood straight up, wobbled first left, then right, then backwards. Almost miraculously, he gathered himself and focused his attention on one step at a time.

* * *

"COOTER, go get him" Hank said. The two had already retrieved the Doctor's buckboard and were waiting in front of the Hotel.

"Damn!" Cooter mumbled, as he jumped off his horse and jogged to the front door.

"What room's he in?" he barked to the Hotel clerk.

"Who?"

"The Doctor, goddamnit!"

"There's always some sort of trouble whenever the Doctor's involved" Beauregard bemoaned to himself.

"He's in room 202. Upstairs".

Cooter ran up the stairs to the second floor, then briskly walked down the hallway for 202. Easy enough to find. The Doctor was able to light his room's kerosene lamp, but left the door open. Cooter peered inside and saw him lying on his back, in his bed, passed out.

"Goddamnit Doctor!" he shouted, causing him to blink open his eyes a few times, but unable to disengage from dreamland.

Cooter thought of just hoisting him over his shoulder and carrying him out, but realized the Doctor's excessive girth would make that nearly impossible. He scanned the room and spied a glass next to a pitcher of water.

The Doctor sat straight up, coughed and spat out the water.

"What the ..." he mumbled, as Cooter scanned the room for the medical bag.

"Get yer' fat ass otta' bed" he yelled, the Doctor still too groggy to comply.

Cooter went to the window. "Hank! Hank! Come on up. I need yer' help".

"What the hell?" Hank stammered, as he slid off his horse and raced to the second floor.

"Grab that bag and help me git' him downstairs" Cooter ordered, as the two scooped up the Doctor by his underarms and half-walked, half-dragged him down the staircase and into the back of the wagon.

Their two horses tied to the back, they high tailed it down the empty street toward the plantation, Doctor Jeremiah Wesley passed out in the back.

9

"**D**ID YOU HEARS?" one of the field slaves asked Tabari as they toiled in the hot sun cutting cane stalks.

"A 'gata done killed Misses Winters!"

Tabari was mostly recovered, but still somewhat exhausted from his forty eight hour ordeal – having been tied to the 'tree'.

"What you's talkin' 'bout? *Who* kilt' Misses Winters?"

"A 'gata. A alligata'. Twelve footer, least 'dat's what I heard".

Tabari couldn't have cared less. Not that the Misses had done him any wrong, but she was married to the Colonel and, as far as Tabari was concerned, they were one and the same.

"Makes no never mind ta' me" he replied, as he continued chopping with his machete.

"Da' Colonel will probly' blame 'dat on me also" he muttered in self-pity. "I's just gotta' get otta' here".

But how? Tom Wilkins and Melba surely couldn't help. Deputy Harley had seen to that. Same with the Jeffersons, and Pastor Jessie and the Reverend Baxter. They were all in a heap of trouble. "Thanks to me" he blamed himself.

He dropped his blade, stood straight up, looked at the sky, then lowered his head. His spirit sank. It was just a matter of time before the Colonel would inflict more punishment. Surely the 'tree' was just an interruption before the real sentencing began.

And now that Mrs. Winters was dead, the Colonel would probably see to it that Tabari was dead as well.

"What you talkin' bout?" the slave standing next to them asked. "Da' Misses ain't dead, you fool. She done been bit bad by a 'gata, but she ain't dead. She's recoverin', in 'da mansion".

"How 'da you knows?" asked the other.

"Cuz' I heard it from Sadie, 'da house nigger, 'dats how. They's called for a doctor to come. She ain't dead. But she did get bit real bad. Might have ta' take her leg off".

Tabari inwardly breathed a sigh of relief. If the Misses wasn't dead, then the Colonel's mind would be focused on her, not him. Sending for a doctor was a good sign. It'd take time for him to get here, and even more time for her to recover, amputation or not. Actually, Tabari was now hoping for her slow, but complete recovery. If her leg wasn't amputated, there'd be less reason for the Colonel's wrath.

"Why, I'll be damned" he chuckled to himself. I guess I'm hopin' 'da Misses *will* be alright. Maybe I'll even get lucky. Maybe 'da Colonel will get kilt' by 'dat same 'gata".

10

TRENT HAD BEEN UP ALL NIGHT keeping watch over his wife. He'd now fallen deep asleep, exhausted, in the rocking chair next to Collette's bed.

It was nearly noon the next day when he heard the commotion in the hallway and started to wake.

"Sadie!" he yelled, then panicked as he looked at Collette and remembered, prayed, that she was still sleeping and not dead.

"I's right here Colonel" Sadie whispered from the corner chair. "I's sooo sorry that I done fainted" staring at the floor, unable to stop a steady drip of tears splashing onto her shoe.

"It's jus' 'dat ... well ... I saws all that blood and ..."

"Shh!" Trent ordered. He bent forward and stretched his back as he stood up.

"In here ... in here" Tolivar motioned as he nudged the Doctor into Collette's room. Hank and Cooter had one hell of a trip. The Doctor had puked at least twice along the way, and once rolled off the back of the wagon when it abruptly bounced up after a wheel struck a large rock.

"Ah, I apologize for my appearance" the Doctor muttered to Trent as he simultaneously tried to pat some dust from his vest and comb his greasy hair with his fingers. "You see ..."

"Enough of that for now" Trent replied just above a whisper. They all stared at Collette and the blood caked bandage that he and Tolivar had carefully wrapped around her left calf.

"Doctor?" Trent's eyes were pleading for him to do something, anything, to heal his wife and remove all her pain.

Still recovering from his hangover, he caught himself mindlessly staring at Collette's leg, then miraculously snapped himself to attention.

"Yes, yes" he finally replied, and started toward her.

Now, some folks say you can't teach an old dog new tricks. For the Doctor, that's certainly been the case. But as he extended his hands to begin unwrapping Collette's bandage, his eyes were drawn to his own dirt caked hands and fingernails. He saw several small twigs still clinging to his sweaty wrist from the fall he took hours ago off the buck wagon.

For perhaps the first time in his life, he felt a tinge of shame. Through the Colonel's generosity, he'd lived the past month or so in splendid luxury, dressed in the finest clothes, meticulous in his hygiene.

Now, he was about to examine this beautiful patient, garbed in a spotlessly clean white nightgown, in a magnificent mansion, and he felt, at least for a moment, ashamed.

The Colonel stood over him and, although his focus was intensely on his wife, the Doctor could feel, almost palpably, Trent's unspoken disgust. He could feel it even in Tolivar, whose habits of personal hygiene were minimal at best.

"Gentlemen" the Doctor stated with a hint of genuine stature, "I must first wash up".

Both Trent and Toliver were momentarily dumbstruck.

"Ah, yes. Certainly" Trent stumbled. "Two doors to your left" as he motioned the way.

When the Doctor returned, he sat of the corner of the bed and slowly and methodically began to unwrap the bandage.

Trent and Tolivar saw the same thing but desperately needed the Doctor's confirmation. They got it.

"It looks ugly but, overall, it's not that bad" the Doctor turned and smiled. "You can see here … and here … where there's going to need some stitchin'" as he moved his finger to visually explain. "That's simple enough to do.

"Then, we wrap it with some slippery elm … well … I mean the special combination of mucilage and calcium oxalate that I developed". Even the Doctor had to wince at this, for he remembered Senator Harrison having pointed out that the Doctor's 'special combination' was no different than the 'slippery elm salve' that the negroe women used to heal cuts of various sizes.

Out of the Doctor's view, Trent shook his head. Not because of the salve. Its healing properties seemed universally accepted and no better remedies were known. It was the Doctor's bullshit that was intolerable.

However, small price to pay after considering the wonderful news just delivered. Collette would be fine.

"We'll regularly remove the bandage to make sure there's no infection. I feel fully confident that the Mrs. will recover in no time".

Trent's eyes filled with tears. Even Tolivar had to use his sleeve to wipe his own nose.

Trent extended his hand to the Doctor.

"Thank you sir. My sincere thanks".

"It's nothing, Colonel. I'm in the business of saving lives".

Bullshitter.

11

DEPUTY HARLEY HAD CAPTURED Tabari and returned him to his rightful owner, the Colonel.

He'd now obtained a criminal complaint against the numerous parties that aided and abetted Tabari's escape. It was now time to extract his revenge.

"I done told you" Harley barked to Freda as she stood on her porch, staring at the lawman sitting on his horse.

"Here's your complaint" he mocked, as he tossed the legal papers toward her. She watched as they fluttered to the ground.

"They'll be a 'commissioner' there to hear the evidence. There ain't no jury. It'll just be you an' me, unless that husband of yours is feelin' well enough to attend" he smirked.

"By the way, how is ol' Frank doin' these days?"

"You cruel bastard" Freda muttered. "Harley, you are a hateful, spiteful man. If I weren't a Christian woman, I'd tell ya' to go rot in hell!"

"Woman, you done brought this on yourself. You and Frank. I told you what'd happen if I caught you aidin' and abettin' a runaway slave. I'm just doin' my duty. I returned that darkie to his rightful owner, and that's my job.

"And now I'm justice bound to see to it that you, you and Frank, be held to account as well. Yup, I'm a man of my word.

"So much so, that I'm off to Marysville, to serve the same complaint on those two, ah, 'men of the cloth'. They're just as responsible for helpin' that nigger escape as you and Frank were. Thirty days, Freda. I'll be seeing ya' in thirty days".

"Bastard" she cried, as she slowly slumped to her knees. "Poor Frank. I can't tell him what just happened. It'd kill him".

* * *

"PASTOR! It's him" Reverend Baxter whispered as he watched Harley dismount his horse. "He said he'd be back".

"Don't panic. Remember, the Lord's on our side".

"Well, well. If it ain't the preacher". Harley remembered Reverend Baxter's face from the brief scuffle with Tabari, but he'd never seen Pastor Jessie.

"What can I do for you?" the Pastor asked, knowing full well why Harley was there.

"Oh, it's not what you can do for me. It's more about what I can do for you. Like this!" as he handed Pastor Jessie the criminal complaint.

The Pastor stared Harley in the eyes, as he nonchalantly passed the papers to the Reverend.

"I've been advised by legal counsel not to discuss this matter" the Pastor told Harley. "In other words, good day to you sir".

"And a good day to you too, Preacher" Harley snickered as he mounted his horse. "I've already served Frank and Freda Jefferson with their papers, and now I'm off to offer my condolences to Tom and Melba at the Herald Beacon newspaper" he retorted. "Yee Haw!" he yelled as he kicked his horse's sides and galloped away, dust swirling after him.

12

THE SUN'S MORNING RAYS FILTERED THROUGH the window, causing Collette's eyes to blink and her muscles to stir, in that most delectable way that only a good night's sleep can produce.

She gave out a lengthy, exaggerated yawn, then threw off the bedsheet that had kept her so warm during the night. That sudden movement caused her severe pain, as she felt the burning sensation coming from her calf wound.

"Oh my" she thought to herself as she remembered the bandage and her vague recollection of all that had happened.

She was wholly relieved to see that the cloth contained no trace of blood, and remained nearly as white as her nightgown.

Sadie was sitting upright in the corner chair, sound asleep.

"Sadie" Collette said softly, so as not to startle her.

Sadie lifted her head, then let it slowly lower back down as she returned to her dream.

"Sadie. I need you to wake up. Sadie".

Her head rose briskly, her eyes opened and closed, and she awoke to the real world.

"Yes 'em Misses. I's right here. How's you feelin'?"

"Mmm. So much better. I would surely enjoy some of the delicious tea you make".

"Yes 'em. I'll be right back wid' some. Pipin' hot".

As Collette waited, her mind kept trying to return to the scene of what had caused all this. She remembered falling into the pond, the gasping for breath, swallowing water, and that most deliriously delicious sensation of nearly passing from this world into the next.

But how was her leg injured? How did she get out of the water? Who brought her to her bed? Struggle as she did, she had no answers. No memory.

"Here's yer' tea, Misses. Like I said, it's pipin' hot" as Sadie placed a napkin, saucer and carafe on the nightstand.

Collette breathed in the delightful aroma as she brought the cup to her lips.

"Is dare anythin' else I's can do for you?" Sadie asked with a genuine smile. Her deep sigh of relief lifted Collette's spirits as she knew that Sadie truly believed she would be just fine.

"Well, yes. Please sit with me and talk for a bit. I have so many questions. I mean, what happened? I remember falling into the pond and nearly drowning. But how was my leg injured? Tell me, Sadie. What happened?"

"You don' knows? Maybe yous got what white folk call 'abneeza'".

Collette looked even more puzzled.

"It was a 'gata, Misses. A 'gata dun pulled you into 'da water. Dat's what happened".

"A 'gata?" Collette mumbled as she stared at the wall, almost in a stupor, horrified by the thought that such a thing could happen to someone. To her.

"How could ..."

"I didn't see it happen. All's I heard was a big slash! You was sittin' in yer swing, just readin' a book wid' no care in 'da world. And all of a sudden … wham!" as Sadie clapped her hands together and completely startled Collette.

"My gracious!" she bellowed, as the sudden thought of actually being pulled into the water by an alligator became real.

"How did I … did it … did someone save me?"

Sadie smiled and nodded.

"Amana.

"Amana saved you".

"Amana?" Collette slowly thought to herself as her eyes unconsciously roamed down to the floor in disbelief. She looked up at Sadie.

"What did she do?" Her mind raced back and forth as she remembered the death sentence she'd given to Mr. Tolivar. "I want her dead" were the very words she'd mouthed, and in the most hateful, venomous tone imaginable.

"My God, what if he's already done it? What if he's already killed her" she tormented herself, almost out loud.

Terrified to ask, but powerless to resist, she asked:

"Sadie … where is she?"

"Amana?"

"Yes. Where is she?"

"Why, she's upstairs. In her room. Recoverin'. Jus' like you".

"Recovering? From what?"

"Misses, you really don't remember anythang'. She got bit too. Jus' like you.

"Lordie, Lordie", Sadie smiled as she slowly shook her head back and forth.

"She dun saw 'da 'gata attack you. She snatched a shovel from one a 'da field workers, as quick as can be, and jumped right inta' 'da water. Lordie, dat's one brave woman, 'dat girl is".

Collette sat dumbfounded.

"How bad … how badly is she injured?" Collette had to know.

"'Bout like you. Only 'da 'gata bit her in 'da ankle and dun broke it. Nasty bite. 'Dat Doctor is wid' her right now. Tendin' to her wounds and all".

"The Doctor? You mean Dr. Wesley?"

"Yes ma'am. He's 'da one 'dat stitched you up and is makin' you all better".

"For Christ's sake!" Collette stammered to herself. "That charlatan!"

"He's a lookin' much better 'den 'da las' time he was here, I must say. He looks … clean. And wearing real fancy clothes. He mus' be doin' pretty good for himself".

"Good for himself! Using my husband's money, the no good piece of trash" she thought.

"Misses, I watched Amana standin' up wid' 'da shovel raised up over her head, and she jus' kept stabbin' and stabbin' into 'da water 'til she found that devil. I'm guessin' she cut him real good!" as she raised both arms and imitated Amana's actions with dramatic flair.

"Ol' Moses, he's 'da one 'dat drug you out a 'da water. I forgets who pulled Amana out, but it was one of 'da 'utter field slaves. But those two was too afraid to jump in while 'dat 'gata had you in its mouth, 'dats fur sure.

"But not Amana.

"Misses, I declare. 'Dat girl dun saved your life. And 'dat's a fact".

Sadie diverted her eyes to the floor, having suddenly realized her own hypocrisy, for she too had been too afraid to jump in.

"Talks 'bout 'da pot callin' 'da kettle black", she silently chastised herself.

Collette wanted to jump out of bed and run to Tolivar's cottage.

"I want you to do something for me".

"Yes 'em".

"I want you to go straight away, to Mr. Tolivar's cottage, and tell him he is to come here. Now! And Sadie, don't dawdle. If he's not there, then find him. It's very important".

"Sure, Misses. I'll do it right away". She scurried out of the room, confused as to why Collette seemed so panicked.

Collette knew that she'd soon have to meet with Amana. And thank her. Thank her for saving her life. But now, as she pondered the past and her husband's likely triste, somehow her hatred toward Amana had nearly, almost instantaneously, dissipated.

She had, quite simply, a new perspective on it all. Her own infidelity with her dear friend, Caroline, and the once unbearable thought of living in the same house with her husband's possible mistress, now seemed at least sufferable.

No matter the circumstance, it's hard to hold a grudge, let alone a death wish, against a person who was willingly prepared to offer their life to save your own.

Suddenly, a calmness descended over Collette's soul. She felt years' younger, as if a huge weight had been lifted from her shoulders. She no longer felt the need or want to carry that heavy burden.

As she took another sip of tea, she looked around the room and breathed in the beautiful ambiance of the sun's rays still illuminating many of the lovely knick-knacks that adorned her special area.

Physically, she'd been a mature woman for some time. But now, this experience, as horrific as it was, had dramatically changed her view of life. Could she ever live comfortably under the same roof as Amana? Time would tell. But for now, she felt young and alive. Alive is good. Her husband and their worldly possessions, they were all good. That load was a light one to bear.

She thought all of these things as she drifted back off to a peaceful sleep.

13

PASTOR JESSIE AND REVERAND BAXTER needed legal representation to fight the criminal complaint that Deputy Harley had served them with. After much prayer, they'd found someone.

"Well, it's certainly not an easy case" attorney Joshua Dickerson told the two clergy as they sat in the lawyer's office, a few blocks from the Church.

"I've only handled one, maybe two, of these types of cases in my career and, I'm obliged to tell 'ya, they didn't turn out very well".

Joshua had practiced law for some thirty years and was a regular member of the Chapel Cross Church. In Marysville, a lawyer had to know a little about a lot. Divorces, real estate, business contracts. The garden variety legal issues that generally pop up in a small town environment. But the Fugitive Slave Act was another matter altogether.

Reverend Baxter spoke next.

"We have faith in you Josh" as he made eye contact with Pastor Jessie for confirmation. "We know this isn't the area of law that you practice. But even if we could pay for an attorney, it's unlikely we'd find one that specializes in … the slave trade" he whispered, uncomfortable to even be speaking about such an abomination.

"I agree" Pastor Jessie said. "There's probably not a lawyer in all of N'awlins that focuses in that one area. That aside, I want to reiterate how thankful we are that you're willing to help without asking for payment.

We certainly can't represent ourselves, and we have no money to offer" he stated, his eyes beginning to water.

"Forget it" Josh responded, his face somewhat contorted as he began to brainstorm the law and facts in the matter facing them.

"We've got thirty days". His eyes then lit up as he remembered why his previous cases didn't 'turn out very well'.

"The commissioner!" he nearly hollered.

"What?" the Pastor and Reverend both asked.

"The commissioner. The cards are already stacked against us. This case will be heard by a 'commissioner', not a judge. And the commissioner gets … a 'commission'. Five dollars if he decides you didn't aid and abet …?"

"Tabari".

"Thank you. He gets five dollars if he finds you didn't provide food or shelter to Tabari, but he gets ten dollars if he decides you did!"

"What?"

"Yea. So how do 'ya think he's going to rule?"

"What's the logic behind that?" the Reverend asked.

"It's total bullshit! Opps, sorry" Joshua apologized.

"It's nonsense, but the rationale is that if the commissioner finds that you *did* violate the law, then he'll have to do additional paperwork. You know, write out a citation for a thousand dollar fine, have the Sheriff serve more papers, stuff like that.

"That's supposedly why he gets five bucks more.

"But if you're not guilty, then he only gets five bucks, period. That's because the case is closed. No more paperwork, nothin' more to do".

"Jesus!" Reverend Baxter mumbled. Pastor Jessie threw him a scolding glance.

"You're saying this case may hinge on a measly five dollars?" the Pastor asked.

"Look" Joshua continued. "This is the real world. At least the real 'legal' world. We're all human, including this commissioner. And for better or worse, everyone needs money.

"Is he a moral individual who wants to achieve justice and will apply the law evenhandedly? Well, wouldn't that be nice?

"Or is he like ninety nine percent of us, who want to do the right thing ... so long as it doesn't cause them to lose money. Look, we'll fight this thing on the law, and we'll fight it on the facts. But as to this commissioner's 'morality', well, we're just not in control of that. I don't know that there's much else to say".

"We understand" the Pastor replied. "Josh, let us know what we can do to help. And again, I can't express how thankful we are for your help".

Joshua stared into space, deep in thought as he began to formulate his legal strategy.

"Ah, yes. Yes, you're welcome" as he snapped out of his concentration. "Obviously, we'll be in touch".

14

DEPUTY HARLEY NEEDED A WITNESS. He needed the slave's owner to testify. And that, of course, was Colonel Trent Winters.

Harley rode out to the plantation to explain the situation.

"So, that's how it's got to be" he informed Trent.

"I know you're a busy man, Colonel, but I need you and Tabari to appear before the commissioner. Without you, justice won't be served.

"This city ... hell ... this country, is based on the rule of law. And it's against the law to aid and abet runaway slaves. If those folks can break the law with no repercussions, then our whole way of life goes to hell in a handbasket."

"I see, I see" Trent replied. He was conflicted. There was no question the Church violated the law. They'd provided both food and shelter to Tabari, and were about to send him on his way to freedom via the Underground Railroad.

But he and Collette were also church goers, and quite generous in their donations. Most of the Christian Faith Church, where they attended, was built through the Colonel's contributions.

The Jeffersons? He didn't know them. He'd heard of the Herald Beacon, but never read the paper.

"Deputy, what about an affidavit? Can't my participation be done with a simple affidavit?" he asked, trying to avoid not only the considerable trip to N'awlins but also the awkward position he'd place himself in by testifying against the Church.

"Sorry Colonel. I wish it could be. But the Church has hired a fancy lawyer to represent them, and there's no tellin' what shenanigans he might pull in front of the commissioner. No, sir. Agin', I'm sorry but I need you to personally appear. With Tabari."

"Understood. I want you to know, I have a great deal of respect for the law" he honestly replied. "And, I have a great deal of respect for, as you put it, the rule of law.

"Deputy, you have my word. Tabari and I will be there to assist."

* * *

"MELBA, I believe we've got to do this" Tom Wilkins somberly said. "It's the only chance we've got".

"My goodness, Tom. We're so implicated in this already. And about to stand trial. And now we're going to publicize this in our newspaper?"

"It makes perfect sense. Look, we're not going to get a fair trial anyway. We can't have a jury, and Tabari has no right to testify. It's not permitted. And you heard what Joshua said. He's tried one or two of these cases, and lost 'em both.

"We need to generate public interest in the case. Enough that, hopefully, we pack that courtroom with plenty of people so the commissioner can't just rule against us because of what Harley tells him. Don't you see? We put pressure on him so he can't make a decision just based on whether he gets an extra five dollars. Five dollars! Do you believe that?"

Melba was nearly in a stupor, incredulous that all of this was actually happening.

"Alright then, let's do it" she agreed. "But how? I think we need to stay far away from citing the actual facts. I mean, we did shelter and feed Tabari. We did transport him to the Jeffersons, for the purpose of moving him to the next 'station'. We've got to stay away from all that".

"No, no ... I mean 'yes', I agree. It needs to be an editorial about the fugitive slave act of 1850, but focusing on the real life impact it has on just regular N'awlins citizens who don't want to be forced to lend a hand to help enforce the law.

"Imagine that. The law gives Harley the legal right to force everyday citizens to help *him* enforce the law. That makes for a compelling article. It's not going to change the minds of anyone who favors slavery. But we don't need that. All we need is to inform regular folks about how the law impacts them, how it can force them to participate, whether they're for or against slavery.

"That's the goal. Write a powerful piece that riles enough folks up that they'll want to attend the trial. That's all we need. That's all we can hope for. Enough interest to convince the commissioner that he can't just sign off without fairly hearing the evidence. All the evidence."

"I agree. Let's put our heads together and bang this out. And Tom, I know we can't afford it, but this edition has to be given away, for free. We need as many people as possible reading it. Besides, if we're not successful ..."

"I know. A thousand dollar fine. You're right. It may as well be a million dollar fine. Either way, we'll be out of business."

15

I T WAS TIME. Collette was restless to get out of bed after four straight days and nights. Merely stretching her muscles wasn't enough. Her body was becoming weak and, painful or not, she needed to rise and walk.

She also needed to address Amana.

"What in 'da world does you think you're doin'?" Sadie barked as she found Collette slowly inching her way up the staircase towards the third floor. "You needs ta' get back to bed, rights now!"

Collette winced as she squeezed the top of the handrail, each rise of her left leg caused tugging at her stitches.

"Sadie, I'm fine" she recoiled, although thankful for the concern. "I need to see how Amana's doing".

"She's doin' jus' fine" she replied. 'Da Doctor's been up there to see her already 'dis mornin'".

Collette stopped and turned to address Sadie, standing three steps down the stairs and poised to catch her if she fell.

"Sadie, take my arm and help me up. I tell you, it feels good to walk. Just give me a little help".

Sadie shook her head in disagreement, but quickly rose to Collette's side and placed a firm grip on her right bicep to help balance. It took three good minutes to reach the outside of Sadie's bedroom door.

"Thank you. I want to spend some time alone with Amana. Now, go back to your chores. If I need you, I'll call".

Sadie again shook her head in disagreement, but turned and walked toward the staircase. "'Dat woman" she fumed. "She needs to be in bed and restin', jus' like 'da Doctor ordered".

Collette softly knocked three times. No answer. She then slowly turned the knob and gently pushed open the door. Amana was lightly sleeping, her left foot elevated on two pillows. The Doctor had splinted her ankle and lower leg between two wooden slats, bound together by tied linen strips. Rest and immobilization were the best remedies.

Collette quietly limped to the rocking chair placed next to the bed, and sat patiently. She, too, quickly fell into a light sleep, exhausted from her sojourn to the third floor.

Amana's dream suddenly shifted violently to the nightmare of the alligator attack. Her heart began to race as she felt herself trapped underwater in its death roll. She gasped for breath, then her left leg jolted and she instantly woke up, gripped with pain and the realization that she was lying in bed with a broken ankle. Her slight scream woke Collette up.

"Amana, Amana my dear. Are you alright?"

Amana stared at the wall for a moment as her garbled senses refocused. She knew someone was seated next to her and, for a moment, thought it was Sadie.

"Yes, Sadie. I's alright. I's so thirsty. Could you fetch me some water? With ice?"

"Amana, it's me" Collette whispered, not wanting to frighten her any more than she already seemed.

Amana recognized the soft voice and at once felt paralyzed and powerless. She knew a moment like this would come, when the Misses would confront her. But how surreal it now was. She couldn't fight, she couldn't run. She was simply defenseless to protect herself. She began sweating profusely.

"Everything's alright" Collette gently reassured her.

"Sadie told me everything that happened. How brave you were. How you … how you saved my life". Collette began to whimper as she remembered the whole tragic event.

"I can see you're in pain. There's no need to move. Just lie still, and we can chat for a while".

Amana couldn't control her panicked feelings. Did the Misses know? Did she find out about the Colonel and her? Would she be tossed out onto the grounds, broken ankle and all? Whipped? Sold?

"It was such a brave thing you did for me" Collette continued. "Jumping into the pond and fighting off that 'gata. I have to tell you, I couldn't have done what you did. I'm just too much of a scaredy-cat".

Collette's nakedly true and spontaneous admission caused her to giggle. Amana too. For a moment, it released their pent up emotions over the entire life-threatening ordeal. Their giggles became contagious, then burst into uncontrollable laughter until it reached a peak, and turned to intense sobbing and crying. All of their suppressed memories came spewing out at once until exhaustion replaced them with a peaceful calm. A calmness that only those who have been to hell and back can know.

Each felt their shared common bond. A sisterhood of sorts. At least for now.

Collette gently took Amana's hand as they both stared out the window. In unrehearsed unison, they both deeply inhaled and let out long gratifying sighs. No words were spoken. No need to.

After a minute of peaceful silence, Collette released Amana's hand.

"When does the Doctor think you'll be recovered enough to start walking?" she quietly asked. "Oh, there's no rush. When you're ready, you're ready".

Amana quickly returned from her near meditative state.

"'Da Doctor said he'd bring by some ... ah ... 'cruxes', you know, some kinda' wooden sticks to hep' me to balance when I walk. I guess that's what I's waitin' on".

"Ah, yes".

Both women now began to feel some tension. About Trent. The Colonel was the elephant in the room. But this was not the right time for Collette. Much of the burden she'd carried had been lifted from her shoulders. She'd eventually have to speak with Amana, but not now.

"I'll speak to the Doctor about your crutches. But for now, get your rest. It takes time for bones to heal".

She gingerly stood up, gathered her balance and began limping to the door.

"Oh, and I'll see to it that Sadie brings you some water. With ice" she smiled.

16

THE TRIAL AGAINST THE DEFENDANTS was rapidly approaching.

The prosecutor was Miles Jenkins, a tall rotund man in his late fifties. He'd tried hundreds of cases, many involving negroes.

Lynchings, runaways, sexual assaults, fraternizing with a white woman, just to name a few. His approach was textbook prosecution. He wanted a one hundred percent conviction rate, and his twenty five years of 'wins versus losses' came close to that.

He's spent several hours counseling Harley on how the case would proceed.

"We've got six defendants. Too many to try all at the same time. I don't want to confuse the commissioner, or the citizens in the audience.

"This case has drawn quite a bit of publicity, much more than it deserves. A runaway nigger, assisted by two preachers, and caught by you, red-handed. It should be simple".

"It is simple!" Harley barked. "The same with the Jeffersons and those two at the Herald Beacon newspaper. They did just as much to aid and abet that negroe as the preachers. They're all guilty as hell!"

"Calm down, calm down" Jenkins ordered. He inadvertently shook his head in reaction to Harley's outburst.

"That's exactly what we don't need. You comin' across like a hot head on the witness stand. Composure, Deputy. Composure".

Harley smiled. He knew Jenkins had a wealth of experience at this and was confident he'd bury all six of them.

"Yes. You're right, of course" he told Jenkins. "And it doesn't hurt that the commissioner gets paid twice as much if he rules in our favor, now does it?" he snickered.

"Now get that out of your mind right now" Jenkins scolded him. "If this were a usual trial, with no publicity and just the slave owner to testify, then I'd agree. But this ain't a 'usual' trial, now is it? You've heard the conversations around town. It's quite likely that courtroom will be packed. And packed with a lot of emotion. Half that crowd will be for us, and half against.

"No, sir. That commissioner couldn't care less about a measly five bucks at this point. He has too much at stake. For us or against us, he'll be the subject of a lot more newspaper articles. Yes sir, he's gonna' be the talk of the town. And he knows it".

* * *

"WELL, the trial starts tomorrow" Jenkins began as he and Harley sat together for the last time in the prosecutor's office.

"We'll try two at a time, starting with the preachers. That's the easiest case for us. If we don't win that one, we won't win the other two.

"If we do win, then we'll try the Jeffersons and the newspaper separately".

"You're the expert" Harley offered. "Aidin' and abettin'. Right?"

"Wrong.

"Treason. One count against each defendant. For treason".

"Treason?" But what about aidin' and abettin'?"

Jenkins could only smile at Harley's legal naiveté.

"Well now, that's really what aiding and abetting the escape of a runaway slave is really about. It's treason. Treasonous to try and prevent you from arresting Tabari. A violation of the fugitive slave act.

"Treasonous to assault you with the intent to rescue a slave. Isn't that what the Reverend Baxter did when he tried to trip you in the Church's basement?"

"You're damn right he did! He tried to grab my legs so I couldn't get to him. Yea. I call that 'treason'!"

"And preparing and distributing writings. Newspaper writings, urging people to resist the fugitive slave act. Isn't that what Tom and Melba have been doing for years?"

"Treasonous!" Harley snickered.

"And the letter that slave woman wrote to Freda Jefferson ... what was her name?"

"Helen. She wrote that from Boston. To Freda, thanking her for helping her escape".

"Yes, Helen. Isn't that proof of treason against Frank and Freda? Another violation of the fugitive slave act?"

Harley just smiled. "Brilliant" he thought to himself.

17

THE COURTROOM WAS PACKED. And hot. And humid. Almost stifling. It smelled like old damp and musty wood. The top rafter held room for about eighty souls, where a smattering of black folks were allowed to view the proceedings. The courtroom almost had the look and feel of a small scale Roman colosseum, the battle of gladiators versus Christians about to unveil.

The newspaper copies would have sold like hotcakes, if they hadn't been given away for free. Smart move on Tom's and Melba's part. They'd started with two hundred fifty copies. Gone. Then another two hundred and fifty. Gone again.

They knew that many of the people who'd read a copy would speak to their friends and neighbors and stir up heated discussion. They were right.

Joshua sat at the left side of the counsel's table, a large heavy law book in front of him, next to a stack of writing paper and three pencils. His brown leather briefcase was fully scuffed and tattered at the edges, full of years' of courtroom stories if only it could speak.

His round spectacles rested on the tip of his nose where he wiped a dangling sweat bead with his handkerchief. All attendees fanned themselves, some using the newspaper's very article that brought them to the court, in a futile attempt to obtain some relief from the muggy air.

Next to Joshua, sat Pastor Jessie and Reverend Baxter.

Harley, the prosecutor, and Trent sat on the other side of the counsel table.

Freda sat alongside Tom and Melba in the front row. Frank wasn't present. So weakened from his heart attack, he was now mostly bedridden.

Tabari was also in the front row, handcuffed and seated next to Tolivar and another deputy from Harley's office.

"All rise!" hollered the bailiff in the deepest and most authoritative voice he could muster, excited to be one of the players on this big stage.

The commissioner was the Hon. Howard B. Cowherd, diminutive in size but tough as nails, partly because of the number of fistfights he suffered through in defending his name against schoolboy bullies. He'd held the position of 'federal commissioner' for only two years, since the 1850 passage of the 'Act'.

He was also well aware of the derogatory euphemism "five dollar collar" that outraged abolitionists would shout when they believed a commissioner would automatically side with the prosecution – just to make an extra five bucks. A phrase repeatedly used in Tom's and Melba's editorial.

Comm. Cowherd took his seat at the bench and scanned the audience as he simultaneously shuffled his papers into order. He was trying hard to hide his nervousness. It would've been easier if a jury were allowed. Let them decide. Like Pontius Pilate, he could then just wash his hands.

No such luck. Either way, it was certain that at least half the courtroom would want his hide.

"Ahem" he cleared his throat. "Ah … the District Court of the State of Louisiana, in the case of the People v. Reverend Baxter Atlee and Pastor Jessie Jerimiah Johnson. Madam Clerk, please swear all parties".

Everyone stood.

"Please raise your right hand" she dutifully instructed them.

"Do you swear that the testimony you give before this court ... er ... commission, shall be the truth, the whole truth, and nothing but the truth, so help you God?"

All agreed, although Harley wasn't so convinced the others would play fair.

"Frank Jefferson" he muttered to himself. "At least he won't commit perjury" he chuckled, safe in the knowledge that his actions had permanently warehoused Frank to remain in his own bed, for good.

"Mister ... Jenkins" the Hon. Cowherd began. "Are you ready to proceed?"

"Yes your honor" he answered, as he nodded to Harley and glanced around the room. He relished all courtroom dramas, particularly with this packed house where he could center himself in the spotlight.

"As the court is aware, the People bring one count against each defendant. The count of treason." Some in the courthouse gasped.

"The State will prove that the two defendants willfully and intentionally assisted a slave ... one 'Tabari'" as he stared at him sweating and handcuffed in the front row ... "and provided him with both food and shelter, and attempted, through a physical confrontation, to thwart the efforts of the Sheriff's Office of this great State, to carry out its mandate to enforce the Fugitive Slave Law, a despicable act of treason!"

More gasps erupted from the audience, enough to intimidate the commissioner to tap his gavel several times to restore quiet.

"Let me be clear" Cowherd announced to the audience so the entire courtroom could hear.

"I will tolerate no outbursts of any kind. This case will proceed in an orderly fashion, and anyone who disrupts this proceeding shall be physically removed".

Initially encouraged with his forceful pronouncement, he now pondered exactly *how* he would be able to physically remove a disruptive soul. The only law enforcement was Harley and another deputy, far outnumbered by the two hundred or so in attendance.

"Please proceed" he ordered the prosecutor.

"Thank you, your honor. The State calls Harley Stafford to the stand".

"You know you're under oath" the commissioner reminded him.

"Of course, of course".

Jenkins began his direct examination.

"How are you employed?"

"I'm a deputy Sheriff, employed by the City of N'awlins under the jurisdiction of the State of Louisiana".

"And in that capacity, are you tasked with the obligation to assist private citizens with the capture and return of runaway slaves?"

"I am".

Harley was good. He'd testified many times before, although never in a 'treason' case involving the Fugitive Slave Act. But he knew just how far he could bend the truth without committing perjury, and he knew how to look the part of an honest and trustworthy lawman in front of a jury or, in this case, before a mixed theater with polar opposite opinions.

"Now, in your own words, tell us what happened".

For the next twenty minutes, the audience remained spellbound as he 'held court' with riveting details of his exploits in this case, methodically recounting his interactions with Tom and Melba, the Jeffersons, Randy and Seth, and eventually Reverend Baxter.

"And did the Reverend physically lay his hands on you?" Jenkins nearly hollered his question.

"You're damned right" he exclaimed. "Tabari knew I had him cornered" aggressively staring at the prisoner.

"So he jumped up, grabbed the chair he was sittin' on, and swung at me wildly as he tried to rush past. I would've had him too, if the Reverend there hadn't punched at my legs and caused me to fall" he half lied.

"By the way Rev', you throw a nice punch" he chuckled, as his intended quip caused many in the audience to laugh, adding to the credibility of his testimony.

The prosecutor smiled inwardly. "Good Harley! Good".

Soon, Mr. Jenkins rested his case.

The prosecutor had presented his case perfectly. Although attorney Joshua objected often, he inwardly had to agree when the commissioner overruled nearly each protest.

There were really three cases, to be tried separately. But it made legal sense to tell the whole story at one time. The facts were inextricably intertwined. The commissioner couldn't know what led Harley to the Chapel Cross Church unless he knew about the Jefferson's participation. And he couldn't know about the Jeffersons unless he knew of Tom's and Melba's involvement.

Jenkins had proven everything he said he would. Tabari *was* a runaway slave. Reverend Baxter and Pastor Jessie provided him with both food and shelter. The Reverend physically assaulted the Deputy and willfully tried to prevent him from enforcing the Fugitive Slave Act, a federal law.

Treason.

"Mister … Dickerson" the commissioner prompted. Joshua was furiously scribbling notes on his paper.

"Mr. Dickerson?" he nearly shouted, as he banged his gavel twice.

"Sorry your honor" he answered as he held up his left hand without looking up and continued scribbling with his right. "The defense is ready" he stated.

"Then proceed".

Harley stood up and began to walk back to his seat at counsel's table.

"No need, Deputy" Joshua informed him and the entire courtroom. "We'll just continue with your testimony. If that's alright with you" he asked sarcastically, earning a few chuckles from the audience.

Two more bangs of the gavel were followed by a stern look from the commissioner.

Harley retook his seat on the witness stand.

"Deputy. You described in painstaking detail the tussle you had with Tabari, but you didn't quite say exactly where this took place".

"In the basement".

"In the basement of the Church?"

"Yup".

"Not in the Church itself? I mean where the sermons are held, where the altar's at?"

Harley was confused. He knew Joshua was up to something, but didn't know what. The answer to the question was obvious.

"The 'tussle', as you called it, took place in the basement. Underneath the Church" Harley answered rhetorically.

"And Reverend Baxter ... did he say anything to you?"

"Yea"

Joshua cupped his hand to his ear, inviting Harley to answer the question.

"He said 'this man's protected from the law. It's a sanctuary, and I had no authority to take him away'. Somethin' like that".

Joshua intuitively sensed this was the moment of truth. All of the facts were against him. It was time to use the first axiom taught in law school: 'If you can't dazzle 'em with brilliance, then baffle 'em with bullshit'.

"Your honor" he began. "This humbug has gone on long enough.

"My learned opponent" as he turned to acknowledge prosecutor Jenkins, "well knows that the historical custom and practice of the United States, and of the great State of Louisiana, in particular, both politically and religiously, has been to acknowledge a church as a safe haven for any runaway slave, particularly when there is no charge against him of having committed a violent act or a sexually accused crime".

"Objection!" Jenkins shouted. He'd anticipated, and was fully prepared for, Dickerson to try and pull this diversionary move.

"This is nothing but a 'red herring'" he stammered.

The commissioner knew the term. Dog trainers will sometimes throw a fish, a 'red herring', far off the trail the dog should be following, to see if he'll be distracted from the true scent where his owner wants him to go.

"Ah ... not so fast Mr. Jenkins" the commissioner stuttered. The courtroom audience sensed uncertainty in his voice and facial expression.

"The objection is overruled. Proceed".

"Thank you, your honor".

"Bullshit!" Jenkins muttered to himself.

Jenkins had been right all along. Dickerson knew full well that not only were the facts against him, but also the law. There had never been a case, from the US Supreme Court down, that acknowledged the legal authority of a church to declare itself a 'sanctuary' and thus not obligated to obey, in this case, the mandates of the Fugitive Slave Act.

But Dickerson also knew that there were many cases where abolitionists had refused to be bound by the Act, and had risked fines, imprisonment and even death rather than violate their own religious and moral beliefs.

This was the strategic risk he had to take. He scanned the courtroom looking for sympathetic eyes and expressions of anger. He certainly

76

didn't want these explosive issues to incite a riot among the citizens sitting in the courtroom, or those outside, waiting for the decision.

But he welcomed the possibility that he could win this case by placing the commissioner in such an impossible situation that he'd have to find for his clients. All six of them.

"Well …" the commissioner almost stuttered. He'd been sweating all morning, but more so now that the gravity of the situation was approaching a climax. His blood pressure soared.

"The evidence and the law present two immediate questions" he began, glancing briefly at the six seated directly in front of him and then looking more sideways at the larger audience in the room.

"It seems to me that the first question is whether the Reverend and Pastor did aid, abet or assist the negroe in question, one 'Tabari'?

"And the answer to that question seems obvious. Ample evidence was presented, and uncontradicted I might add, that the two provided him with food, clothing and shelter in a dwelling located on church property, located below the main structure, that is, a basement."

"Jesus!" the Reverend and Pastor both muttered audibly.

Joshua patted Pastor Jessie's left knee a few times, and held his index finger to his lips, extolling them both to remain quiet. "I need to hear this" Joshua whispered.

"The second issue … presents … a more difficult analysis" the commissioner continued, looking like he was passing a kidney stone.

"And that is, of course, whether such acts constitute treason against the United States."

"Jesus!" the Reverend and Pastor again both muttered.

"Now, it is true, as pointed out by the learned counsel, Mr. Jenkins, that there has never been a case, from the United States Supreme Court down, that acknowledged the legal authority of a church to declare itself a 'sanctuary'.

"In other words, neither the federal government, nor the great State of Louisiana, both long steeped in tradition and exulting the very embodiment of the rule of law and steward guardians of civilization, has granted a church the right to disregard federal law and, of course, that applies to the particular law in question, the Fugitive Slave Act."

Smatterings of 'groans' could be heard from those in the higher rafters, long tired of listening to legal mumbo-jumbo from politicians and lawyers who loved to hear themselves pontificate from on high.

Pompous asses all.

"On the other hand, the very term "treason" connotes an utter disrespect, not only for the rule of law, but for the very constitutions that govern our Country and great State.

"The Chapel Cross Church, a Christian and legal entity, has never been accused of such an atrocious act against the State or Federal governments.

"But an entity is an idea. A concept. Live human beings are responsible for the 'entity' and, of course, we are here speaking about the Reverend and Pastor.

"As was ably pointed out by the learned counsel, Mr. Dickerson, there are many cases where abolitionists refused to be bound by the Act, and had risked fines, imprisonment and even death rather than violate their own religious and moral beliefs. The acts of these two clergy must be considered in this context as well.

"In other words, were their acts directed against the government itself, or were their actions focused on preventing, what they considered, an illegal intrusion ... 'nay' ... an unjust perversion ... of their devout Christian beliefs? That is, their lifelong commitment to the teachings of our Lord, Jesus?"

The audience leaned forward to hear the final verdict.

"It is not this tribunal's function, nor do I have the legal authority, to make rulings on the validity of the relatively recently passed Fugitive Slave Act.

"But as both counsel will surely acknowledge, there is no dispute that every man has the right to life, liberty, and the pursuit of happiness."

The commissioner stopped to gather his thoughts. "Where am I going with this?" he admonished himself. He, too, then remembered the age old adage: "If you can't dazzle 'em with bullshit ... or was it the other way around?"

No matter.

The important thing was to get out of this case without adding fuel to the fire and exciting a possible riot.

"That being said, and having thoroughly weighed all of the evidence and justly applied all of the law, it's the finding of this commission that, although the defendants did aid and abet the escape of a runaway slave, their actions were based upon their firm belief in their religious doctrines and their God given responsibility to resist laws that oppose those principles, whether they ultimately prevail or not.

"Therefore, it is the judgment of this commission that the defendants did not commit treason. The decision is in favor of all defendants. The cases against them are hereby dismissed."

"Jesus! Thank you Jesus!" the two men hollered as they hugged their attorney and looked at Melba, Tom and Freda, all smiles and tears of joy.

Jenkins sat dumbfounded, as did Harley. They turned and looked at each other, but neither spoke a word. The prosecutor dropped his glance to the floor and slowly shook his head in disbelief.

"Well" Jenkins muttered to Harley, "at least we can't call him 'five dollar collar' Cowherd."

18

SENATOR JEB HARRISON WAS RELAXING in his den, enjoying the latest copy of the New Orleans' Centennial, one of several newspapers he religiously read to keep up to date on issues affecting his constituency. Buried at the bottom of page three was an article that immediately drew his attention:

"Gata attacks wife of wealthy plantation owner.

Collette Winters, wife of wealthy sugar cane plantation owner, Colonel Trent Winters, was attacked and seriously injured by a ten foot gata in the property's twenty acre pond, reported an eye witness.

"It was at least a ten footer" Jim Bob Cooter told the Centennial. Cooter works as an overseer at the plantation. "Her leg got pretty torn up. We've been dredging the pond to make sure we find and kill it" he reported.

Mrs. Winters is recuperating at home".

"My God!" Jeb shouted. He bolted from his chair and jogged to the kitchen where his wife, Caroline, was busy washing dishes.

"What's the matter?" she asked, her eyes remaining focused on the task at hand.

"Read this!" he bellowed, as he thrust the paper towards her.

"My, my. What *is* the hurry?" as she stopped her progress and reached for a towel to dry her hands. Jeb stood still, controlling his excitement. He wanted to see his wife's reaction to this unbelievable report.

Collette took the paper and scanned page three, not knowing what she was looking for, or where to start reading.

"There! Right there" Jeb almost shouted, as he put his finger on the paragraph. He watched as she read.

"Collette … 'gata … oh my God! Did you read this?" the shock of the story made her forget the obvious.

"What do we do? We've got to go there. Now! That poor dear". She began sobbing and threw her arms around her husband.

"There, there" he comforted her. "The article says she's recovering. That's a good sign" he said, trying to reassure his wife.

"But it also says her leg was badly injured. Oh, Jeb. We've got to go to her. Now!"

"Yes, my dear. I'll have Jacob ready the carriage. Now gather your necessities. We'll be out of here in no time".

* * *

They arrived at the Plantation early that afternoon. Sadie met them at the door.

"Misses Harrison! Senata' Harrison! Why I's so happy ta' see y'all. Come in, come in. Oh my stars, 'da Misses will be so happy. Let me get da' Colonel. Please, has a seat in 'da parlor. I's be right back". She scurried down the hallway as Caroline and Jeb took a seat.

"Well, Jeb! Caroline" Trent bellowed as he entered the parlor. "I can't tell you how glad I am to see you both. It's been too long".

They both stood. Jeb extended his hand which Trent enthusiastically shook. Caroline threw her arms around Trent, uncontrollably sobbing. She looked up at him, trembling.

"She's doing fine, my dear. She's doing fine. She still needs rest, but the Doctor is confident of a full recovery". As he referred to the 'Doctor', he sheepishly look at Jeb, knowing that he viewed the Doctor as a mere charlatan.

Jeb looked down, his eyebrows up and a slight smile on his face.

"That's wonderful news, Trent. You hear that Caroline? Collette will be just fine" as he put his arm lovingly around his wife's waist.

Caroline smiled at Trent, her trembling subsiding.

"Can I see her?"

"Of course, of course. Follow me".

They whispered as they walked out of the parlor and down the hallway toward Collette's room.

"My God, man" Jeb stated to Trent. "How could this have happened? I've lived in Louisiana my whole life, and never saw such a thing. I mean, we've all heard about 'gata attacks, but I've never seen one.

"Saw some close calls, but never saw someone get bit" he remembered out loud, then felt a tinge of shame for speaking so matter of factly about a subject that was still raw.

"No, I agree" Trent whispered back. "It's unimaginable". He saw what they both were about to ask, so he continued.

"She was just sitting on her swing, the one I had custom made, at the pond. Just sitting there with Sadie. And that damned monster grabbed her".

They stopped half way down the hall, intuitively knowing that the retelling of the story should be done out of Collette's earshot. Caroline and Jeb were spellbound for more.

"I was on the other side of the house and heard the screaming. By the time I got there, one of the slaves had already pulled her out of the water". Trent started to openly sob.

Jeb put a firm hand on his shoulder, and Trent regained his composure.

"It got her on the left calf. But Dr. Wesley did a good job on stitching the wounds. There's no infection. She's even starting to walk around some". He paused as he fought back more emotion, then looked sternly at Caroline who started to cry.

"Caroline, the worst is past. Collette doesn't need to see you crying. I want you to see her, but be strong. She needs to know that you're strong for her".

"I will be" she replied, and gathered herself. She was now calm, and looked to Trent to escort her to Collette's room.

"My dear" Trent whispered as he stepped into the bedroom, past the open door.

Collette was in bed, sitting up and reading.

"You have some visitors".

Caroline and Jeb followed inside.

"Oh, my goodness" Collette gushed. She set her book down and frantically tried to arrange her hair and nightgown.

"Of my, I must look like a mess" she frowned, then dropped both hands to her side and smiled, surrendering to the reality of the impromptu visit.

Caroline scurried to the bed and immediately sat in the rocking chair, taking Collette's hand into both of hers, remembering that she must be strong.

"You look wonderful" she honestly told Collette. "I half-expected you to be near death. Why, your skin is as radiant as ever. You look marvelous".

"Thank you" Collette whispered, then looked at Jeb to convey the same warmth. "I feel pretty good".

"I guess that 'gata tussled with the wrong woman" Jeb teased.

"It was Amana" Collette offered.

Caroline and Jeb looked puzzled.

"It was Amana, our house servant. She saved my life".

Jeb and Caroline looked at each other, wanting to hear every detail of this amazing ordeal.

Trent smiled, overjoyed that Amana was now in his wife's good graces, even though the catalyst came from a near tragic event.

William Congreve once wrote that hell hath no fury like a woman scorned. Collette remembered reading that, and how it had reflected, perfectly, her hatred of Amana. She remembered how it felt when her hatred caused her to ache in places she didn't know existed. No matter how many 'fruit' juices she drank, or imported dresses she bought, the incessant thoughts of Trent's infidelity, and even her own, had continued to haunt her dreams.

But that was now passed. At least for now, she'd made her peace with Amana. There was no need to relive the past, or seek counsel from Caroline. She had harmony.

"She jumped into the water and stabbed that monster until it let go of me. Then it bit her, too. And broke her ankle".

"My, God" Jeb blurted. "We heard about this just this morning, when I read an article in the newspaper. We got here as fast as we could".

"I'm so glad for that. It's just wonderful to see you" Collette warmly responded.

"Senator, why don't we leave the ladies to themselves for a bit? You and I have some catching up to do" Trent said, as he put his arm around Jeb's shoulder.

"Yes, yes. We certainly do. And Collette, don't let Caroline talk your ear off. You still need your rest" he joked, as the two walked out and left the women alone.

The two best friends looked lovingly at each other for a moment. Then suddenly, they both diverted their eyes, each remembering the last night that Collette had stayed at Caroline's house while her husband was away. Ever since, Caroline had desperately wanted to talk with her about their physically intimate evening, but now was definitely not the time.

Obviously, 'gatas and intimacy don't make good bedfellows.

"Now, do as Jeb instructed" she quietly said to Collette.

"Jeb and I will stay as long as you'd like. For once in a long time, he doesn't have any pressing legislative matters to attend to. My, it's nice to have him home for a while".

"Yes, I do think I'll rest. And Caroline, I'm truly happy that you've come".

She quietly left the room, closing the door halfway behind her.

19

HELEN AND MAX DONOVAN had lived their entire lives in Baton Rouge, a stone's throw from the Mississippi River. A modest cottage, similar to the many smaller homes that lined the winding shore.

Helen would sit in her favorite chair, a rocker that made the most annoying creaks and squeaks, except to those fortunate souls who'd witnessed the countless seasons come and go while Helen knitted or crocheted, all the while counselling and nurturing family and friends with her wisdom and kindness. She was as non-judgmental as an angel, with a peaceful countenance earned through enduring all that life could throw at one's self, both the horrific and the beautiful.

And so, the rhythmic sound of her chair became like soft inviting music, alluring all within earshot to come, sit a spell, and take comfort, knowing that their spirits would be lifted and their lives better off for having visited with this wonderful woman.

For now, she was busy in the kitchen, making delicious concoctions from every imaginable fowl, critter and plant that called this land home.

"Get 'otta that flour" she yelled at one of the many young'uns that scampered back and forth from kitchen to bedroom, crawling over and under tables and chairs.

"You, Zebadiah, put that chicken wing down. It ain't been properly cooked yet. Ya' wanna' get the worms?"

Their sons, daughters and grandchildren were all there for an annual family gathering, more souls than one could count. And Helen loved every moment, despite her repeated warnings and chastising.

"Alright. I've had it. Everyone out! You young'uns get outside until supper's ready. If I catch one of you dawdlin', your grandpa will tan your hide so you can't sit 'til next Sunday!"

Each one stopped dead in their tracks, staring at their grandma to see if she meant it. When she raised her frying pan over her head, they began running. First into each other, then the furniture, until they hightailed it out, two by two through the front door, laughing and giggling all the way.

"My dear, you sure have a way with those children" Max lovingly complimented her, as he continued reading his newspaper.

Helen smiled. "What are ya' readin' about, my beloved?" letting out a deep sigh of appreciation that quiet had finally descended on the house.

"Laws" he answered.

"What kinda' laws?" she asked, meticulously cutting green beans and potatoes for the venison stew.

"Says here that regular citizens ... ah ... that includes you and me" he teased, "have to offer assistance to any slave owner whose slave dun' run off".

He kept the paper in front of his eyes, pretending to still be reading, but he listened intently to hear his wife's response.

She stopped her slicing and dicing, placed both hands on the tabletop, and stared at the wall for a moment.

"I could never do that!" she almost shouted, as she turned around toward her husband, now holding her cutting knife in one hand and unconsciously pointing it at him.

"Not for one minute!" then spun back around and resumed her culinary craftsmanship.

This startled him completely, for it was entirely out of character for Helen to become upset, let alone lash out in anger.

"Well, now, I think I must disagree with you" he replied, not wanting to upset her more but curious to judge the degree of her irritation.

"We obviously don't own any slaves, and never will, but I'm a man who respects the law. I don't write the law and I don't always agree with the law. But if the law says I have to do somethin', then by God I'll obey it. It's my duty".

She stopped and grabbed a towel to wipe her hands as she quietly walked to where he was sitting.

"Max, you don't really mean that, do you?" she asked softly. "I've been married to you for forty two years, and never heard you say such a thing. Do you mean to tell me that if a hungry, thirsty, lost soul, even though he's black, came to our house seekin' help, you'd deny him food or drink? You'd turn him in to the law?"

"I'd have no choice".

"Why, I've never ..." she stammered, and stormed back to the kitchen.

He put the newspaper down.

"Now look, my dear. I'm a Christian man. A God fearin' man, I am. And I believe it's a Christian man's duty to obey the law, pure and simple".

Helen and Max truly loved each other. They'd raised their children to be upright productive citizens, respectful to others and their property, and abide by the Golden Rule.

But this new law, the Fugitive Slave Act, was beginning to effect society as a whole, and now individual families. Most folks didn't know the law existed. And some that did, didn't care. At least not until some unexpected situation, some circumstance, thrust the law into their lives.

Helen just couldn't let it go.

"Max, if some poor negroe soul came by our home, seeking his or her freedom, and simply asked for a blanket to keep 'em warm, you mean to say that you'd not give one to them? I don't mean a brand new blanket, but not even an old ragged one that we were going to throw away anyway?"

"Helen, I'm sorry that this upsets you so. But my mind's made up on the subject.

"Look, society's accepted this abomination for centuries. I've never been in favor of it. But there are folks, mostly rich folks, and some Christian, who have a different view. They've relied on their workers to run their businesses. Couldn't survive without slave labor.

"And, right or wrong, they don't see them as equal to themselves. They see them as a shiftless, ignorant, and lazy tribe. Unable to care for themselves. Just mentally inferior. Unable to rise up and understand and appreciate the progress that society reaps.

"To them, they're like little children. They need to be taught, punished when bad, and given whatever luxuries are needed to feed and clothe themselves".

Helen sighed deeply, her concern palpable.

"Max, do you believe that they have souls? I mean, when they die, will they go to heaven?" she asked, praying that the answer was 'yes'.

Max was becoming tormented. But he'd come this far on the topic and, respecting his wife, he continued to engage her.

"I do. I do believe they have souls. And those who've done the right thing by God, will rest with the Lord. And those who haven't, well, just like us, they'll be banished, forever.

"Don't you see Helen? Society, such as it is right now, needs these poor fellows, as much as they need society. They can't fend for themselves. They're uneducated. They can't read or write. How would they survive? How would they build homes and roads? Create businesses?

"The answer is, they couldn't. You see, they need masters as much as the masters need slaves".

Helen fought back to control her sobbing.

"Oh, Max. That's exactly why they need our help. If they *are* like little children, then it's our Christian duty to teach them. Educate them. And yes, feed and clothe them.

"Don't you see? If we do these things, then, in time, they'll be able to appreciate and contribute to our society".

"A nice thought" Max mused to himself.

"Helen, many of the blacks were living in grass huts before they came here. They've no concept of how to organize themselves into a labor force, how to take inventory of crops, how to sell and ship them. The list goes on.

"They can't add or subtract, and obviously couldn't write out or understand a contract. They're just not capable of understanding or benefitting from any of the industrial inventions that we're experiencing, right here and now.

"What I'm trying to say is, they're just not evolved enough. Yet.

"In other words, if they had our brains, then they'd have our place".

Helen was nearly traumatized, listening to her husband's emphatic views on slavery and the condition of negroes in general. It was almost more than she could suffer.

Max just stared at the floor, upset with himself that this topic ever popped up, or that he unwittingly provoked such an intense response from the woman he loved.

"Should'a kept my mouth shut" he chastised himself.

"I'm gonna' check on the young'uns" he quickly stammered, then stood and walked out the front door.

She knew when to back off.

"Patience" she thought to herself. She knew her husband well enough to know he was a charitable and honorable man. If, and when, the need arose, she knew he'd see it through to do what the Lord demanded. And so she prayed on it, as she set herself back on preparing those delicious concoctions that were beginning to fill the house with the most pleasant aromas.

20

"**Y**ES, MR. TOLIVAR. IT'S A DONE DEAL", the Colonel stated. "I've sold Tabari. I think you'll have to agree that he's no good here.

"He burned the Doctor's house down, costing me thousands of dollars. I had him whipped, and he escaped. I had him tied to the tree until he should've died. Now he's back in the fields, and Hank and Cooter have both told me he's been disrespectful. No sir, the writing's on the wall. It's just a matter of time before he tries to escape again.

"Mr. McKenzie's overseer will be here in two days to take him. Based on everything that's happened, I had to sell him cheap. But I fear I'd lose even more if I kept him here. Please see to it that he's ready to be shipped off. I want no further trouble from him".

"Yes sir, Colonel. I understand completely. I'll see to it that Mr. McKenzie's overseer picks him up. Yes sir".

Mr. McKenzie was a plantation owner, like Trent. But he'd added another facet to his business. He was also a 'speculator', one who purchased negroes solely to resell them for a profit. Purchasing Tabari was a risk, him being a grown man and a runaway. But he had enough experience that he was pretty sure he could turn a profit.

Most of his 'speculating' involved children. Children almost always returned a handsome yield on investment. So much so, that he'd purchased two negroe women he used solely for breeding purposes, to churn out babies.

At the ripe age of three, they were sold. Their mothers eventually accepted the fact. Their first two or three babies took the largest emotional toll, having their toddler torn away and sold, never to be seen again. But a human being, no matter the maternal bond, can only take so many whippings.

"Damn, that poor devil" Tolivar thought to himself. He hated all slaves, but he almost felt a slight bond between himself and Tabari, considering all that they, and the Doctor, had been through.

"Ah, well. It's otta' my hands. Maybe his new master won't be so hard on him".

An hour later, he informed Hank.

"That's right. McKenzie's overseer will be here on Wednesday to pick him up. Don't tell him, obviously. You can pack up what few clothes he has once he's in McKenzie's possession. You got it?"

"Yes, sir. Wednesday. McKenzie. So long, Tabari!" Hank laughed.

It didn't take long for the news to travel. The Colonel had informed Tolivar, who informed Hank, who told Cooter, who told … who knows?

Pretty soon, many slaves heard of the sale and, naturally, Tabari found out.

"Sold?" he muttered to himself. "I's don't knows any mass'r named McKenzie. Damn! Well, 'dats it. I gotta run. But it sure ain't gonna be to N'awlins.

"No, sir. Already dun' tried 'dat away. Oh Lordie! If'n only Miss Melba or Mister Tom could hep' me. But that ain't gonna happen. Surely, once 'dey know I'm missin', ol' Tolivar will be hightailin' it 'ta N'awlins. Ain't goin' 'dat way agin".

Tabari remembered that even the Underground Railroad 'conductors' didn't know the exact route that would take him to freedom. The 'plan' could change day to day, or moment to moment, depending on information, availability, and just plain unpredictable circumstances.

But one place stuck in his mind. A country. A country called Canada.

He didn't know where Canada was, but he knew it was 'north'. A long ways north.

"'Dat's where I'll head. North. All 'da way north, to Canada. They's ain't no slaves in Canada" he told himself.

Besides, he'd long ago made up his mind. No food, no water, no direction, it didn't matter. Death was much preferable to whippings and hard labor until his last breath. He'd find his freedom, or die trying. It was that simple.

"'Da Mississippi" he shouted to himself. He didn't know how far the river ran, but he knew it was a very long river. And it flowed south, meaning the upriver end was north. He'd follow the Mississippi upriver.

"'Dat gives me fish 'ta eat and water 'ta drink. And lottsa plants and tall grass to hide in". His spirit rose.

* * *

THIS time, no one knew of his escape plan. He'd gathered as much gruel, bread and water as he could reasonable carry, unnoticed by his fellow prisoners. He knew that the overseer, working for a master named McKenzie, would arrive the next morning. It was time to leave.

The mighty Mississippi was right at his door step. He thought about crossing over to the east side, thinking that Tolivar's 'posse' would most likely ride along the well-travelled west side of the river's bank. But then he remembered that, most likely, they'd first gallop to New Orleans and search there. He could always cross the river if needed.

* * *

IT was the beginning of the fifth night, and Tabari had seen neither hide nor hair of the Colonel's 'posse'.

As evening began to set in, he watched the many lanterns and candles flickering in the windows of the Baton Rouge homes as he approached closer. It had just become the capital city, though its population was only around four thousand.

He longed for a hot meal. So much so, that even some nasty warmed gruel would be preferable over the raw catfish and crawdads he'd scavenged along the bank.

"Damn!" he muttered out loud, as he slapped another mosquito on his neck.

Louisiana's always thick with the 'no see-ums' in the summer, but especially along the river bank, and especially at dusk. As small as it was, that little pest was nearly to cause his undoing.

Solitude can be a wonderful thing, so long as it's invited. But when it arrives unwelcomed, dark thoughts of despair and loneliness can descend, sending otherwise stable men into severe depression with near suicidal thoughts. So it was with Tabari.

Exhaustion began to garble and twist his judgement. It began an incessant chatter in his mind, causing him to relive the beatings, whippings, and near starvation he'd endured while laboring in the hot cane fields.

But this struggle was his alone to endure. There were no fellow slaves to tend to his wounds, listen to his story, or commensurate with. His will to live was dwindling.

But all of these experiences had also developed and fortified his most valuable attribute: determination. He wouldn't give up. He couldn't give up.

And so, his stamina forced each foot to keep moving forward, always unsure of the next location, but always sure of the final destination: Canada, and freedom.

* * *

"I can't take no mo' of dez' 'Gud' ... damned ... mosquitos!" he yelled out loud as he went to slap another off his neck. His anger completely focused on the mosquito, and not the precarious surface of the slippery bank. His foot slipped off the top of a smooth and unsteady rock. As he fell backwards, the back of his head struck another rock, knocking him out cold.

* * *

"GRANDMA! Grandma Helen, come quick!" Zebadiah cried as he and his twelve year old brother came bursting through the front door, panting and frantically waving their arms in frightened excitement.

"Oh, you gotta' come quick. Thar's a man down by the water. A darkie. And he may be dead!" Zeb hollered.

"Yes 'em" said the older brother. "He don't look good. We both nudged him, but he didn't move". The brothers' eyes as big as saucers, they looked at each other to confirm the truth of what they just saw and did, so scared and excited at this once in a lifetime experience.

"Now young'un" she anxiously looked at Zeb's brother. "You go and fetch your father. He's over at Mrs. Hamilton's, helpin' her with her garden. Tell him to come right quick. And bring some more help.

"Did you hear me? I said go!" she hollered, and then tried to compose herself so as not to frighten Zeb any more than he obviously was.

She gathered herself, and with a softer voice said: "Now Zeb, take me to him. If we can help him, we'll do so". This calmed the boy considerably, knowing that his blessed grandmother was in control and always made everything right.

* * *

"SET him there" Helen told her son, a strong muscular man in his late twenties. He'd carried Tabari from the shore, still unconscious but very much alive.

"On the guest bed. I guess you'll have to sleep in another spot tonight if we can't fix 'em up for travel. My, my. He's smelly and exhausted. Poor man".

Tabari opened his eyes, looked at her son and then Helen. Too exhausted to fully wake, he slowly closed his eyes and peacefully surrendered to whatever might be. Just too drained to care, at least for a short spell.

"Jake" she instructed her son. "Take his shirt and pants off. I'll wet some hot towels to clean him up".

Jake did as told, while Helen searched for some replacement clothes. She pulled open her husband's dresser drawers, hesitating to dare select any one such piece, remembering what he'd said about not giving a runaway slave even a throw away blanket: *my mind's made up on the subject*".

But surely, when he saw how helpless this man was, colored or not, his Christian calling would show him the way.

* * *

MAX had been shore fishing along with one of the many grandkids home for the family reunion.

"Susan, my dear" he softly said to the six year old, "I think it's time to head back". He watched in amusement as she furrowed her eyebrows and squinted her eyes, her tongue slightly protruding between closed lips, intensely focused on threading a large night crawler onto a hook.

"Aw, Grandpa" the little one sighed. "I'm just gettin' started" she replied, proudly dangling the finished product for his inspection and approval.

He smiled as he observed the well hooked worm, prideful that this feminine young'un showed no signs of squeamishness at all.

"Besides, I've only caught two fishes" she bemoaned.

"Well, that's two more than me" he chuckled, happy to see her face light up as she began to appreciate her accomplishment.

"Besides, your Grandma will most likely have breakfast about ready. Let's see … mmm … eggs, grits, and maybe some of those sweet cakes you like so much".

She pondered only a moment, then remembered the smell of Grandma Helen's cooking.

"Maybe I am a little hungry" she thought out loud, then immediately began to gather her hooks, sinkers, and stuff all things fishing into her basket.

Max stood up and watched her as she began briskly walking toward the house, now oblivious to anything besides a warm breakfast.

"Ah, Susan?" he called, holding the two fish behind his back, dangling on a string.

"Did you forget something?" as he held them in front of him.

"Oh, yea. Don't forget to bring them" she said matter of factly, as if it was obviously her Grandpa's job, then quickly spun around and continued her brisk pace toward the house.

He shook his head lovingly as he followed after her, admiring the self-assurance his young granddaughter possessed.

* * *

HELEN sensed their approach, and closed the door to the bedroom where Tabari lay. She needed time to gently disclose the presence of the unexpected guest to her husband.

"Well, how was the fishing?" she gushed as she bent down to hug young Susan, then patted her dress to remove some of the dirt and twigs still clinging to her.

"I caught two fishes!" she exclaimed, looking to her Grandpa to confirm the accomplishment.

"That's right" he replied, smiling ear to ear. "I say, that young'un makes for a good fisherman" he boasted to his wife as he held up the two catfish for all to see.

"Oh my, those are nice fish". She turned to her son, Jake, and asked him to take the fish outside to clean. Jake stood cautiously still, contemplating how his mother was going to explain Tabari's presence to his father.

Helen gave her son a worried look, then scanned the room, looking for something, anything, that she could use to divert her husband's attention. She knew this would simply avoid the inevitable, but she couldn't think of any alternative.

"Oh my" she said with feigned excitement, as she found a temporary solution to further her deception.

"Just look at that pillow" as she hurriedly moved toward her husband's chair. "I hadn't noticed before" she lied. "It's all tattered!

"No worry, I'll get my sewing kit and have it good as new in no time" as she looked to her husband.

They'd been together too long for him not to sense something serious was bothering his beloved wife. Through all their long years together, he'd learned all of her expressions, her body language, and her muscle tensions. No, something was wrong.

He stepped toward her, cupped her hands into his, and looked lovingly into her eyes, which slowly dropped downward to the floor.

"What is it my dear?" he whispered, now conscious that Jake and Susan were closely watching. Susan sensed the tension between her grandparents, and waited spellbound to learn the secret that seemed certain to be revealed.

"I ... have ... to ... tell you something" she blurted out, unconsciously looking at her son and granddaughter, then back to her bewildered but concerned husband.

"Zeb was down at the shore a while ago, and found a man lying unconscious" she truthfully told him.

"I had Jake carry him here" as she looked toward the bedroom door. "I think he's going to be alright, but he's resting in the guest room".

"Well" Max pondered for a moment, not knowing what to say or do next.

"Why was she trying to conceal this?" he asked himself, remembering how she just made a fuss over a tattered pillow, rather than come right out about the injured man in their bedroom.

His eyes looked directly into hers, compelling her to explain.

"Oh, Max" she started. "I'm so scared. I remembered what you said about the fugitive slave act, and how you'd refuse to help someone in need" she began to openly sob.

Max didn't need to respond. His expression of disbelief said it all. But he did.

"Helen, are you telling me that the man in the other room is a runaway slave?"

"No, no!" she stammered. "I mean, I don't know whether he is or isn't" she honestly stated. "But I do know he's black!" as she looked to her son, pleading for his support that she was doing the right thing.

"Grandpa?" Susan asked, looking up at the man towering over her.

"Aren't you going to help this man?" she innocently asked.

Funny thing about little ones. Innocence. They haven't yet learned that life has teeth. That prejudice exists. That the color of a person's skin matters. That human beings can be bought and sold, all under the guise of laws that legitimize the businesses of slave traders and owners.

No, sweet little Susan didn't know about any of that. But her rhetorical question to her beloved grandfather cut to the heart of the Golden Rule and, at least temporarily, silenced the natural disposition of grownups to discuss and debate such issues.

Simply put, she melted her grandfather's heart.

Max looked down at Susan, and smiled softly.

"Of course we're going to help him" he lovingly reassured her, then looked to his wife.

"My dear" he began. "I know what I said before" he began to explain, just above a whisper.

Helen's loving reaction enveloped the room. Unconsciously, Jake slowly sat himself down in his mother's chair, and began to rock back and forth until the soothing creaks and squeaks calmed each one's soul with that familiar rhythmic sound that brought immediate comfort to all.

"We'll take care of him".

He looked back down to Susan.

"We'll feed him, clothe him, and help in any way we can. After all, that's the Christian thing to do. Isn't it Susan?"

She reached up and wrapped her small arms around his legs, and watched as her father continued to rock back and forth, eyes closed in prayer with a peaceful smile.

"Let's see how he's doing" Max told his wife as she led the way to the bedroom.

As she slowly opened the door, Max asked: "What's his name?"

"His name?" Helen though to herself. "Why, I rightly don't know" she thought out loud. "I haven't asked him. He was so exhausted, he just fell back to sleep. We really haven't spoken yet".

Max chuckled to himself when he saw that Tabari was wearing his clothes. Not new clothes, but certainly not ones that Max was ready to throw out. He looked at Helen.

She sheepishly smiled, then stared at the floor.

"Old worn out blanket?" he teased.

"Oh, Max. He was so cold and wet. I couldn't …"

"I'm kidding, my dear. I completely understand.

"Where are his shoes? Does he have shoes?"

She looked at her husband, somewhat puzzled by his question, then smiled a grateful and appreciative thank you. She knew he'd do the right thing. "Patience" she remembered herself saying. "Patience".

Little Susan was busy rummaging through the closet.

"Here's some shoes!" she shouted.

"I don't think they'd fit him very well" Helen gently told her. "Besides" she whispered, "They're for ladies".

Susan looked at the shoes and realized her grandmother was right.

She tossed them haphazardly back into the closet and continued her frantic search.

"I think I know where there's some shoes that might fit him" Max stated. "We're probably about the same size". He reached up over Susan, as she watched in admiration at the tall man's range, and saw him grab a shoebox way up on the top shelf.

Helen was delightfully spellbound. Those were her husband's brand new shoes. Never worn. They'd planned on wrapping them as a Christmas present to open in front of the whole family.

* * *

"EVERYTHING?" Helen couldn't believe what her husband had just instructed.

"Everything!" he replied. "Why not? Let's have a feast, and show this stranger what it's like to have a banquet among new friends. Let's go all out!"

She hugged him so hard he almost winced.

"And tell the Hamiltons to join us. And the Menards. And the St. Johns".

"My, my" she responded, grinning and giggling.

The Hamilton, Menard and St. John families were old friends and had been part of the Baton Rough community for many years. They were a close knit 'clan', regular church goers and devout abolitionists. There was no fear that any of these friends would harm Tabari in any way. To the contrary, they'd all offer their devoted assistance to guide him on his way to freedom.

Tabari was scared, but intuitively believed that this group of white folk truly did intend to help him. He knew how much assistance Tom and Melba, the Jeffersons, and the Reverend Baxter and Pastor Jessie had provided, risking their own lives to obtain his freedom.

He desperately hoped these new friends wouldn't experience the same injuries the others had, but he had no control over this. But he made a point to disclose the unexpected dangers that his previous escape had produced, and wanted to make certain that these new friends fully understood the risks.

* * *

MARGO Menard was the first to arrive to help with the feast, and immediately began placing plates, forks and spoons on the table, and making sure the delicious buttermilk and sweet potato pies she brought were properly wrapped and stored away, to ward off not only pesky insects but mischievous young'uns as well.

The trading and selling of slaves was a personal issue for her. Several years ago, she'd gone to New Orleans to visit her sister. Her return brought her on board the steamboat *Princess*, one of the most luxurious of its time.

Both top and lower decks were filled with excited passengers, many of whom appeared quite wealthy. Bales of cotton were stacked seemingly everywhere, and on top sat small groups of slaves, some shackled at the wrists, while a smattering were unfettered and free to roam the ship.

On the top deck sat a young female negroe with a small child on her lap. Not more than three years old. The woman wasn't dressed like a slave. She wore a rather fashionable dress, and costume jewelry hung around her neck. The toddler was certainly a handful, demanding all of her attention as he pulled on the necklace and repeatedly poked her cheek.

Margo watched the mother lovingly reprimand her son but, with infinite patience, twisted his curly hair in her fingers while planting soft kisses on his face.

She then noticed two men engaged in serious discussion but, about what, she couldn't hear. But they continuously looked at the young woman, making it apparent that she might be the topic of their conversation.

The older man, squat and rotund, seemed to have a sully disposition and repeatedly flipped the pages of a little scratch pad back and forth, pointing out something of importance to the younger, well-attired gentleman.

There was something about the older man that disturbed her. He appeared well-dressed but, on further inspection, she could see that his pants were old and somewhat soiled, and his shoes had long ago lost their shine.

The younger man held an air of superiority, certainly educated, and showed the other no respect for his advanced years. Clearly, they were discussing something of importance, most likely involving business and money.

Margo gave it no more thought, as she focused her attention on the west and east shorelines of the Mississippi River, enjoying the light breeze on such a wonderful day. White puffy clouds kept the air cool, and she found the small homes scattered along the shore to be quite quaint, almost romantic with their picket fences and manicured vegetable gardens.

She then returned her gaze to the two men, and watched as they put their signatures to a piece of paper and vigorously shook hands. A moment later, she saw the older man approach the young woman and speak loudly in her face. The woman began violently shaking her head from side to side, then began to cry uncontrollably. This heated conversation quickly drew the attention of other passengers who began to gather around the two.

As some pressed in, an unintentional barrier was momentarily placed between the woman and her toddler. In the blink of an eye, Margo saw the younger man scoop the child into his arms and disappear through the crowd.

The older man slapped the woman hard across her face to silence her hysteria. The onlookers were appalled, but not enough to intervene between a slave owner and what was apparently his property.

The small crowd began to disperse, and the young woman looked up to confirm that the unbelievable had occurred. Her son was sold and taken from her.

Margo watched as she slumped off her bench and onto the ship's deck, wailing from the depth of her soul as she curled into a fetal position.

"My dear, my dear" Margo tried to console her, as she knelt down next to the stricken mother. No soothing was possible. What mother could find peace when their only beloved child was stolen in front of their very own eyes?

"Oh Misses" the mother cried hysterically. "Dey's stolen my child! Dey's stolen my only child! Pleeze hep' me. Oh dear God, pleeze hep' me".

"I'll do what I can" she said, trying to reassure the woman. "I'll find the man who bought your son, and I'll talk to him. I'll tell him what a terrible mistake he's made. I'll do everything I can to get your baby returned to you".

The woman stared into Margo's eyes, desperately pleading for her help, but now too hysterical to speak.

"Now, gather yourself up and sit back down on this bench. I promise you, I'll do all I can".

"Oh, pleeze" she whispered. "Pleeze hep' me get my baby back" she begged.

* * *

"I saw what you did!" she forcefully confronted the young gentleman. "I saw you scoop up that child and steal him from his mother" she scolded.

"Ma'am. What you saw was the conclusion of a business transaction. Nothing more. I purchased that boy and have the bill of sale to prove it. Perfectly legal. And quite frankly, you're butting in on matters that are none of your business. Good day to you".

"None of my business?" she scolded him again. "Since when is it not the business of a Christian woman to help a poor innocent child? What you did may be legal in the eyes of the law, but not in the eyes of the Lord. I demand … I implore (she softened her tone) … you to do what's right before God and return that boy to his mother".

"Ma'am, I don't mean any disrespect. But you have no right to interfere with my business. That boy is my property now. Not yours, not his mother's. It's as simple as that.

"What I can offer you, is my personal assurance that no harm will come to him. So long as he honors his Master, he'll be treated fairly, like I treat all of my property. Now good day to you. You can share that good news with his mother".

Devastated, Margo turned away and began to sob.

"How can a human being treat another human being as mere property?" she asked out loud, not caring that no one was listening or able to answer her rhetorical question.

"My Lord, my God" she prayed. "Please bring this boy back to his mother. Please take away all of her pain. Please. Please".

* * *

EMOTIONALLY exhausted, Margo adjourned to her little cabin, undressed and prepared for bed. She neatly folded her dress and placed all of her items away for the evening. A small cabin closet, miniature by any standard, provided just enough space to stow her personal things.

The cabin, though cramped, was comfortable. She appreciated having it all to herself, as the Ship's owners generally required at least two passengers per room in order to increase revenue.

A petite dresser, twin bed, two paintings of the river, a mirror hung on the wall, and the small closet. Not causing her any claustrophobia, but tight enough that she was looking forward to landing at Baton Rouge.

Night passed without much sleep. She tossed and turned, trying to think of a way, any way, to right this wrong. Did the Lord intervene during the night? Had the young man seen the light and returned the child? she lamented.

The sheets felt nice. The cotton stuffed mattress and pillow were comfortable enough, but not so much to allow her to mind to unwind and forget about the day's emotional strain.

Eventually, she began to drift off and begin to enjoy some of the dream world that leaves one rejuvenated come morning. She dreamt she was back in her childhood, strolling along the river with her father, picking flowers in the cool afternoon without a care in the world.

But she heard a tapping noise. Her dream shifted to see a Pileated Woodpecker, a marvelously colored bird, perched high in an oak tree. The rare sight always enthralled her and her father. They'd sit on the bank and listen to its loud ringing call and watch the graceful creature peck away until a rectangular pattern had been chiseled into the trunk.

It remained a mystery, to them both, why a woodpecker would be so fixated on hammering away on a tree.

But the sound caused Margo's eyes to drowsily open. She realized that the sound was in the present moment. Her mind had incorporated it into her dream, but in reality, there was a real tapping noise taking place.

"It's coming from the porthole" she thought.

"But how can it? How can someone be tapping on my window?"

This bothered her greatly, as she turned to find the pocket watch she'd carefully placed on the dresser next to her. She stared at the timepiece for a moment, until her eyes began adjusting to the darkness.

"Three o'clock" she read.

She heard the tapping again.

"Who's there?" she asked out loud, slightly above a whisper.

"How can someone be tapping on my window?" she wondered again. She remembered looking out the porthole earlier the previous afternoon, distinctly noticing that there was no walkway underneath. Nothing to obstruct her view of the river's never-ending shoreline.

She desperately wanted to light a lamp to see what could possibly be tapping at her window but, in the near pitch black, couldn't see well enough to remember where the lamp was in the unfamiliar room.

The tapping came again.

"It's not the porthole" she thought. She felt the small hairs on the back of her neck rise, and began to tremble.

"It's coming from somewhere else".

She was now too terrified to pull the sheets over her head in the frightened hope this unwanted intruder would simply vanish and leave her undisturbed. Her hands began to shake as she reached to return the watch to the dresser.

"Tap tap tap … Tap tap tap …"

"Who is it?" this time yelling out loud, sitting straight up and staring at the wall where the sound now seemed to emanate from.

No reply to her terrified demand.

She couldn't just lie there. By now, her eyes had adjusted enough that she could make out the silhouettes of the furniture in the room. The dresser, the end of the bed, a picture frame on the wall. And the mirror.

"My God!" she screamed to herself. "The tapping … is coming from inside the mirror!"

She kept her eyes trained on the mirror as she slid her legs off the bed and felt her feet touch the cold floor.

She stood, and used the bed's edge to feel her way toward the wall where the mirror hung. She slowly slid one foot at a time across the floor, while fanning her arm in front of her, waiting to come in contact with the panels.

Finally, she felt the wooden boards with her fingertips, then placed her hands on the wall and inched sideways to locate the silhouette of the mirror.

There it was, hung just slightly above her head. She lifted her body with her tippy toes and peered deeply into it, trying to see her reflection in the darkness.

Slowly, the image appeared, blurry at first with the edges of her face more shadowy than clear.

Then the image gradually took shape, until the face was clearly defined.

But it wasn't her face. It was … the face of the young negroe mother whose toddler had been stolen from her.

Margo stared at her in disbelief. Any thoughts of the outside world vanished, as she concentrated on the contorted look of the lovely black woman who clearly seemed to recognize her.

It was the painful expression of a lost soul. Eyes widened in excruciating sorrow, the look of a wailing mother, pleading for the return of her small child.

Margo began screaming hysterically, then slowly slumped to the floor as she fainted.

* * *

"OH my goodness!" she cried out loud as the sunlight breached through the porthole and cause her eyes to open.

"I need to tell that mother what the bastard told me. Her son won't be treated harshly".

As she quickly dressed, she repeatedly turned to see if the apparition was still inside the mirror. Had it been just a nightmare? A horrible dream that seemed real enough to cause her to faint and awaken on the floor?

She briskly walked the entire lower and upper decks, but couldn't find the woman.

"I've got to search more thoroughly" she told herself. "Every nook and cranny".

She began her search again, this time meticulously starting at the bow of the lower deck, first along the starboard, then port sides, behind every cotton bale, cubby hole and every conceivable space where a body could fit into.

"Ma'am, I see you're intently looking for something" a middle aged white man stated, drinking his morning coffee and smoking a particularly pungent cigar.

"Why yes. Yes, I am" she answered as her eyes continued to scour the deck, seeking for even a glimpse of the young mother.

"I'm looking for a woman. A young black woman. She had a son. No more than three years old. When I last saw her, she was on the top deck.

"Oh, it was terrible. Two men. One young and one old. They sold her son. Sold him right from under her. Oh, she was so distraught, the poor thing. I'm trying to find her".

The man's glance left Margo's eyes and focused on the deck below his feet.

"You haven't heard?" he softly asked, knowing her answer would be obvious.

"Heard what?" she replied. As she spoke those two words, time seemed to suspend itself. He was about to answer her, and she intuitively knew the news would not be good.

"She's gone. In the middle of the night. Jumped overboard. Not a trace. I'm so sorry to be the one to tell you".

Margo couldn't respond. Yesterday's nightmare raced through her mind as she stared incredulously at the deck. The two men. The stolen child. The inconsolable mother. The ghostly apparition in the mirror.

Her last words to her: "I'll do everything I can to get your baby returned to you".

"Did I cause this?" she silently tortured herself.

"I prayed for the child's return, but I also begged the Lord to take away all of her pain. 'Please, Please' I begged Him. 'Please take away all of her pain'.

"Is this how He answered my prayer? Is this how He ended her pain?"

Nearly stuporous, she unconsciously slumped into the nearest chair, face buried in her hands as she cried uncontrollably.

21

"IT REALLY IS GOOD THAT you and Caroline came" Trent told Senator Harrison as the two relaxed on the third story veranda, enjoying another round of rum, with ice of course. Jeb and Caroline had stayed nearly an entire week, ever vigilant to comfort Collette as she recovered from the alligator attack.

Jeb was thoroughly enjoying the peace and tranquility of the plantation life, at least from his present vantage point as a sort of 'vacationer' this past week. The sun had dipped below the tall oak trees, now offering a reprieve from the oppressive heat that lingered just moments ago.

"Ah" he sighed, as he felt a slight cool breeze fan across his face.

Trent, eyes closed, mimicked the sigh, also enjoying the relief.

Jeb was feeling rather good, enjoying a slight inebriation, in addition to the burden lifted from him this past week from his responsibilities as a member of the Louisiana Senate. Those duties remained, of course. But he'd found time to take leisurely strolls through the plantation with Caroline, and he and Trent spent nearly an entire day fishing. He was truly beginning to unwind and relax.

Those strolls also kindled the depression he and Caroline shared over the whole issue of slavery. Watching the workers toil in the hot sun, watched over by armed overseers, and the comparatively squalid conditions of their housing, left the two disenchanted and somber. Neither approved of slavery, but Jeb represented citizens of Louisiana, the majority of whom relied upon the slave system, directly or indirectly, as a vital part of their livelihoods.

There was hardly a family who didn't benefit, even though there was no direct involvement. The clothes they wore, the goods they purchased, all came from enterprises related to the slave industry.

Caroline didn't pressure her husband with her abolitionist views. He knew them well enough. Although she was a woman of means, having inherited a small fortune from her father, she knew that she could never experience the unique lifestyle that a US Senator's wife is granted. Her world was filled with the rich and powerful, society's movers and shakers. She even once met President Millard Fillmore, an 'indecisive thumb-twaddler' as Jeb referred to him.

But the two knew, and shared, each other's view on the issue. Inevitably, slavery was bound to collapse. The number of folks who still truly believed that people were merely property, to be bought, sold or traded like cattle, was dwindling.

They'd try to defend enslavement by misdirection, playing on unsophisticated minds by reminding people how 'Christian' they were, and how they'd sacrificed their businesses by upholding the fifty-two year old Federal law that prohibited the importation of slaves.

Half-truths are more insulting than outright lies. Banning the importation of any more slaves was meaningless, as the U.S. slave population had by now increased to nearly four million. How?

Babies.

Slave traders and owners wanted strong males and females to work the fields, but a young female who'd produce many more children was most valuable. Some owners purchased females for that very purpose. Breed them and sell the babies as soon as they were ready.

But the time for totally abolishing slavery had not yet come. Jeb and Caroline knew this. And taking a hard line stand on the issue would only see Jeb voted out of the Senate.

Unacceptable.

So, Jeb played the diplomatic card whenever possible to make sure he stayed in office. But when a bill came up for consideration that in any way would move toward impeding the slave trade, Jeb would nudge here and there, try to put his finger on the scale, to obtain its passage. Caroline was proud of his efforts.

But right now, the rum's effect was coaxing Jeb's thoughts toward more titillating feelings.

"Trent" he almost whispered. "I've been meaning to ask you something. Something rather personal".

"Of course my friend".

Jeb paused for the right words to come.

"It's about Caroline".

"Yes?"

Jeb looked up and down the balcony to make sure no one could eavesdrop.

"I've been having an affair" he whispered.

Trent's face contorted like he was passing a kidney stone.

"You've been having an affair?" he whispered back, almost embarrassed that he'd simply reiterated what his friend had just confessed.

"Yes" Jeb replied with a tinge of shame, his eyes now focused on the floor below.

Trent waited.

"My secretary" he blurted.

"Oh, she's not married" he hurriedly pointed out, as if her unmarried status made his infidelity more honorable.

"Jeb, you don't need to explain ..." Trent replied, a pang of guilt arising as thoughts of his own infidelity with Amana, his house servant, suddenly sprang to life.

"No, no. I want to say this. You see, Caroline and I haven't been .... intimate ... for some time now".

"Jesus!" Trent bemoaned silently.

"It's not that I don't love her. I do!" he almost shouted, as if he needed to defend his commitment to his wife. He took another long sip, swallowed, and then smiled as he reminded himself to relax.

"Jeb, you're among friends here. Our conversation doesn't leave this veranda".

He patted Trent's knee and smiled.

"I know, my friend. I just felt I needed to tell someone and, well, I guess you're it".

"It's fine" Trent responded, not knowing if he should ask a question or simply wait for Jeb to continue.

"I know Caroline's concerned. Oh, not about my affair" he whispered. "She hasn't the faintest idea. But ..."

"Go on".

"It's about our ... intimacy ... or lack thereof. Ever since I've been with her, my secretary I mean, well, I just haven't been sexually aroused by Caroline".

Trent had never thought about Caroline in an intimate way before. But having just heard his friend say this, made his thoughts race to picture her beautiful face and voluptuous body. She was different, but just as gorgeous, as his own wife, whom Trent had longed to make love to.

"How could you not …" he almost blurted out.

"Jeb, you don't find Caroline attractive?"

Jeb stared out onto the lawns.

"I … I do" he honestly replied. "But this other woman. We have *so* much more in common. We've worked together, nearly side by side, for two years now. She's totally committed to all of my legislative matters.

"And she's very well read. Hell, if she were a man, she could be a lawyer".

They both chuckled.

Trent studied Jeb's expressions, trying to determine if his relationship with his secretary was truly one of admiration, or whether it was purely lust, disguised as appreciation for her legislative assistance.

"I mean, well, she's so much more intellectual than Caroline. Caroline's well-read also, but … it's just not the same" as his eyes started to tear up.

Trent didn't know how to respond. He thought of his own wife, Collette. Certainly not an intellectual, but very smart in her unique way. They got along wonderfully. She as a wife and homemaker, he as a businessman and breadwinner.

Then he reflected on his own education. No formal college, but he could certainly read and write well and, as far as business intelligence went, well, just look around at the splendor of his magnificent plantation, the mansion, the quality and cost of … even the very chairs they were sitting on. Much grander than anything Jeb had accomplished.

But, then again, Jeb was a US Senator. He was quite educated, a lawyer, and held court on a daily basis with the most prominent politicians of the day. Not just local and statewide issues, but national, even international issues, were part of his everyday business. Maybe, to him, it *did* make a difference that Caroline, as beautiful as she is, was still a mere housewife and didn't have the added attractiveness of a political confidant.

"I'm not sure what you're asking me" Trent broke the silence.

"I'm not sure either" Jeb mumbled. "I guess I'm just wondering if this is natural. Maybe a middle age crisis" he smiled then took another long sip.

Trent was becoming antsy. He wavered between delving deeper into the subject with Jeb, and retreating because of the emotions involving his own affair with Amana. An encounter caused by the exact opposite of what Jeb was feeling.

It was Collette who lacked sexual interest, not he. If Collette had wanted intimacy, he'd never have turned to his 'servant'.

With Jeb, it was the reverse. It was he who rejected his wife's advances.

"My God" Trent lamented. He looked at his glass.

Empty.

"Damn" he thought to himself. "I need another drink", then filled both his and Jeb's glasses to the brim.

While Jeb watched Trent refresh his libation, he privately reminisced about the first dalliance he'd had with Roxanne, a curvaceous redhead nearly ten years his junior. Beautiful, articulate and highly ambitious, she relished every opportunity to stand toe to toe with any politician and engage in heated debate, never curbing her argument in deference to the masculine sex.

This was, well, unheard of. Women were relegated to domestic work, plain and simple. Cooking, cleaning and child-rearing. Wife, mother and homemaker. Total deference to their husbands or, if none, their fathers. Politics were for men. Period.

But Roxanne had no desire to take a submissive backseat to any man. At that time, a woman had zero chance of running for office, let alone actually getting elected. So, she volunteered to assist Senator Harrison as one of his staff. She brewed and served coffee, brought daily refreshments in the form of pies, sweet cakes and fruit, and ran errands of all sorts to keep his office running as smoothly as possible.

For Roxanne, this was the beginning pathway. First, get to know Jeb on a personal basis. Then, gradually infiltrate herself into his inner circle. Slowly and methodically become a trusted and welcomed political confidant.

She knew how to sparkle her bright green eyes directly at her male prey, so mesmerizing was her attractiveness that the victim was powerless to resist her seductive invitation.

Her conversation and company quickly became desired, not only by Jeb's staff, but by many of the exclusive male officers of the Senate and House of Representatives.

Their meetings, mostly impromptu, could never be held on the legislative floor, of course. That solemn ground was reserved for men only. But the hallways weren't off limits, nor the private meeting rooms and offices that abound throughout Baton Rouge's Capitol Building.

Her time had come. It was time to break through that proverbial glass ceiling. She needed to penetrate that wall of male dominance, the one where only masculine creatures were allowed to decide society's fate.

Now, she'd be one of the masters that created laws. Nothing monumental, at least not on her first try. But something big enough, something impactful and, most importantly, a law that could actually be passed.

She meticulously researched the acts that the Legislature had passed during the last three years. She laboriously read, studied, and consumed not only the actual laws, but their initial proposals, committee reviews, amendments and all things historically leading up to their passage.

Then her epiphany moment came as she tossed and turned in bed late one night.

"Money!" she shouted to herself. "That's what'll get their attention. Give them what they all clamor for. Money!"

"And my law will see to it that there's money enough for me, as well" she giggled.

Until recently, Roxanne was always an unpaid volunteer. The Legislature had no allocation of money for mere 'interns' although, being a female, she could never have acquired such a haughty title anyway.

Fortunately, whether through gratitude for her helpful political insights, or simply banal lust to ensure her continued physical presence, Jeb had begun paying her a small weekly 'allowance' as encouragement for her sustained assistance.

But now, she'd found an idea that could possibly allow her, a woman, to receive an actual salary, as well as line the pockets of the Legislators who'd most certainly vote 'yes' for such a new law.

* * *

"HMM ..." she began to write.

"An Act for the Great State of Louisiana.

"No, no, no" she reprimanded herself.

"C'mon woman, you know better than that" as she remembered all of the laborious reading and research she'd done.

"Acts

of the

State of Louisiana"

"That's better" she smiled and continued.

"No. 1.

An Act to provide for the payment of the members, officers and contingent expenses of the General Assembly".

"Mmm ... 'contingent expenses of the General Assembly' ... That's me!" she snickered out loud.

Her 'Act' went on to state that the sum of forty thousand dollars would be appropriated for the purpose of paying per diem, or daily expenses, plus mileage, to each member of the Senate and House of Representatives, along with their 'officers'.

Payments that could be used for her own salary would come from the 'contingent expenses' of the Senate, a la Senator Jeb Harrison.

"Genius!" she congratulated herself. "Brilliant in its simplicity" she patted herself on the back.

"Now, I can't submit this Act with my name on it" she lamented. "It'd be dead on arrival".

"Hmm ... I need ... a 'pseudo' name. A man's name. Or at least a name that has no obvious gender.

"Let's see ... how 'bout the initials 'R.A.' ... for Rox Anne?" she chuckled.

"Alright. My last name will be ..." she slowly looked about her desk until her eyes came to rest on a rose petal.

"Flowers" she stated matter of factly, delighted in her creativity.

"R.A. Flowers" she whispered, quite satisfied in her clever, yet harmless, deception.

* * *

"AH, Roxanne" Jeb enthusiastically welcomed her as he sat behind his desk, cleared of all clutter except a few papers neatly stacked together.

"Please come in and have a seat" he offered, a slight smirk on his face as he alternated his glances between Roxanne and the papers.

Rarely a daytime drinker, Jeb felt a small celebratory sip or two was certainly warranted, anticipating the unexpected pile of money about to be dumped in his lap.

As she moved to the chair in front of his desk, he coyly whispered:

"Or should I call you 'Miss Flowers'?" grinning like a Cheshire cat who'd just been spoon fed an extra helping of milk and cream.

The Act would no doubt be passed unanimously. What legislator could turn down his slice of the forty thousand dollar pie?

"Why, whatever do you mean?" she coquettishly teased, as she slowly slid two fingers across the desk, finally resting on top of the papers.

Jeb blushed as she sat on the desk's edge and crossed her legs in front of him, her thin cotton dress seductively accentuating the curves of her buttocks and thighs. She leaned forward across the desk as if to examine the papers in front of him, but the world at large knew her intent was to torture his carnal instincts, adding another arrow to her quiver.

Just as she knew, he couldn't resist staring at those voluptuous breasts, the temptation all too natural to ignore.

She took pleasure in how easily she could manipulate men by deploying a little sexual suggestiveness. It didn't take much.

But she felt her real pleasure from the thrill of matching wits with these powerful politicians. The excitement of having introduced her first legislative bill, though done surreptitiously, was euphoric.

She knew a basic truism: The way to a politician's heart wasn't through his stomach, but through sex. Or money. Quite basic and simple. And very effective.

She watched amusingly as Jeb finally became aware of his lustful gaze, and returned his stare to her.

"I must say" as his blushing began to dissipate.

"Impressive. Quite impressive, indeed". He took another sip.

Supremely proud of her accomplishment, and with no need to continue to play coy about the bill's author, she reached over, took Jeb's snifter glass, and downed it in two large swallows, unconcerned about the elixir's content.

Jeb was momentarily stunned. Then instantly aroused. The confidence this beautiful creature demonstrated was mesmerizing. She could instantly transform from an intelligent political strategist to seductive harlot without the faintest sign of remorse.

Roxanne rarely had sexual urges. But when she did, they came hard and fast. And uncontrollable.

She looked at Jeb, having momentarily forgotten her accomplishment. Jeb saw her breasts heave, and her eyes glaze over, the aura of sexual desire saturating the space between them. She smiled wide, running her slippery tongue across her top teeth.

He was powerless to resist. No thought of his wife, no thought of the repercussions if they were discovered by an uninvited intruder into his office.

Hardly taking his eyes off of her, he slowly walked to the door and quietly locked it.

"Jeb? … Jeb?" Trent leaned forward and loudly whispered, as if his friend had been in a trance.

The Senator's smile disappeared as Trent's voice brought him out of his lustful dream.

"She's that good, eh?" Trent teased, chuckling at Jeb's unspoken but obvious delight in reminiscing about his liaison with Roxanne.

"Oh … well … yea" was all Jeb could muster, his smile returning.

"I don't know what to add" Trent said. "If she's that alluring, and Caroline won't find out, I guess there's no harm" he thought out loud, inwardly debating the cost of his own marriage if Collette ever learned of his infidelity.

"She won't" Jeb reassured himself. "She can't. Roxanne lives in Baton Rouge. Caroline's met her once or twice but, of course, only when I've taken her to the Capitol. Hardly ever".

Trent's confusion caused his face to contort.

"What does he expect me to say" he thought.

"Does he want my verbal approval?"

Jeb could read his face and mind.

"I'm not seeking your approval, or forgiveness, my friend. I only wondered if you've experienced anything similar".

"Good God" Jeb chastised himself. It sounded as if he wanted Trent to confess to an affair of his own, in order to justify his own infidelity.

"Trent, I didn't mean to ..."

Now it was Trent whose mind had retreated into a trance, his thoughts racing incessantly between the pleasure Amana had brought him and the true love he still felt for his wife.

"Look, Jeb" scanning the veranda to make sure no one else could hear.

"I've had my thoughts ... of another woman ... like I suppose most married men have" he started, unconsciously thinking it more acceptable if he believed that infidelity was a natural trait of the male gender.

Trent was beginning to feel a bit drunk, and about to engage Jeb in that macho barroom banter that liquor has a tendency to stir up in men.

He almost began to tell Jeb about his affair with Amana, but stopped suddenly when he observed Jeb's facial expression, coaxing him into revealing his innermost secrets, all to relieve Jeb of his own indiscretions.

124

"No, no" Trent demanded to himself. He could sense what Jeb wanted. Not just a salacious tale, but a confirmation that Jeb was somehow vindicated for his extra-marital affair. If Trent was guilty, then Jeb's shame could at least be partially erased.

"Listen. It's simply not my place to say whether you and ..."

"Roxanne".

"Whether you're doing the right thing ... with Roxanne. I know you and Caroline have been married for a long time. You've always seemed like a perfect fit. I understand what you're saying, but ..."

Trent didn't know what to say. This conversation started with Jeb confessing that he had no sexual interest in his wife.

"How the hell am I supposed to respond to that?" Trent anguished inwardly.

"Jeb, all I can say is that you've got to work this out. I mean, like I said, if Caroline doesn't find out, and you find Roxanne so attractive, well, maybe things will work out alright. Assuming Caroline never finds out".

"My God!" he thought to himself. I could just as easily be listening to the same lecture from Jeb. "*As long as Collette doesn't find out, just keep screwing Amana!*"

Jeb was relieved just enough to know this topic had been exhausted, at least for now. He'd released some of his burden, a secret that had haunted him for too long.

He was no different than any other of our species. The number of times that he actively had to hide the fact of his intimate relationship with Roxanne was minimal. Although they spent countless hours working together, their physical encounters were rare.

The number of times he *thought* about the secret was an overwhelming burden. That heavy load incessantly chattered in his mind, day and night.

Sharing the secret with Trent lifted that weight. It didn't remove it entirely but, involving him, a trusted confidant, with the details reduced Jeb's stress considerably.

"I think Sadie will have dinner ready soon. Perhaps you'd like to freshen up?"

Jeb just smiled as he stood up and walked with his best friend back into the house.

22

"MY DEAR, YOU'RE LOOKING like a million bucks!" Trent gushed as he watched Collette walk into the dining hall with hardly a limp.

Collette was near to a full recovery. The Doctor had actually done a good job. He'd meticulously applied his slipper elm concoction to the wound and, somewhat amazingly, the scar tissue was barely visible. Collette's slight limp would completely vanish as she continued to walk and strengthen her calf muscles.

The alligator attack still haunted her dreams, but was beginning to subside. Feeling more relaxed and composed, she'd enjoyed a luxurious bath and pampered herself with scented oil and lotion. She wanted to return to her former self, and put on her favorite 'crinoline' dress for dinner.

"Why thank you, Colonel" she coyly cooed, lifting her dress hem slightly as she passed by her husband.

"I must say, I'm feeling so much better" as she inhaled the sweet scent of her perfume.

Jeb and Caroline were already seated at the table, both admiring how beautiful and gracious Collette looked. Always the gentleman, Jeb stood to show his respect for this lovely southern belle, while Caroline nearly popped out of her chair and quickly shuffled to greet her friend with a loving hug and kiss.

"You look just marvelous" Caroline gushed, water beginning to fill her eyes. "I can't tell you how magnificent you look" she genuinely fussed.

"My, my" Jeb also began. He looked at Trent. "Colonel, your wife is as radiant as ever.

"Collette" Jeb addressed her directly. "Caroline and I are ever so happy to see that you've made a full recovery. That ugly memory will probably haunt you for a bit, but I assure you it'll soon be forgotten. It's been wonderful to spend the past week or so with you and Trent".

Collette was genuinely moved.

"Thank you. Thank you both … for being here and for being such good friends". She looked to Trent and almost began to cry.

"Well, let's enjoy a quiet evening. Among friends" as he motioned all to sit at the table. I do believe Sadie has prepared quite a feast".

Collette nearly bolted from her chair.

"Oh goodness! I almost forgot".

She walked briskly toward the kitchen, then nearly hollered back: "We're having one more for dinner".

Trent appeared confused. Jeb and Caroline just smiled, wondering who Collette's surprise guest could be.

* * *

DAYS before, Collette spoke with Amana.

Amana had received her 'cruxes' from the Doctor, and quickly became skillful at balancing her bad leg using the two sticks to adjust her weight. She only had one near fall, when one of the prosthesis slipped on a wet spot in the kitchen. Other than that, she'd learned to nearly whirl in a circle, provided she wasn't deterred by the pain in her ankle.

Sadie was with Amana in the kitchen, washing some pots as the two chatted, when Collette walked in.

"Amana, I'd like to speak with you" Collette softly stated, in more of a question than a command.

"Sadie, would you give us some time alone?" she asked.

Sadie nodded her head as she dried her hands with a nearby towel, then scurried out the door.

Amana froze. "Is 'dis when it happens?" she asked herself. "Is 'dis when 'da Misses is gonna' let me have it?" she anguished.

The talk they'd previously had went well enough, but Amana was certain that Collette would seek to extract her vengeance once enough time had passed. Collette had been truly thankful that she'd saved her life, but surely, over time, that appreciation would dissipate and be replaced by the need for revenge.

Amana's head was about to explode. She couldn't go on like this, not knowing whether Collette knew, didn't know, or only suspected, that her husband had an affair with her.

It was torture. Emotional torture. The same that Jeb had experienced. Amana hadn't actively had to hide the fact of her triste with Trent. Collette had never confronted her about it.

But, like Jeb, it was the *number* of times that she thought about the secret that carried such an overwhelming burden. Day and night. "Will I be sold? Will I be whipped? Beaten? Killed?"

But unlike Jeb, she had no one to share her secret with. No one to lift that weight. No trusted confidant.

"Amana, please, come sit next to me.

"I know that there's been some ... tension ... between us" she started.

Amana hung her head, her body tightening like a spring. What was worse? Slaving in the hot fields, filthy clothes, disgusting food, smelling like a wild animal?

Or living a life of relative leisure, clean garments, delicious nourishment, and regular baths?

Given those physical facts, the answer was obvious, of course.

But the *non*-physical facts were just as real. Her expectation of future harm was just as real. Her inner turmoil of anticipated events was just as real. Amana had experienced this tortuous anxiety for weeks now.

And now, with Collette about to reveal her intentions, her pent up anxiety immediately turned to fear.

Collette wasn't sure how to broach the forbidden subject, but could no longer keep it inside her. She, too, needed someone to share her burden with. Even if it meant her rival.

Amana wasn't going to admit to anything. She couldn't. She detested lying, but the repercussions for telling the truth could well be a matter of life or death for her. No, lying was perfectly justifiable in this situation.

"For some time now, I've had these awful, terrible thoughts, and I think you may know why. I don't know why I've had these feelings" she lied.

She knew damn well why. She'd watched as her husband ogled Amana's breast and backside one morning while she washed dishes in the kitchen. She'd found Trent's hair in Amana's bedsheets. She smelled her own lilac scented perfume in those same sheets.

She certainly didn't expect Amana to admit to having an affair with her husband. No woman in her right mind would do so, even one from such an inferior race. But by merely broaching the subject, perhaps she'd be able to glean the truth, perhaps from Amana's eyes. Her body language. Something.

Amana was thinking the same thoughts, but her concentration was focused around concealment, rather than revealing the truth. There was no way this white woman was going to trick her into divulging the sordid truth about her dalliance with Collette's husband.

"Let me say it this way" Collette continued.

"I've had these horrible ... intuitions ... that you and the Colonel ... well ... have had an intimate relationship ... behind my back".

"There! I've said it" Collette congratulated herself inwardly, while outwardly examining Amana's every blink and twitch to detect whether there was the slightest truth to her accusation.

Amana was ready. She'd now steeled herself for this very moment. There was no way the Colonel would tell. She was certain of that. What other evidence could Collette have? It didn't matter. Amana would improvise any alibi needed.

She looked Collette directly in the eyes, expressing complete disbelief at what she'd just heard.

She started to speak, but then paused, waiting to gauge Collette's thoughts. She was anticipating, hoping, that her own facial expression of incredulity would convince Collette that her suspicions were ridiculous.

No such luck. At least, momentarily, Collette's accusation remained steadfast.

"Misses! I has no idea what you's talkin' 'bout" as she stared directly into Collette's eyes, never flinching in her adamant denial.

"Da' Colonel? 'Da Colonel and me?" she almost shouted, convincingly persuasive that she'd heard what Collette had just said, but couldn't believe her ears.

"I wud' never ... not in a 'millin' years" she piously proclaimed, as she whipped up sufficient tears and forced her body to tremble.

"I wud' never ..." she began to sob uncontrollably, covering her face with her hands.

And it worked.

Collette suddenly felt sorry for this young woman, whom she'd obviously just wrongly accused of adultery. She also felt huge relief.

"All the times I thought about Trent's infidelity. About Amana's betrayal. About the two of them ... together. Oh! Oh how I wasted those precious hours. How I unnecessarily tortured myself!" she rejoiced inwardly. She looked Amana in the eyes with a loving and repentive smile.

"But wait! What about Trent's hair? What about my perfume on her bedsheets?" she asked herself.

She looked at Amana, who'd placed her hands at her sides, still sobbing, exposing herself in complete innocence. She looked like a naïve little child, wrongfully accused of the most atrocious horror.

Why would Collette pursue interrogation? The presence of her husband's hair could be explained simply enough. Any static electricity could have attached it from the hallway floor to the bedsheets lying crumpled in a pile, waiting to be washed.

But the perfume? How could her perfume's fragrance be on Amana's sheets? Collette relished closure on all these tortuous topics of infidelity, but she knew that without exhausting all questions, the ordeal would continue to haunt her.

"Amana, what about my perfume?

"Remember when I ordered you to wash my clothes before you washed your own? You dropped your bedsheets on the threshold of your bedroom door and walked away. I picked them up. The sheets. And I smelled my perfume!"

Amana anticipated Collette's question as soon as she heard the word 'perfume'. This would be easy.

"Misses" she began. "I has a confession ta' make".

Collette panicked as she thought Amana was about to plead guilty to her crime.

Amana saw right through Collette's expression.

"No, no Misses. It ain't got 'nothin ta' do wid' 'da Colonel" she emphatically announced.

"I … I … went inta' yer' bedroom and sprayed some of yer' 'purfume' on me. I shouldn't a dun' it … I knows … Lordie, I knows. But I jus' wanted ta' feel … pretty. Dat's all. I jus' wanted to smell 'feminum'" as she openly sobbed, her face once more planted in her hands.

She again looked like an innocent little child, being punished for an adult crime that really wasn't a crime at all.

Collette was convinced. Such a simple explanation. Such an innocent act. Like a young child, wanting to act like a grown up. A little squirt of perfume. Yes, it was simply explained. And believable.

Collette almost blushed, so relieved that the unthinkable was no more than a figment of her own perverted imaginations. She'd projected her own guilt over her triste with her dear friend Caroline. Projected that remorse onto Amana.

"Pathetic soul" she rebuked herself.

* * *

"WE'RE having one more for dinner" Collette had announced as she walked from the great dining room to the kitchen door.

Trent appeared confused. Jeb and Caroline just smiled, wondering who Collette's surprise guest could be.

Collette slowly opened the swinging door to the kitchen. She'd had Sadie turn down all of the lamps so only a soft glow emanated, just enough to now reveal the silhouette of a woman dressed in a formal ball gown. A beautiful dress, the neckline open with a drawstring ensuring a tight fit to secure voluptuous breasts.

Trent couldn't be certain because of the dim lighting, but he could swear he'd seen the dress before, but not the feminine creature that adorned it.

Jeb and Caroline were enthralled by the way Collette had orchestrated this dramatic scene. This mystery dinner guest.

Collette held out her hand, motioning with her fingers for the unknown woman to move forward into the light of the dining room.

Trent immediately recognized Amana, and nearly spit out his sip of champagne as she gracefully took a few steps toward the dinner guests.

Jeb and Caroline had no idea who she was, but were excitedly intrigued to see it was a black woman. Young, light skinned, and beautiful.

"Senator Harrison, Caroline, I'd like you to meet one of our house servants, Amana" Collette beamed, feeling both gracious and proud to display one of her human 'properties'.

Jeb immediately rose from his chair and walked briskly to greet their new dinner guest. Caroline was enthralled to see this lovely negroe woman grace the Colonel's dining room, creating a beautiful mix of eclectic company.

"Amana, it's so nice to meet you" Jeb gushed, as he took her gloved hand and gently kissed it. Of course, Amana had never worn such a magnificent dress, let alone felt the luxury and refinement of wearing such elegant gloves.

Trent was dumbfounded. He knew that Collette had warmed to Amana ever since she'd learned that Amana had saved her life. But this! Dressing her in Collette's favorite ball gown? Inviting her to dine in their own home? With the company of white folks? Dignified, educated, and powerful white folks, at that!

"Amana, it's so nice to meet you" Caroline warmly greeted her, with a genuine smile of affection.

"Amana, come sit at the table" Collette gently instructed her, then led her to the chair next to her own. Trent's seat, as always, was at the head of the table, with Collette seated to his immediate right. Jeb sat to Trent's left. She purposely placed Amana across from Caroline, so Collette could have an unimpeded view of Trent's every eye contact and expression. She still remembered him lecherously ogling Amana during that unforgettable breakfast encounter.

Trent was much conflicted. He liked the energy that Amana's presence brought to the table, Jeb's and Caroline's excited interest almost palpable. A slave woman. With experiences that neither Jeb nor Caroline had ever fathomed. Both titillating and educational for them.

But he couldn't understand how he would fit into this conversation. Every eye contact, every word he'd speak to Amana, would include a pregnant pause, one that would conjure up, for each, images of their lustful encounter. Thoughts that had to be kept secret, set aside and unspoken, while the conversation among the dinner guests continued.

"Is she doing this to punish me in some way?" Trent asked himself silently, as he studied his wife's face to see if any signs of vengeance surfaced.

"Does she expect this to be a regular occurrence? Having dinner together? With or without other guests?" He almost shook his head at the absurdness of such a dilemma.

"Amana" Caroline began. "I have so many questions I'd like to ask you". She looked at Trent to see if he'd be uncomfortable or disapprove. It didn't matter. Her genuine interest in this slave girl was overwhelming.

"Please. Tell us how you arrived in N'awlins".

All eyes focused on her. Trent and Collette were now also intrigued. They'd never once asked Amana how she got here, where she came from, what her life had been like. It was unimportant. She was a slave, an owned property, whose only duty was to do the bidding of her masters.

Amana was a fish out of water. She'd never worn such beautiful clothes, or sat at a table with wealthy white people, let alone conversed with them on an apparently equal basis. Too much, too soon. Her lack of education, social skills, inferior class status, left her feeling helpless. She nearly bolted from the table in disgrace and shame.

Caroline moved to comfort her.

"Amana, it's alright. You don't have to talk about it if you don't want to. We understand".

Jeb rushed to the rescue by changing the subject.

"Colonel, I've been talking with some plantation owners about the effect from the recent weather. It seems …"

"It's alright" Amana stated, staring at the silver forks, spoon and knife in front of her. "I don't minds' talkin' 'bout it" she blurted out, still unsure if she should speak without being instructed to do so.

All eyes again focused on her.

She thought of her Martinique home, the times she'd been sold or traded, the horrendous ocean voyage, stuffed in the belly of a rancid ship, of the long hours toiling in the hot sun on the Winters' plantation.

"I come here on a slave ship" she began to explain.

"I remembers' it all" as her eyes began to water, still staring at the table, unable to muster the courage to see herself as the equal to these people and look them directly in the eye.

"It was horrible. Truly horrible" she remembered out loud.

Then, deafening silence. Their hope that Amana would continue her story was dashed, as they all realized her memories were still like exposed nerves, raw and painful.

Caroline felt awful, having probed about issues she knew nothing about. She felt ashamed, asking a slave to relive their horrid past, in order to entertain some rich white folk at Amana's expense.

Collette then broke the silence.

"I asked Amana to join us this evening as a sort of celebration. A warm hearted 'thank you'. A thank you for having saved my life".

All felt immediate relief by Collette's skillful intervention. A much appreciated change of conversation.

"As you know, it was Amana who jumped into the pond and wrestled that 'gata" she continued.

"I was about dead" she explained. "Drowned. Do you know what it's like to nearly drown?" she asked, but to no one in particular. It was like asking one's self a question, only out loud.

"It's quite peaceful, really. You get a very warm, comfortable feeling. Like a dream, but the dream is real. I don't know how to explain it. It's like you know you're about to leave this world, but there's no fear. No fear of the unknown. It's almost as if you're going home. To a wonderful place that you've always known, but only forgotten. I …"

She stopped in mid-sentence, like emerging from a trance, for the first time seeing all eyes focused on her every word.

"Oh, please. Go on" Caroline begged. The others silently concurred.

"My, my. I don't know that there's more to tell. Like I said, I was drowning. I do remember, though, feeling my toes touching … the mucky bottom, then slightly pushing off. I felt myself slowly propelling to the surface. I also remember not caring. Not caring if I made it to the surface. I remember I was quite content, almost wishing, that I would continue to travel into that most enjoyable journey to … where? I don't know".

"My goodness" Trent declared, wiping a teardrop.

137

"All I can say is thank God you decided to stay with us".

"Amen" Jeb and Caroline said in unrehearsed unison.

"But, again" as Collette looked directly into Amana's eyes.

"The reason I've asked you to join us tonight is to thank you. Thank you for saving my life" as she wiped her own teardrop.

Amana felt suddenly empowered. Collette's soliloquy spiritually uplifted her.

"I's jus' so happy to be here" she gushed as she looked directly at them all, momentarily feeling an equal.

"An' Misses, you's welcome" she giggled, as they all laughed together, the humor being contagious.

Trent smiled, briefly forgetting the tension he'd felt when Amana first sat down at the table. He reminded himself not to look her directly in the eyes, sure that his wife would be keeping a vigilant watch to discover any sexual indiscretions.

And so the evening went on. Sadie's delicious dinner was served, course by course, and enjoyed by all.

At one point, Caroline thought of offering one of the ladies' 'fruit juices' to Amana but, having silently looked to Collette for approval, concluded it was not a good idea.

Soon, the men excused themselves and retired to Trent's den, brandies and cigars in hand.

Amana began to help Sadie clear the remaining dishes and silverware. Collette started to stop her, but then reconsidered. Enough impromptu events and emotions had transpired for one evening. It was best not to encourage Amana into thinking her position as house servant would change in any way.

"Amana, go ahead and help Sadie clean up. You can wash my dress and gloves in the morning".

"Yes 'em ma'am", as she resumed her accustomed tasks. The clock had struck midnight. Like the table candles, her Cinderella fairy tale was dowsed.

23

THE TABLE WAS SET. True to his word, Max Donovan had pulled out all the stops to prepare a feast in honor of Tabari.

The Hamilton, Menard and St. John clans were all there, dressed in their Sunday best, the young boys whining to their mothers about their legs itching from their scratchy wool pants.

"Everyone outside! Now!" was their mothers' collective reply.

"Stop complainin' or I'll give you somethin' real to complain' about!" Mrs. Hamilton hollered at her young'un, a boy with disheveled curly red hair, somewhat resembling a mop.

Tabari looked splendid, dressed in Max's new shoes and the cleanest shirt and pants he'd ever worn. And there was more. The invited guests arrived with their own contributions, enough clothing to keep Tabari comfortable during the hot summer and warm enough to endure the coldest winter.

The ladies tried hard to outdo each other with their fondling, fussing and genuine concern for his well-being. He was nearly full before dinner, being handed cake after sweet bread and all sorts of treats prepared for the feast. Although still nervous, he was beginning to relax and feel trusting of these new 'friends'.

The young'uns' table was set up in the small living room area, their plates being prepared by each one's mother, who knew what and how much their child would eat. The older ones, of course, fended for themselves, but nearly all piled extra helpings of chicken and molasses to top the sweet bread cakes.

Tabari, of course, was the center and topic of attention. One by one, the ladies asked him questions. "How did you get to N'awlins? Where were you born? What's happened to your family?"

Finally, Max stepped in to end this well-intended, but oppressive, interrogation.

"Ladies, ladies, please! The poor man can't even chew his food, what with your rapid fire questionin'. Let the fellow eat and enjoy his dinner. There'll be time enough for questions and answers".

Tabari smiled and nodded his head in appreciation.

"Oh my goodness" he replied. "I dun' know when I's ever ate so good. Well, 'dat ain't so. Truth is, I's never ate so good".

The ladies giggled, sure he was telling the truth. Then, almost in unison scooped another spoonful of whatever dish was closest and piled more onto his plate, each again trying to display the sincerest devotion to their forlorn victim.

Max and the other men smiled at each other, observing how each of their wives were behaving like little mother hens, obviously trying to outdo each other in wrapping Tabari under protective wings.

Dinner completed, the women began clearing the table, washing and drying all things necessary, and preserving the leftovers for future feasting.

The men stayed at the table with Tabari, their conversation turned serious, just above whispers but enough that the women folk could hear every word.

"Tabari" Max stated. "We've been discussing your predicament" as he looked into the eyes of the concerned men seated around him.

"Yes" Daryl Hamilton interjected. "There's a lot of people, like us, concerned about folks in your plight" he continued.

Daryl and his wife were devout abolitionists. His small lumber business provided plenty of work to meet the local timber demands, and kept him and his family relatively well-off. In time, his business would boom as the Northeast and Midwest regions depleted their own supplies of lumber and large swaths of timberland in Louisiana could be purchased cheap to fill the demand.

But for now, Daryl's business caused him to travel extensively, at least as far north as Winnipeg, Canada. Along the route of the Mississippi River, he'd made business contacts and friends all the way to Minnesota, then a booming US territory.

"Tabari, not every white man believes in slavery" Daryl stated.

"There's lottsa' folks who can't stomach the thought of a man being sold or traded, like he was just a piece of property".

Tabari's eyes began to water.

"I knows 'dat's true" he stated to them all, looking into their eyes to convey his genuine understanding. He then slowly glanced toward the women folk, knowing they were intensely listening to every word.

And they were. Having momentarily stopped their household chores to listen in on the conversation, they instantly began scurrying about, dusting, rearranging pillows, whatever chore they could do to act as if they hadn't just been caught in the act of eavesdropping.

Helen didn't care. She walked right up to the table, pulled out a chair and sat down behind Tabari.

"Mr. Hamilton knows what he's talkin' about" she told him.

"And all of these men, and us women included, we're all here to help you. We want to help you become a free man".

Tabari was overjoyed, but wouldn't abandon his promise to tell these decent folks about his prior escape attempt, and how Tom and Melba, the Jeffersons, and the preachers nearly lost everything when they tried to help him.

And so, he told them all. How the Doctor and Mr. Tolivar lied about the fire that burned the Doctor's house to the ground. His whipping by the Colonel. How he'd travelled by foot to N'awlins. The newspaper that Tom and Melba owned. How they'd taken him to Frank and Freda Jefferson, and eventually to the Chapel Cross Church. Being tied to the 'tree' and nearly taken for dead.

He told them everything.

The women no longer pretended to be preoccupied by their chores.

The stood or sat, mesmerized by Tabari's tales of travel from Africa, his escape from the plantation, his capture, and his determination to find freedom, or die trying.

The men looked at each other, no longer with sympathy for Tabari's horrific experiences, but with a set resolve to help this man fulfill his dream.

"Gentlemen" Daryl stated, looking at all but focusing on Max.

"I believe I have an idea. Give me a day or two to mull this over. Max, with your permission, I'd like us all to meet here in two days, say around two o'clock".

"That's fine" Max replied, then looking to his wife for confirmation.

Helen smiled affirmatively. Two of the other women slightly sobbed with joy.

"Agreed". "Yes". "Certainly" was the unanimous reply of the other men, all anxious to lend whatever assistance they could.

* * *

DARYL'S plan was brilliant in its simplicity, and equally dangerous in its execution. Take Tabari up river to Minnesota or, more specifically, to Minneapolis, as Daryl's personal valet. From there, travel into Canada, maybe toward Winnipeg. Who knows? So many intangibles could happen. Correction. *Would* happen.

Sounded so simple when Daryl and Max put their heads together to work out the details. Dress Tabari in gentlemen's fine clothes. Top hat, burgundy colored cravat (tie), vest, pocket watch with chain, the works.

No one would mistake him for a runaway. He'd simply be Daryl Hamilton's personal attendant. Carrying his impressive brief case, a pearl handled carpet bag, filled with important looking documents. For all intents and purposes, Tabari would be a sort of sophisticated 'step and fetch' that wealthy Louisiana men routinely brought along on business trips.

But Max and Daryl also had to consider that one pesky inconvenient fact: That Tabari *was* a runaway slave whose new owner might likely be searching for him this very instant.

Tabari was very clear to divulge everything that happened to him, including the fact that the Colonel sold him to one Mr. McKenzie which, of course, was the reason Tabari escaped.

"Damn!" Max almost shouted. "That damn fugitive slave act".

He looked at Daryl who, seconds earlier, had already begun pondering the same problem.

"Hmm … yes … that is a problem" Daryl reiterated the obvious.

There were many ways a man could violate the 'Act'. Some much more punishable then others.

One might simply remain silent about the known whereabouts of the runaway. Nothing too criminal there. Just keeping quiet. Not hiding anybody, not providing clothing or shelter. Just not telling.

Then again, other ways were much more felonious. Like giving food and comfort to the 'enemy'. Actively participating is his escape. Much more serious than merely keeping quiet. And the resulting punishment obviously greater.

But here, Daryl was taking many risks. He'd need some type of bill of sale. Something to prove that he did in fact own Tabari, should the need ever arise to prove such ownership.

This would be much akin to horse-stealin'. Taking property that you knew damn well didn't belong to you. That would take some real explaining to do.

Any bill of sale would be an outright lie. Daryl would have to make up the name of the 'seller', then forge his signature on the document. He'd have to make up a city where the sale took place. The document would have to be real legal looking, not just some handwritten scribbling on the back of a piece of paper.

And, of course, the sufficiency of the document would be dependent on the perceived authority of the person making the inquiry. If it was Mr. McKenzie, or one of his posse, no paper would suffice.

All of this was discussed between the two men, who became less and less convinced of the genius of their plan. The further they thought on it, the more depressed they got.

Daryl, particularly. He remembered Tabari's expression of hope when Daryl told him that he 'had an idea'. Now that expectation might be dashed.

Or would it?

"What if?" Daryl began thinking out loud.

"What if that McKenzie, or one of his men, did find Tabari with me?"

"You'd be caught red-handed, that's what".

"Would I, now? What if they did confront me? I'd simply show them the bill of sale. Then I'd say …

"Look gentlemen. This here is a bill of sale. Says right here I bought this slave from Mr. Sam … or whatever his name is. Bought him right in N'awlins. On August thirtieth. Says it right here!" as he forcefully pokes his finger at the phantom document.

"And I paid him two-thousand dollars. Cash!" as he shook the imaginary paper.

"You see Max! What are McKenzie's men gonna' say?

"They'd say 'No you didn't. This here slave's the property of Mr. McKenzie. He bought that nigger from some Colonel and he ran away. His name's Tabari'.

"So what?" Daryl continued. "I listen politely and eventually pretend to realize that I've been duped by that no good N'awlin's slave trader. He sold me someone he didn't own. I'm out some two-thousand dollars, I tell them.

"I act like I'm all mad and furious and swear I'm high-tailin' it right back there to get my money back and have that no good sonofabitch thrown in jail".

As Daryl's explanation began to wind down, Max's grin got wider and wider. Talk about a snake oil salesman. Max was fully convinced. It *was* brilliant in its simplicity. Well, at least this scenario.

They both knew the plan was extremely risky, but then any plan to help a fugitive escape to freedom would be inherently dangerous.

And so, the two met at Max Donovan's house with Tabari and the other men to lay out the blueprint of the strategy.

* * *

"DARYL, I think there's one thing you've left out" George Menard, Margo's husband, pointed out.

"You've regularly travelled up the Mississippi on business. There's alotta' folks that know you. What if one of them, say Millard Coffey for instance, is also travelin' on the boat at the same time as you and Tabari? He knows you're an abolitionist. He knows you don't own any slaves. How're you gonna' explain Tabari to him?"

"Good question" Daryl replied.

"Already thought about it. And you're right. It's possible that someone I know could spot me and Tabari together.

"The plan is to distance ourselves from such a possibility, as best we can. And that means leaving from, say, Fort Adams. That's a good five hours from here. And on a Sunday, as late as possible. Least chance that anyone from Baton Rouge, or any place nearby, will be travelin'".

George and the others looked concerned.

"Look" Max stated. "There's no easy way to do this" looking at Daryl.

"That's just one of, maybe a hundred, things that could go wrong" feeling his own concern that his good friend was taking on a risk that might prove devastating.

"I know all of that" Daryl said matter of factly. He became calm, almost spiritually reflective.

"I'm nearly sixty. The Mrs. and I have raised our children to be God fearin' good Christians. I've had a good life" he stated, then realized he may have sounded like he'd developed a defeatist attitude about the outcome of the plan.

"No gentlemen" he sought to reassure them. "I have no intent on snatching defeat from the jaws of victory" he chided, to a chorus of muffled laughter.

"What I'm saying is … what I'm acknowledging … is that I *want* to do this, risks and all. If we're successful … *if* …" he looked at Tabari to emphasize the uncertainty of a successful journey.

"Then I've made a small contribution to the cause. I know that getting one slave to freedom won't change the course of our Country. I understand that. But it's kinda' like … if not now, then when?"

The others all felt a certain bond had been created. A pledge to each other that each would do his part, however big or small, to assist in this act of kindness to another human being.

"I have a fine set of clothes that my wife, Rebecca, will be glad to tailor for him" offered one of the men.

"I don't have the money for the steamboat fares, but I'll give what I can" added another.

"I can cover much of the cost" offered a third man. "Why, I suspect Daryl here may actually make a profit" he teased.

"There's still much to do" Daryl reminded them.

"If we leave by next Sunday, and all goes well, Tabari and I should arrive near Minneapolis within two weeks or so. The ship's schedule will tell us that.

"From there, we'll travel to the Canadian border. We don't have to make Winnipeg, but Tabari will need at least a secure temporary place to stay, and I know several folks who'll be glad to help.

"Of course, it's possible that we'll find assistance just over the border. That'd be great. But we need a 'for sure' plan, just in case.

"Gentlemen, that's it in a nutshell. I can't think of anything else, for now.

"Tabari, God willin' and the creek don't rise, you'll be a free man soon enough!"

Tabari clasped his hands together as if in prayer.

"I dun' know what ta' say" his shaky voice whispered, tears welling in his eyes. "All I can say is thank you. God bless ya'all and thank you".

With that, the meeting adjourned.

24

THE DOCTOR WAS STILL miffed, having been respectfully requested to complete his residence stay at Mr. Tolivar's modest but comfortable abode, instead of the luxurious accommodations of the mansion.

The Colonel made the request three days ago after, once again, the Doctor embarrassed the Senator and his wife during the Winters' formal dinner, not to mention the Doctor's patient, Collette.

The conversation was blunt.

"Doctor" Trent began his justified reprimand as the Doctor was finishing the next morning's breakfast feast.

"I … don't know where to begin" he honestly stated.

"On the one hand, you've provided great assistance to my wife. And for that, I'm truly appreciative. Your medical support and care assured her full recovery.

"On the other hand, you've embarrassed my wife, Senator Harrison and his wife. Completely unacceptable!"

The Doctor knew he'd screwed up.

"Now, Colonel" he began his excuse.

"Rarely is the occasion when I indulge in alcohol in any form, except of course, for medicinal purposes" he lied.

"You can ask any of my colleagues ... or patients!" Of course, his offer meant nothing, as he had neither colleagues nor patients, other than Mrs. Winters.

Trent had lost his patience with the deceitful excuses. The very first time the Colonel met the Doctor, he'd personally witnessed him slam down multiple shots while amputating the leg of Gabe, one of his slaves.

He and Jeb had to carry him to his room before finishing that evening's dinner, the Doctor having become so smashed that he'd fallen off his chair and broken Collette's expensive vase.

In fact, Trent couldn't recall a time when the Doctor didn't smell of booze, except during breakfast when he was recovering from the night before.

"I've never been inebriated a day in my life!" the Doctor continued. "The appearance of such, the other night, was the result of a cold flu I had. The alcohol obviously exacerbated my symptoms" he went on.

Trent was incredulous. He hadn't even yet told the Doctor *why* he was being evicted from the mansion, yet here he was, defending himself against his drunkenness.

"Doctor, Doctor, enough! I'm in no mood to argue.

"Again, I'm grateful to you. But the fact is, you have one patient here. Mrs. Winters.

"When the Senator and I have to pick you up off the floor, like we did last night, well, I'm just beside myself, sir. Collette, my wife ... your *only* patient ... watched in horror as you passed out in front of our guests. Her own doctor!

"Understand. I'd like you to stay on for a few more days. Mrs. Winters is healing nicely, but Amana still needs attention. Based upon the circumstances, I'd simply prefer that you stayed at Mr. Tolivar's residence".

The Doctor stared at the floor. Even he couldn't come up with an argument that would convince the Colonel that his eyewitness account had been mistakenly interpreted.

"Colonel, I understand" he regretfully admitted. "Although I haven't been inebriated a day in my life" … he stopped. "I recognize that my delight in your wife's recovery, and that of Amana, may have contributed to more merriment than would otherwise have been expected".

"Did he just say that I'm punishing him for celebrating my wife's recovery?" Trent dubiously asked himself.

Confusion, misdirection, deflection. The Doctor was good at all three. But not enough this time to convince Trent that he was the bad guy here.

* * *

TRENT met him at the mansion's front door. The Doctor knew it was time to go, and decided it best to initiate the farewell before he was asked to leave.

"Colonel" he began. "I know that Mrs. Winters will be just fine. Amana's ankle is healing well, and she should recover nicely.

"And so, with your permission, I'll be taking my leave now" as he admired his three luggage bags, packed and ready to go, examples of even more 'gifts' via the generosity of Colonel Trent Winters.

"Of course, should the need arise, I'm always available at a moment's notice to return".

"Why, that's much appreciated Doctor. And yes, I agree, the Misses and Amana are doing fine now, thanks in no small part to your medical skills" he added, thinking there was no harm in extending a courtesy compliment, even though it was an exaggeration.

The Doctor reached for one of the luggage bags, then looked helpless as he stared at his buck wagon.

"Oh, here! Let me give you a hand" as Trent gathered the two additional bags and placed them in the back of the wagon.

Trent dreaded the next anticipated topic.

"And, by the way" the Doctor started. "My new home's about finished. Your construction engineer, Brock, has done a marvelous job. And quickly too, I might add".

Trent couldn't muster an immediate reply, still fuming about his out-of-pocket costs in rebuilding the Doctor's house, providing food and lodging in a luxurious hotel, new clothes, and now the piece de resistance.

"Furniture. Now, I'm a man of my word, Colonel" he lied again. "I've promised to keep the costs down, and that's exactly what I'll do. I won't be replacin' any furniture except what I lost in the fire. And it won't be of any better quality, I can assure you of that".

Trent had plenty good cause to believe the Doctor was fleecing him.

Supervising the construction, Brock had pointed out that the charred wood cleared from the Doctor's lot wasn't nearly enough to constitute a two story house. But the Doctor had represented, matter of factly, that that's what he had before the Colonel's slave caused it to burn to the ground.

Mr. Tolivar was of no help. He'd told the Colonel that he'd arrived at the Doctor's home after dark, and hadn't noticed whether it was a one or two story structure, let alone the amount and type of furniture inside. He'd been in awful pain, the result of having broken his arm while protecting Mrs. Winters from the lynch mob on their way to New Orleans. Most of what he'd remembered was the fire, and that Tabari had accidentally started it.

Trent couldn't bring himself to further interrogate Tolivar. He was eternally grateful to him for saving Collette's life from that gang, and risking his own in the process.

No, the Doctor had him over a barrel. How could Trent retaliate against the man who'd sewed up his wife's leg, saw to it that the scar tissue brought on by the 'gata's bite was nearly invisible, and overall brought her back to health?

Not to mention Amana. She too needed stitching, immobilization of her broken ankle, and enough 'doctoring' to restore her well-being.

Besides, he'd given his solemn word that the Doctor would be fully compensated for his loss. Losses caused by Trent's own slave. A slave who'd run away twice and was still on the loose. Too many intertwined events had occurred to renege on his gentleman's promise, as hard as it was to swallow.

"Doctor, I trust your ... honesty" Trent replied, the last word sticking in his craw.

"I'm sure you'll do the right thing. Replace what's been lost. It's only fair.

"Other than that, I believe you've performed your services ... admirably. I wish you a safe trip back to N'awlins".

"Good enough" the Doctor thought. Hell, even Mrs. Winters had offered him her genuine thanks. Several times.

"Well Colonel. I bid you adieu".

Trent shook his head slowly as he watched the Doctor steer the buck board away.

"This must be the last time" he vowed to himself. "I've got to get to N'awlins and find a real doctor". He jogged up the steps to look in on Collette.

25

THE TICKETS WERE PURCHASED. Daryl Hamilton and Tabari were about to embark on their journey to Canada, with many stops and diversions in between. Some planned, most not.

They'd leave from Fort Adams, as hoped, but not on a Sunday night like they'd planned. The latest departure was seven at night, on Tuesday. The sun didn't set until almost nine o'clock, so their very first 'plan' of leaving under the cloud of darkness wasn't met.

Oh, well. In the grand scheme of their universal objectives, this unexpected change in plans was small potatoes. They had much bigger fish to fry.

On the bright side, Tabari looked magnificent. If ever there was a negroe 'personal valet', he was fit for the part. Three-piece suit, personally tailored by one 'Miss Rebecca', gold watch and chain donated by Daryl's friend, and shiny dress boots given by another.

A tall silk top hat finished the ensemble.

Max's carriage ride delivered them to the Fort Adams landing, arriving a good two hours before departure. The plan was simple, but strict. They'd need to stick to their roles, without diversion.

They'd rehearsed it numerous times, with many participants playing different parts. Their goal was to identify every conceivable contingency that might be encountered, and play out the scene, giving both Daryl and Tabari confidence that they'd be prepared to safely react.

That included the possibility that one of Daryl's acquaintances would recognize him along the way, knowing that he'd never owned any slaves and that Tabari's accompaniment must be false.

Perhaps a violation of the Fugitive Slave Act.

"Why, if it isn't Daryl. Daryl Hamilton! How are you my friend?" one of the male protagonists asked as they secretly rehearsed a scene.

"And who is that handsome negroe with you?"

Daryl's whole body tensed as he quickly grasped the importance of this rehearsal. Had there been no trial run, and this scene was playing out for real, he'd have stuttered out some drivel that would've obviously given their true intentions away, and possibly set the stage for the unwanted visitor to contact the Sheriff at the next port.

"This, my friend, is Lazarus. My dear brother, James, sent him to assist me on a lumber business deal we're working on.

"It's quite a business opportunity" he whispered to his role player, leaning in to deliver the story in a confidential and animated explanation.

Daryl continued with his enthusiastic explanation as he regaled his 'friend' with just enough details of the trade venture to divert his interest in questioning him about his negroe companion.

Before long, the 'friend' was so curious about the lucrative potential of the lumber deal that the thought of a negroe valet seemed completely unimportant. It appeared as a perfectly natural relationship needed to carry out the many tasks needed in such a business excursion.

Particularly since 'Lazarus' was simply on loan from Daryl's brother, ipso facto a slave owner himself.

"Good, Daryl. Very good, Tabari" Max and the others smiled as they praised the two men.

Tabari was fully grinning as both intuitively felt the naturalness, and necessity, of acting out such a perfectly acceptable explanation.

And so the rehearsals continued, until every possibility had been summoned forth and then fully exhausted.

* * *

WELL, not *every* possibility.

Tabari faithfully followed his orders to remain in the boat's cabin, only exiting to relieve himself and then, only when the normally crowded deck was as empty as possible. He ate, slept and stayed in his room, never wavering from this necessary regiment.

The men's lavatory was on the below deck. Some of the wealthier travelers had their own bathroom, but the '*Grand Princess*' steamboat was old, as steamboats go, and their last minute ticket purchase left them with one of the only remaining cabins available.

Still, pleasant accommodations nonetheless.

'Deck passengers' had no pleasant lodging. Their fares were a fraction of the tickets paid by the 'upper deck' travelers. The large dining room, restaurant, and gambling saloon enjoyed by the wealthier patrons were off limits.

The 'low deckers' could travel for as much as a quarter of a penny per mile, sometimes less, depending on the amount of space available after the cargo and livestock were brought on board.

In fact, they lived with the livestock and among the cotton bales, barrels, and other crates that made the bulk of profit for the steamboat's owners. Passenger fares were almost an afterthought.

The 'low deckers' basically lived outside, exposed to rain, wind and cold. They slept mostly on the cotton bales, hopefully one that rested against a cargo crate piled higher, so there was some protection against the elements.

Cheap transportation certainly, but a palatable way to travel west, or north, hopefully to a better life and sometimes a new beginning.

Having averaged about five miles per hour steamboat time, the Grand Princess would arrive in Cape Girardeau, Missouri by morning.

* * *

"MISSER' Daryl! Misser' Daryl, I's jus' gotta' go!" Tabari whispered and half yelled as he hopped back and forth, desperately needing to pee.

"I's so sorry" as he cupped his crotch, his face straining to control his bladder.

They were both dressed in their pajamas. Daryl knew Tabari couldn't wait long enough for them to both change into their business attire disguises.

"Alright, Alright! Hold your water, man. Let me make sure the coast is clear" Daryl instructed.

He cracked open the cabin door and looked down the walkway. Not a soul present.

"Come on, now. Follow me".

Daryl leading the way, the two tippy-toed toward the stairs leading down to the deck.

"Damn!" Daryl grunted. "My room key. I left it in the cabin".

He turned to retrieve it, but then saw Tabari's contorted expression, still hopping back and forth, pleading to get to the men's room before his bladder burst.

As they walked down the hallway, two obviously intoxicated young men approached, stumbling back and forth as they made their way toward them. Tabari and Daryl leaned their backs against the wet wall to avoid being bumped into.

"Hey old man!" one of the lads called back and yelled to Daryl. "Where ya'all goin' with yer nigger?" he laughed.

"Yea!" hollered the other. "What's yer hurry?"

"Ignore them" Daryl said. "We don't need any trouble.

"It's slippery" Daryl warned as they began descending the steps, the guard rails wet and slick.

Daryl stopped mid-way. He could see a gathering of deck passengers, twenty or thirty, obviously enjoying an impromptu party under one of the lamps that created a festive ambiance.

Many were dancing to the up tempo music being played with an accordion. Nearly all were enjoying some inebriation, some singing, some clapping, and all having quite the merry time.

Except one. A little girl of five or so. No other children were in attendance, their parents having put them to bed long ago.

A petite girl, with blonde hair and wearing the prettiest white dress her parents could afford. She'd danced with her father, being slowly twirled about until he gently dipped her, then playfully laid her on the deck as the crowd watched and cheered their delightful waltz. Her mother had clapped the loudest, admiring her precious little girl and the genuine love her husband shared for their child.

But that was an hour ago. She'd since become bored with the grown-ups' conversations, and began to unconsciously wander slowly away, fascinated by the fire flies blinking on and off along the shoreline.

Her parents were momentarily oblivious to the child's drifting, instead allowing their full enjoyment of the festivities to occupy all of their thoughts.

The girl placed her hands on top of the upper pipe railing, then stepped onto the lower railing with first one, then the other foot.

Barefoot. First her left foot slipped, then her right hand. The wet railings and her weight was too much for her handgrip to hold on. She fell to the deck, the steamboat listing slightly downward as the weight of the livestock and cargo hadn't been evenly distributed.

As they reached the next to last step of the stairs, Tabari saw her slide the foot or so to the edge and then disappear.

He momentarily froze, dumbstruck with fear. Did anyone else just witness this? Did her parents see this?

With terrified eyes, he looked at Daryl for help. He hadn't seen it. He'd just stepped off the last stair and was about to turn right to the men's lavatory.

It was as if Tabari's mind suddenly split in two.

"Will dis' end my escape?" he screamed to himself as he made a mad dash to the spot where the girl went overboard.

"All 'da plans, all 'da rehearsals … is dis' what I gets?" he cursed to himself as he felt his feet leave the deck and his body hurl through the cool night air and into the cold water.

Daryl looked back to see where Tabari was. He hadn't seen what happened.

"Jesus!" a man screamed as he jumped off a cotton bale and pointed to the spot.

"Help me! Help me!" he hollered as he rushed to the railing, looking to the water swirling at the back of the paddle wheels.

"Oh my God!" screamed the girl's mother, as she frantically sought her daughter's whereabouts, the unthinkable now becoming a surreal reality.

"William! Oh, William" she wailed, as her husband yanked off his shoes and prepared to dive in.

"Sir, don't do it!" a man yelled. "Someone already dove in after her!"

The terrified husband looked at the man, wishing there was a way out. He then looked at his wife, her face contorted in pain, not wanting to lose her husband but unable to tell him not to save their daughter.

He dove in.

"I'll get the Captain" someone hollered, then ran toward the wheelhouse.

Tabari's only focus was to keep swimming as hard and fast as he could. No thoughts of losing his freedom, of having his prayers dashed.

He stopped, and treaded water while he franticly inhaled as much air as he could, scouring the river's surface for any sign of the child.

"Young'un! Young'un!" he screamed, desperately listening for any sound, looking for any movement, so he'd know which way to keep swimming. As he bobbed up and down, he saw the lights from the steamboat in a straight line, slowly sailing away from him and the little girl.

"Is 'dis how I's gonna' die too?" he pondered in despair, as he swallowed a large gulp of water. He knew there would only be a moment or two left before the river covered the girl for good.

But as he watched the ship steam away, the moonlight's gleam on the surface illuminated something white, bobbing up and down with the rhythmic motion of the water.

Tabari fervently swam toward the object, desperately wanting to believe it wasn't just some trash or log floating aimlessly.

He stopped within an arm's reach.

It was the girl! Face up, floating in her white cotton dress, arms stretched out, motionless, her legs dangling down.

"Oh, baby girl! Sweet angel!" he said softly as he gently put his arm around her neck.

To his utter amazement, she calmly replied back.

"I can swim. I can swim, you know".

"Yes 'em. Yous' sure 'nuf can" he answered, breathing hard as the two smiled at each other.

Tabari stopped treading and began to slowly kick his legs and paddle with his free arm. But which way? To which shore? Both were far away, as the boat was in the middle of the river when the child fell overboard.

"They're coming back" the child stated matter of factly. "Look! They're coming back".

Sure enough, Tabari saw the ship's lights begin to move clockwise, making a wide right turn.

"Goddamn 'low deckers'" the Captain had grumbled when told that one of the 'lower deck' passengers had fallen overboard.

"They got no common sense. Shouldn't even be on a boat. There should be a no alcohol policy for those folks" he fumed.

"This here back-trackin' will cost me a cord of wood to keep that damn boiler hot!"

Tabari's adrenalin rush had stopped. He was thankful he didn't have to make the swim to the distant shore, but just treading water made him begin to shiver. He held the girl tight to him to maximize body heat.

"What's yer' name?" he asked, both out of curiosity and to keep her from panicking.

"Lisa. My names Lisa, and I'm five years old".

"Well, Lisa. I's glad to meet you" as they both chuckled.

After what seemed an eternity, the *Grand Princess* slowed and came within earshot.

"Are you alright? Are you both alright?" a crewman hollered.

"Yes, sir. We's both fine" Tabari hollered back.

There was no lifeboat, no rowboat on board. The Captain brought the big boat to a stop, a rope was slowly lowered. First Lisa, then Tabari, were hauled on board.

"Oh my baby! Oh my baby!" Lisa's mother cried as she dropped to her knees and wrapped a blanket around the shivering little girl.

A small army of women nearly tripped over each other, attempting to comfort both child and mother.

A gathering of men stood in a semi-circle, staring at Tabari, dripping wet, as Daryl put a blanket across his shoulders. Tabari gave his friend a half-grin, shaking from the cold and wet but very much glad to be alive. His grin quickly ended, as he saw the panic in Daryl's eyes as these men began to examine them both.

A middle aged well-dressed gentleman stepped forward and, with a stern look, faced them directly. They knew they had cause to fear the worst. This was one of those 'possibilities' they hadn't considered. Or rehearsed.

"Sir, let me shake your hand!" the gentleman requested as he held his hand out toward Tabari. "That's the bravest thing I've ever seen!"

Tabari looked nervously at Daryl, then extended his hand. The gentleman grasped it with both of his and vigorously shook, his smile revealing a full set of teeth, his face nodding up and down in genuine delight.

Two of the women had helped lift Lisa into another woman's arms, and four or five of them whisked her away to a warm and safe cabin on the upper deck.

Now, her mother sat on the deck, still shaking and exhausted from the ordeal.

A crew member joined the women, and kneeled next to Lisa's mom. A private, whispered, discussion ensued. Then silence.

The mother then began to wail, a blood curling cry and gnashing of teeth that only comes from a soul when a beloved husband and father dies young, unexpectedly and tragically.

Several women knelt down beside Lisa's mother, consoling her over the loss of her husband, after they'd learned from the crew member that they couldn't find his body in the river.

She looked at the crewman, tears streaming down her cheeks as she pleaded that the Captain continue the search.

He fought to find the words.

"Ma'am, it's just too dark, and too much time's passed" was the best he could offer. He knew the Captain wouldn't budge. The heartless bastard.

He'd already pleaded with him.

"No, goddamnit!" the Captain shouted back. "That'd cost me another cord of wood to heat my boiler. The river takes many lives. The river don't care. Why should I?"

* * *

"LOOKING good, Tabari" Daryl complimented him as he watched him carefully put on his top hat, completing his wardrobe attire.

"We've got to change boats this morning. The *Grand Princess* is headin' back to N'awlins.

Tabari was clearly worried. The last time he left the cabin nearly cost him his life.

"It's alright" Daryl tried to reassure him. "We'll step off, grab some coffee, and sit a spell on the other side of that hill. We'll just wait there 'til the new steamboat arrives later this morning. Nothin' to worry about".

A crowd of passengers was causing a bottleneck at the boat's exit platform.

"Hmm ... what's this about?" Daryl whispered.

"I's don't know" Tabari replied.

"Come on, move along. Keep moving!" the Captain hollered, trying to disembark his passengers as quickly as possible. He needed to unload all cargo and then restock with new freight and passengers to begin his trip back down river.

They were sardined in, bodies leaning against each other as the crowd pushed forward ever so slowly toward the exit.

Finally, it was their turn to step off.

"Just a moment" snarled a middle aged man, short and rotund, wearing a white cowboy hat. "I need to have a word with you" he ordered, motioning for Daryl and Tabari to step to the side on dry land.

Daryl instantly noticed the badge pinned to his shirt. A lawman. A Sheriff Deputy, accompanied by a tall, lanky officer.

"Shit!" Daryl groaned silently. He looked at Tabari and, with unspoken words, told him to keep quiet. They'd rehearsed this possible scene many times.

"We're checking for illegal contraband" the Deputy stated, suspiciously eyeballing Tabari from head to toe.

"As in runaway niggers" his companion sarcastically added.

Daryl straightened his back and stood tall as he could, then stuck both thumbs inside his vest pockets, exposing his gold watch chain to display his obvious social prominence.

"Well, gentleman. I have a great respect for the law" he mostly lied as he consciously tried to convey an air of superiority.

"How can I be of help?" he asked, knowing they would want written proof that he owned Tabari.

"Well, let's see your papers".

"Papers?" Daryl replied, as innocently as possible.

"Yea. The papers showin' you own this nigger" the taller officer snarled.

Daryl smiled. "Why of course, Deputy. You must mean the *bill of sale*". He accented the last three words, condescendingly educating the Deputy on the correct use of legal terminology.

Daryl's confidence showed, as this was one of the very first rehearsals they'd practiced, in case one of Master McKenzie's men confronted him about Tabari.

In preparation, Max, Daryl and the others had drawn up a very legal looking document, signed by a made-up slave trader, one Sam Thomas, showing that Daryl had purchased 'Lazarus' (Tabari) for two thousand dollars on August 29, 1852 in New Orleans.

"Good thinking" Daryl smiled to himself. Although the bill of sale was prepared to rebut a confrontation with one of McKenzie's men, its purpose would now suffice perfectly to thwart the clash from this Sheriff's Deputy.

"The papers are right here" as he assuredly reached into his vest pocket.

He stopped as his fingers felt the pocket empty. His blood pressure began to rise.

He reached into his other vest pocket.

Nothing. He began to sweat profusely.

"I ... I" he mumbled, as he frantically reached into all of his pockets, one by one.

"My wallet! My wallet! Where's my wallet?"

Panicked, he looked to Tabari to see if there was anything he could offer. Tabari could only divert his eyes, and stared at the ground.

"Those thugs! Those two drunks" he mumbled out loud.

The two Deputies smirked at each other, then at Daryl, thinking to themselves that maybe they'd caught their man.

"Deputies" Daryl began to stutter. "Last night, my ... personal assistant" as he looked to acknowledge Tabari.

"We'd left our cabin, momentarily, and were walking to the men's room when two drunken passengers stumbled our way. I didn't have my room key. I didn't lock the door. Those two musta' entered our room and stole my papers. And my wallet! Look, my wallet's gone! All my moneys gone!" he stammered as he opened his vest to reveal his empty pockets.

The Deputies continued to smirk, enjoying the panicked and pathetic look their suspect was conveying.

"Well, well now" the taller one began. "Let's see here. What we've got is a darkie, travelin' with a stranger in these parts, up the Mississippi, without any papers. Now, don't you think that looks a little suspicious?" as asked sarcastically.

"It's not suspicious at all!" Daryl argued, still patting his pockets in desperation to find the missing paper.

"I've already told you! Two thugs musta' stolen it. And my wallet!"

"Well sir, that may be. And maybe it ain't that way at all. This is Missouri, my friend. And in Missouri, a black man's presumed to be a runaway 'lest he has papers to show otherwise. That's the law".

Daryl was beside himself. He'd had the proof, even though the bill of sale was impersonated. But the Deputies wouldn't know that. But those damn thieves! Because of them, he didn't have the proof.

Daryl looked pleadingly at the rotund lawman. He seemed less of a hard ass than the taller one, although not by much.

"Mister, we're takin' your boy with us" the lankier Deputy stated. "Now, if'n you can come up with the proper papers, you can come by the Sheriff's office and we'll have more to talk about".

Daryl felt like an animal trapped in a corner. His hands involuntarily clenched into fists, but he quickly relaxed, knowing that an aggressive move would find them both in jail.

Tabari was beginning to shake, sweating profusely. Starting to panic, he looked every which way for the easiest path to start running, but knew it'd be futile. He'd tried that before on his previous escape attempt.

"Stand still, just stand still" he convinced himself. "Mister Daryl will figure somethin' out".

The shorter lawman motioned for his partner to step to the side to speak in private.

"Look, Barry. We don't have any space to house this nigger" he whispered.

"What are you suggestin'? We just let 'em both go their way?"

"No, no". He looked back at Daryl, recognizing that he and Tabari were dressed much finer than a runaway and white abolitionist would normally be. He took this into consideration, not wanting to jeopardize his career if Daryl turned out to be a wealthy businessman with contacts in high places.

"These two are obviously well-heeled" he pointed out. "Look at how the nigger's dressed. He's ain't no field slave. What if he does have proper papers, and knows men in high places? I don't want no trouble with the mayor or anyone else. I like my job too much.

"So, what are you suggestin'?"

"Keep your voice down" as he looked back at Daryl.

"We'll tell him to find his papers, and bring the darkie to our office tomorrow morning".

"What?" the lanky one almost shouted. "I don't agree. Let's take 'em both with us. Right now!"

"For Christ sake! Lower your voice" he ordered.

"How long you been a lawman?" the short one asked.

"You know damn well. Two years".

"And how long for me? Ten years. Ten years, cousin Barry. And I'm tellin' you. One … there's no room in the jail cells. And two … I'm not riskin' bein' wrong about this fella'. Runaways and runaway 'conductors' don't dress that fancy. Most likely, he *is* his property. If so, he can bring a heap of trouble on us. No, you're gonna' do as I say, *cousin* Barry".

He walked back to Daryl, who'd been nervously pawing the dirt with his shoe, anxious to learn the Deputies' verdict.

"Well sir, here's what I'm willin' to do" the rotund one began. "I'm gonna' give y'all a chance to prove that this here's your property. As my partner said, Missouri requires that a black man has gotta' always have papers in his possession. Always.

"For whatever reason, you ain't got 'em. And I understand you think you've got a good excuse. But I need proof.

"So, bring your man to my office tomorrow morning, along with your proof. If you ain't got it, then you can fill out an affidavit, under penalty of perjury, attestin' that he's your property".

"Tomorrow morning?" Daryl protested. "We're leavin' on a boat in two hours!"

"Can't help ya' there" the Deputy replied. "Besides, you couldn't get to my office, and back here, in two hours. That's the best I can do. You want the alternative?" he sarcastically asked, meaning that Daryl and Tabari could be escorted to a jail right then and there.

"I … I …"

The Deputy had him over a barrel.

"So, let me get this straight" Daryl tried to fight back his anger.

"I've got to get a hotel room. One that'll accept a negroe.

"Yup".

"Then get to your office tomorrow morning. Sign an affidavit".

"Yup".

"Then figure out when I can get two more tickets for a steamboat?"

"Looks that way".

"How am I gonna' buy two more tickets when all my moneys been stolen?"

"I saw you're sportin' a nice gold watch" the smaller one answered. That otta' buy you your tickets".

Both Deputies then tipped their hats, turned and walked away as they chuckled.

* * *

"WHAT we gonna' do, Mister Daryl?" Tabari asked, nearly in a panic.

Daryl didn't immediately respond. Too deep in thought.

"Tabari, this is all gettin' too hot" he finally replied.

"The little girl almost drownin', her father dying, our papers bein' stolen, and now the law's breathin' down our necks".

He looked serious at Tabari.

"Remember how we all discussed that plans could change at a moment's notice?"

Tabari nervously nodded.

"Well, our plans are a changin'.

"If we stay here tonight, there's more chance we'll run into trouble. If we go to the Sheriff's office in the morning', there's even more chance we'll be in trouble. No".

"Whadda' we do?"

"Illinois!" Daryl thought out loud.

"Illinois? 'Dat's another state".

"Yes. But it's a free state. A free state, Tabari!

"And guess what? It's right across the river. It's right there!" as he pointed east.

Tabari looked to the other side. How could it be? How can one side of the river be a slave state, but the other side a free state? There's no markers, no boundary lines, no fences or walls. How do white folks make these rules? His confusion was palpable as he thought these things.

"How does we get ta' 'da 'udder side?" he asked.

Daryl was pondering the answer before Tabari asked the question.

The river was full of working boats. Sailing ships, steamers, fishing boats, small row boats. This wouldn't be a problem. He watched two ferries that appeared to be carrying passengers, cargo and livestock to and from Cape Girardeau and the other side.

Daryl couldn't see clearly to the other side, the river being quite wide at this point and the sky overcast. No town was present. The Illinois landing appeared to be vacant land, with maybe some shacks built along the shore and some livestock pens.

"Follow me" Daryl gently ordered.

They walked over to another landing, a short distance from the *Grand Princess*.

"Hello sir" Daryl addressed a young man who appeared to be in charge of a small tugboat type vessel, loaded with cattle and sheep on a flat deck.

"Yes, sir. What can I do for you?" he asked as he concentrated intently on a scratch pad, most likely an inventory list.

"Well, me and my 'valet' here would like to board your vessel to take us across river" he answered, looking at Tabari to acknowledge his well-dressed companion.

The kid continued to scribble on his paper.

171

"We don't take passengers" he stated matter of factly. "This here tug's only for livestock" he replied, still not looking at them.

Tabari leaned in toward Daryl's ear.

"How's we gonna' pay for fare?" he whispered. "Yer' money's all been stolen".

Daryl gave him a dismissive look and spoke again to the young lad.

"I understand" he continued. "But it's very important that my companion and I reach the other side. We have important business in Clear Creek Landing".

"Clear Creek? Why, you must mean McClure. Thar' ain't nothin' thar', 'cept a post office" the lad pointed out, for the first time looking up at Daryl and seeing him and Tabari, duly impressed that they were dressed like wealthy gentlemen.

"I understand, son" Daryl stated, anxious to persuade the youngster to take them on as passengers.

"My business *is* livestock. Well, livestock and cotton" he lied. "We simply need a ride to the other side. That's all. I know you need payment. I can assure you, money's not an issue" he said, waiting for the boy's reaction.

The young man smiled, the thought of making some unexpected cash a pleasant surprise, enough to lessen his arduous work and the constant smell of animal dung.

He looked around, making certain his boss was nowhere in sight. 'Boss man' would either forbid taking any passengers, or pocket the fare himself.

"Well, alright" the youth whispered. "It'll be one dollar apiece. And there ain't no seats. You gotta' stand up the whole way". He nervously looked to see Daryl's reaction to the overpriced fare.

"Deal!" he exclaimed.

He reached into one of the luggage pieces, retrieved a small 'buck' knife, took off his jacket, and gingerly cut the thread that Miss Rebecca had sewn to conceal a secret lining.

"Here you are, sir" as he handed the boy two dollars, then slowly turned to Tabari and secretively gave him a wink and a smile.

It was all Tabari could do to disguise his own smile. "Lost all yer' money, eh?" he chuckled to himself. He remembered the discussion during their rehearsals about bringing along some concealed money. Just in case.

26

AFTER COLLETTE'S 'SURPRISE' DINNER was concluded, the Senator and Trent had excused themselves and retired to Trent's den, brandies and cigars in hand. As Amana helped Sadie clear the table and wash dishes, Collette and Caroline adjourned to the parlor, their favorite 'fruit juices' in hand.

Caroline seated herself on one of the luxurious sofas, and patted the space next to her, inviting Collette to join.

Collette took another sip, then noticed Caroline's loving and focused smile, looking deeply into Collette's eyes.

She felt Collette's uneasiness, and looked away.

She then broke the uncomfortable silence.

"My, I don't think I've ever been so touched as when I listened to your story. At the dinner table tonight.

"Hearing how that terrible 'gata … almost …" she fought back her tears.

Collette gently grasped her hand.

"You know? It *was* hard to relive that experience" she reflected.

"But now that I've told the story, it no longer has the power over me that it once did".

Caroline listened intently, her loving smile returning.

"And Amana! Just incredible how that girl jumped into the water to save your life! Just amazing!"

Once again, Collette's relationship with Amana welled up. Although she'd pushed most negative thoughts to the side, suddenly she almost desperately needed to confide in someone. She forced herself to refocus.

"Yes. Oh my, yes. I've told Amana, if the roles had been reversed, I'm pretty sure I couldn't have done what she did. I'm too much of a 'scaredy-cat'".

Caroline uncontrollably giggled, a tacit admission that she too would've been too afraid.

"She looked beautiful in that dress. It was very kind of you to let her wear it. I could see how wonderful she felt".

Collette stared at the wall and took a long sip.

Moments passed.

"Collette. Are you alright?"

She let out a deep sigh, then took another long sip. She turned and looked Caroline intently in the eyes.

"Caroline, I want to tell you something. But I'm too ... 'tormented'. I suppose that's as good a word as any".

"Tormented?"

"Yes. Oh God! I've just got to tell someone!" she whispered loudly.

Like Jeb, like any of us, the incessant thoughts that we keep secret can burden our minds to the point of disease, unless the cause is confronted and then shared with another soul.

"Several weeks ago ... I think several weeks ago ... I seem to have lost track of time". She looked at both parlor doors to confirm no one else was within ear shot.

"I think Trent's had an affair. With Amana!" she blurted out.

"There! I've said it!" she screamed to herself, then took another long sip.

Caroline just stared into her eyes, jaw dropped.

"Trent?" she stammered back. "Your Trent? With Amana?" she whispered in disbelief. She took a long sip.

"I ... I think so. I've thought so for a long time. While I was away" she guiltily looked at Caroline. "With you. I think it happened then".

Caroline stared at the floor, not able to focus on two intimate scenes at the same time. Trent with Amana? She'd never conceived such a thing could be possible. How could he betray her beloved friend? His own wife? With one of his own slaves for Christ sake? Impossible!

But what of Collette's own affair? With her? What was the difference? An affair is an affair, regardless of the responsible party. Or is it?

"Collette, calm down. Are you sure? Are you sure of this?" she quietly asked, unable to answer her own conflicting questions.

"Mostly. Oh my Lord, Caroline. There's just too many coincidences that point to it.

"I saw Trent's hair on Amana's bed sheets. I smelled my perfume on those same sheets. My own perfume!" she stammered, the corners of her mouth trembling.

Caroline tried to envision how hair and perfume could equal an affair.

"Could there be another explanation?" she asked.

More silence, as Caroline stared at Collette, who gazed off into space.

"There can. I've told myself a hundred times. Amana dropped her bedsheets on the floor. She was gathering things up to wash. It's possible that static electricity simply attached one of Trent's hairs to the sheets. It's certainly possible" she acknowledged.

Caroline waited for an explanation of the perfume.

"I ... actually confronted Amana about it. Not the 'hair'. That seemed silly. But she confessed to going into my bedroom and spraying my

176

perfume on herself. She knew it was wrong, but she admitted it and asked for my forgiveness".

Caroline listened intently.

"That's it?" she asked, almost incredulously. "Caroline, please share with me. There must be more to it than that. That's not enough to believe that Trent had an affair. Surely there's ..."

"There *is* more. A lot more.

"So many times, I've caught Trent ogling Amana from a distance. At breakfast one morning, I watched him. He was so ... focused ... on staring at her backside, he couldn't raise his fork to eat his eggs! I thought he was going to choke when he glanced over and saw me watching! Oh, God, Caroline. I could go on and on". She reached for the carafe to pour another drink.

Caroline listened, and thought. Then thought some more. She remembered how Collette had revealed her lack of interest in having sex with her husband. She knew Collette still had an interest in *some* physical intimacy. She knew that from personal experience.

But there was much more here, below the surface. If she truly had no interest for her husband, then why would his having an affair be of concern? Why not just go about your normal business, being a devoted housewife and homemaker? There was no question they still loved and supported each other. There was so much to lose. Their wonderful mansion. And the money. Oh, the money. Enough to live an incredible life.

Jealousy was the obvious answer, but a convoluted one. 'Intimacy' can take many forms, both physical and non.

That her husband would share his deepest secrets and emotions with another woman would certainly be cause for righteous jealousy. Certain topics should be faithfully reserved between husband and wife, not a relative stranger. They should be held inviolate, a confiding trust that mustn't be abridged.

But that's not what invaded Collette's mind. She hadn't even thought about Trent sharing secrets with another woman. No, it was the physical act that tortured her.

But to withhold sex from a spouse, purely the result of disinterest, certainly places a different twist on the emotion of jealousy.

Caroline pondered all this, but still couldn't form a cohesive response. Her situation was similar, yet different. It was she who wanted intimacy with her husband. He was the disinterested party. Was she wrong to seek pleasure in another, even of the same sex? Would her own husband have the right to be jealous?

"Collette, let's slow down" she whispered, taking Collette's hand in hers.

"I don't know how to say this, so I'll just start. You told me before that you weren't interested in … intimacy … with Trent. Is that right?"

Collette took another sip, then hiccupped as she wiped a tear away, her eyes twitching from anxiety.

"Yes. I did tell you that" she confided again. "And I told you that I love him dearly. I still do. It's just that I don't have the … desire … that I once had. You know, before my baby boy died and … the miscarriage" she blurted out these painful memories as her sobbing increased.

"It really isn't fair then, is it?"

"What do you mean?" Caroline asked.

"That Trent should have to go through the rest of his life without … what most men desire … physical intimacy" she answered.

Caroline didn't know how to respond, again realizing the same scenario could be asked of her. Should she go throughout life without sex because her husband wasn't interested?

And Collette wasn't just a 'relative stranger'. She was her best friend, the one person she'd shared her deepest secrets and emotions with. If Jeb ever found out, he'd certainly be justified to feel jealousy. Perhaps not because of the physical infidelity, although that question was still unresolved by their discussion.

But surely the intimate sharing of thoughts and emotions that are sacred between a husband and wife.

"I know the same can be asked of you and me" Caroline finally responded.

Collette waited for more explanation.

"You just said it wasn't fair. That Trent should have to go through life without sex" she whispered.

"Well, what about you and me? Is it fair that I can't find happiness because my husband isn't interested in me? That I'm not allowed intimacy?" she asked herself out loud as she stared into her glass.

"And the same goes for you" she whispered, leaning in toward Collette's face.

"I know ... from personal experience ... that you have desires" she went on.

Collette looked afraid.

"Oh, I'm not talking about just you and me, silly. It could be anyone. I'm simply saying that we're all human beings. We all have needs. It's not a matter of right or wrong. It's a matter of ... 'life, liberty, and the pursuit of happiness'" she giggled, holding her glass high as she jokingly toasted the Declaration of Independence.

"And here's to the French!" as she lifted her glass high, some 'fruit juice' spilling as Collette joined in and clicked the vessels.

"I told you before. The French don't have these problems ... men, women, mistresses. They see sex as a natural impulse, to be enjoyed, not fretted on with overbearing emotions of jealousy and guilt".

They both realized they'd been contemplating all of this through the filter of alcohol, but this intoxication couldn't solve all of the world's problems, let alone their personal demons.

"I can't think straight" Caroline blurted out, having much surpassed her limit.

She grasped Collette's hand and placed a gentle kiss.

"Merci beaucoup" she whispered. "I need to retire for the evening. I'll see you in the morning".

A minute later, Collette was fast asleep on the couch.

27

HAVING PAID THE LAD the two dollar fare, Daryl and Tabari boarded the vessel. The tugboat trip across the river was uneventful. There was plenty of time for them to figure out their next 'plan'. The livestock, wind and splashes made enough noise that they could speak in regular volume without concern that their 'captain' could overhear them.

Tabari remained silent, watching Daryl's face as he pondered their next move.

"Tabari, it's true that Illinois' a free state. Been that way for a long time now.

"But" he continued. "There's still pockets of slavery. It ain't legal, mind you, but there's still some folks who rely on it, even though it's against the law".

Tabari looked even more worried.

"Our goal is still to get you to Canada. But you can see, our situation's changed".

His pressing concern now was how they'd get transportation once they reached the other side. They hadn't rehearsed for this predicament.

"Well, you're here" the youth bellowed the obvious as the tug slid gently forward onto the soft sand of the shoreline.

Tabari and Daryl stood at the front, lookin down to see if they could step off the boat without sinking into the wet sand. No such luck.

They tossed their carpet bags as far onto shore as possible, then took a few steps and leapt as best they could. Their shoes sunk in, then sucked up mud as they stumbled forward toward solid dirt.

Two men jogged down to the boat and began chatting with the 'captain'. They shared notes from their scratch pads, confirming the livestock inventory they were about to unload.

Daryl and Tabari cleaned up their shoes, as best they could, then surveyed the landscape and pondered how they'd get to the next town.

As the two men were securing the livestock into pens, Daryl approached the older one.

"Hello, sir" he began. "I can certainly see you've got your hands full".

The cow poke didn't even look up, as he continued to herd the animals into their various quarters.

"May I inquire? Where's the nearest town?"

The man stopped his work, obviously annoyed at the stranger's intrusion.

"Mister, can't you see I've got my hands full?" he barked, repeating Daryl's previous observation.

"Why, yes sir, I can" he replied. "I'm simply looking to obtain some mode of transportation for my fellow and myself" he said, looking toward Tabari.

"Town? Did you say town?" as he cracked a stick across the backside of a cow to encourage its forward progress.

"Why, thar' ain't no town here!" he chuckled, thinking the neatly dressed newcomers were likely just wealthy simpletons.

Daryl surveyed the desolate landscape, acknowledging the obvious.

"I understand. But I've heard there's a post office somewhere nearby. Perhaps in McClure?"

"That's right. Thar's a post office alright. But that's it. There ain't nothin' else. Mister, what's you lookin' for?"

"A ride, plain and simple. We want to get to the post office".

"Well, I can arrange that for ya'. Be about an hour or so".

"Mighty grateful to you, sir. Of course, I'm happy to pay".

"Well, let me finish here. Tell 'ya what. A buck apiece. That sound fair?"

"More than fair. We're ready whenever you are".

"Buck apiece. Idiots! Jus' because they're rich don't mean they got common sense" he chuckled to himself, then returned to herding the livestock.

* * *

"WELL, this is it!" the cowpoke shouted as he pulled the buck wagon in front of the post office.

"Hey Tom! Tom! You in there?" he yelled toward the wooden shack.

They could hear rustling and glass breaking from inside, and the voice of a man swearing at someone or something.

"Get otta' here you varmint! Get yer' ass otta' here!" the man yelled.

The front door flew open, the unwanted intruder running for his life, and an angry man, wildly swinging his broom in hot pursuit.

"Ya' sonofabitch!" he hollered at the possum critter, followed by the cowpoke's laughter.

"Why, Tom! Now, that's no way to treat one of yer' best customers!" he wisecracked, Daryl and Tabari trying hard to control their own laughter.

"That no good possum! I just broke two jars of my wife's peaches chasin' that no good bastard!" he shouted.

Tom watched the marsupial disappear into a wood pile, then looked up at Daryl and Tabari, two of the best dressed aristocrats he'd ever seen.

"Excuse my language, gentlemen. That damn creature steals into my office and ransacks everthin' he can. I know he's got kin to feed but, god damnit!" he groaned.

"No excuse necessary" Daryl offered, he and Tabari having stepped off the wagon and set their luggage on the ground.

The driver having been paid, left the three of them to conduct whatever business they might have.

"Well, I know you're 'Tom'" Daryl began the introductions. "My name's Daryl, and this gentleman is my personal valet. Tabari".

"I'm pleased to meet you both" as he patted dust off his vest and reached out to shake hands.

"Welcome to McClure" he cheerfully offered, sweeping his arm and hand as if to visually present the remoteness and quiet beauty of the countryside.

"Well, welcome to the post office at least. I'm Tom, the postmaster. Course, I ain't officially the postmaster. That honor should rightfully belong to my wife. She runs the place" he chuckled, a gleam of happiness permeated his aura, making Daryl and Tabari quite glad to have met him.

His figure was near to a diminutive Santa Claus. Bald head except for a white band of hair that ran the back of his head, nearly from ear to ear, and meticulously trimmed, presumably by his wife. He had a closely cropped beard and moustache, as white as his hair, and a full set of teeth that almost glistened when touched by the sun.

"Letters, mail, stamps, yes sir, we do it all here" he offered, obviously proud of his work and station in life.

"How can I help you?"

"Well, we don't need any of those, at least not right now" Daryl began to explain.

The sound of horse hooves drew the attention of all three, as a buck wagon came into view.

"Why George! If it ain't good ol' George" Tom exclaimed, obviously happy to see his old friend.

"Best checkers player this side of … the Mississippi" he bellowed out, slapping his thigh and laughing hysterically.

Daryl and Tabari caught the joke, and found themselves smiling to see this jolly old man so happy.

Seated next to George was a black man, the darkest man that Tabari or Daryl had ever seen. He wore a light blue farmer's bib, a suspender over each shoulder and plenty of pockets.

Seated in the back of the wagon were the black man's three young'uns, two boys and a girl. Her dry frizzy hair sported many braids, each one pointing outward without rhyme or reason. Certainly not a stylish look, but her smile and twinkling eyes showed she had little concern in making any sort of fashion statement.

"Whoa!" George ordered his horse as he pulled back on the reins.

"How the hell are you, Tom? And the misses? It's been at least a couple a weeks".

"Sure 'nuf, my friend. The misses is fine. You just missed all the action" as he looked to the wood pile and then at his new acquaintances.

"I'm thinkin' it's that possum again, eh?" he laughed. "Why don't you just take him an' his family into the fold? Like some kinda' pets?"

"Pets!" Tom scoffed. "If'n I catch that critter, he'll be the main course for dinner!" he laughed.

"Well, where's my manners?" Tom exclaimed.

"George, this is Daryl and …"

"Tabari" Daryl refreshed his memory.

"Ah yes. Tabari. Gentlemen, this here's George. My good friend.

"And his most valued employee, Luke" as he acknowledge the dark man seated in the wagon.

Luke had been a slave his entire life, save the last three years, when his owner died and his Christian wife granted his freedom. Not only his freedom, but his wife and children also.

They'd travelled from the plantation where they'd lived in Memphis, Tennessee, up the Mississippi to the Illinois side of Cape Girardeau. It was there they met George.

George and his wife owned a large tract of wheat fields, always in need of laborers. Devout abolitionists, they employed nearly thirty workers, both white and black, and provided their families with modest housing for which their laborers paid rent.

Tom returned his attention to his new acquaintances, as George and Luke strode past and entered the office.

"Gentlemen, how can I be of assistance?"

Both men desperately wanted to confide in Tom. Having to travel in secrecy, concealing their true objectives, was exhausting. Tom seemed to be a genuinely good man, yet they'd only met. But having seen his interaction with George and the dark skinned Luke, their confidence grew.

"Tom, we need transportation" Daryl began to explain. "Transportation ... north" he almost stuttered, anxious that this revelation might have tipped their hats, too soon.

"North, you say" Tom replied, his eyebrows furrowed as he stroked his beard.

"How far north?"

Daryl looked at Tabari, who nervously stared at the ground. A pregnant pause ensued, Daryl not sure how much information he should reveal.

Tom knew. He'd never involved himself as a 'conductor' of the 'Underground Railroad'. But he knew. He had several friends who'd regaled him with stories of the 'Railroad', and how they'd provided assistance, all the way 'north' to Canada.

"I think you might want to chat with my friend" he offered with a knowing smile. "George might be of some help" as he took Daryl's arm and escorted he and Tabari into the office.

George had been leafing through some pamphlets, waiting for Tom to enter.

"Oh, hey Tom" he said as they entered the building. "Say, are you 'getting' those newfangled stamps the government's been issuin'?"

"Yea. Pretty fancy, eh? I'll show you some of what we've got" as he stepped behind the counter and reached down to set a sample on the table.

"Ah … George" Tom began. "Daryl and Tabari here are lookin' for some help in transportation. They're tryin' to get 'north'. Way north" he said with a twinkle in his eye, looking at Daryl and Tabari, both of whom appeared quite anxious.

"North, eh?" George repeated the statement, turning around to look directly at them both.

Daryl intuitively felt this the opportune moment to cautiously add more information. To hold back would simply leave them in limbo. He had to take the risk.

Luke was in the corner, pretending to examine the jars of peaches that Tom's wife had arranged on a shelf, a little side business to generate some additional income to supplement their postmaster's salary.

His eavesdropping was obvious. All knew that he'd heard every word.

"Well, perhaps I could be of some help" he offered. "Perhaps.

"Why don't you and Tabari ride back to my place? You can spend the night. The misses would love to have you. Besides, there's no hotel here, obviously. It doesn't look like you have much choice" he chuckled.

Daryl and Tabari nervously chuckled back.

The two looked at each other, then Daryl spoke.

"That's mighty nice of you, 'neighbor'. We have no other place to stay. Nor do we have any transportation. It's very kind of you. We accept. Right, Tabari?"

"Yes, sir. Mighty nice of you" Tabari responded, still nervously staring at the floor.

George turned to Tom. "Well, I'll be back soon with the misses. She's gonna' want to ogle some of those stamps, that's for sure. I do believe she's already started a 'stamp collection' book. You believe that?" he laughed. "Stickin' expensive stamps into a book, instead of an envelope! Ah, well. Peace, I say. Peace at any price" he chortled.

"The women folk do seem to enjoy them" Tom replied. "I look forward to seein' you both, real soon".

George and Daryl sat in front, Tabari, Luke and the young'uns in back. The horse's hooves, the wind and rattling noise the buck wagon made was loud enough that the front and back seat passengers could speak in relative private.

Luke was a large strong man. His muscles weren't the result of arduous labor in George's wheat fields. They were natural to him, whether he toiled in manual labor or not. His jaw was set tight, eyes piercing like a bird of prey. Conversation wasn't his forte, but when he spoke, each word had purpose and the listener paid attention.

With his peripheral vision, he eyed Tabari suspiciously. He'd never seen such a well-dressed black man before. Something odd about his appearance. He saw Tabai's calloused hands, obviously the result of hard manual labor. The opposite of what a 'personal valet's' hands would look like.

And those clothes! Gold chain, shiny shoes and a silk top hat to boot. Just didn't match up.

Tabari sensed Luke's quiet suspicion.

"You're a free man?" he asked, slightly above a whisper.

"Yup" Luke replied, staring straight ahead.

Tabari let out a deep sigh. He'd been told umpteen times to let Daryl do all the talking. Just be patient. Don't say anything that might give yourself away. So far, Mister Daryl and the other white folks had been so kind to him, and he was much appreciative for that. But he longed to speak with another black. To be able to commiserate with a person who shared a common background. He yearned for that.

"You always been free?" he asked.

Luke sensed Tabari's longing and uneasiness.

He turned slightly and addressed Tabari directly, with that predator's stare.

"I was a slave for near my whole life" he began. He looked Tabari up and down, almost undressing him of his disguised garb.

"Jus' like I think *you* was" he stated matter of factly, locking his eyes on Tabari's callused hands.

He self-consciously turned his palms over and placed them on his thighs. He knew. He knew that Luke knew.

"I'm still a slave" he whispered, staring straight ahead and beginning to fight back some tears.

"Mister Daryl here, he's hepin' me get to Canada".

Luke stared intently ahead, then just slowly nodded.

"I knew you ain't no 'personal valet'" he stated. "Least not one that don't do no manual labor. Jus' lookin' at your hands tells me 'dat.

They sat silent as the wagon bucked back and forth down the dirt path.

"Dat's what we's hopin' for" Tabari continued. "'Dat Mister George can hep' us. Well, hep' *me* 'dat is".

Luke remembered the years he'd spent as a slave. Not as bad of conditions as many, though. His master at least allowed his family to stay together. Not one of them sold off to another owner. For that, he'd been plenty thankful. That was always his worst fear. Not the beatings, not the whippings, but the fear of losing one of his own. He'd rather have died than suffer such a loss.

"Can't speak for Mister George" Luke said. "But I can tell 'ya, he's a good and fair man. Don't have no slaves. Never did. Ever one 'dat works for him is an 'em-poy-ee'. Whities and darkies. Makes no difference ta' him.

"But I tell 'ya this. If'n ever there was a man 'ta trust, it'd be Mister George. He and his misses always been kind, and fair, to me and mine. 'Ta ever one".

That caused much needed relief to Tabari's psyche. Knowing that a no nonsense man like Luke would offer such glowing praise for Mister George gave him much comfort.

* * *

DARYL felt the same, having conversed with George throughout the ride.

"That's about all I can tell you" Daryl said, having exhausted the details of the excursion so far.

"My, my. To think of all that man's been through" George pondered.

"You know, I've never been formally involved with the 'Underground Railroad'" he confessed with a whisper. "Tom and I've talked about it.

Many times. We both know of good, decent white folks who've had some experience, though.

"Canada, eh? That's gotta' be, oh I don't know, six hundred miles or so I reckon'"

"Six hundred miles!?" Daryl reacted. "No, no. It's more like a thousand miles" he said confidently.

"Suppose that depends on what part of Canada yer' planning on goin' to".

"Well, the plan is to travel to Winnipeg" Daryl responded. "I've been there a couple of times, on business. I don't have any good contacts there, but I do in Minneapolis. 'Bout half way between here and Winnipeg".

George stroked his beard as he thought further on the matter and pondered the geography of the Country.

"Well, you can take the Mississippi River about as far as Minneapolis, I reckon. But then your Winnipeg's still a far ways away I believe.

"Have you thought of headin' towards Detroit? That's about six hundred miles, give or take. Canada's right there. On the border.

"And" he continued. "They're all free states you'd be crossin'. That's the remainin' problem we have here, in Illinois. We're a free state, but there's lotsa' folks who still harbor slaves. They should all be free. Hell, a few years' back, we changed the Constitution. Illinois banned slavery altogether.

"But here's the rub. Harborin' a fugitive slave is still against the law. The 'dadgummed' US Supreme Court just said so. Recently!

"Now ..." George continued his thoughts on the most logical plan.

"If you went to Detroit, you'd have to travel through ... let's see ... maybe a small part of Ohio, and then through Michigan. Both of them are free states.

"Conversely" he continued his learned analysis. "If you go to Minneapolis, you've got to travel through Iowa. Again, a free state" he instructed, privately congratulating himself on his knowledge of geography and history.

"But, ya' still might have to deal with Missouri. Assumin', of course, you continue to boat up the Mississippi. And you just told me about the problems you've had with the Sheriff there".

Daryl stared at George, spellbound. How did this old man know so much about all these states, and their history and present situations regarding slavery?

"Pretty impressive, eh?" George read Daryl's facial expression.

"Tom! Good ol' Tom. You know, the postmaster".

"Ah, yes" Daryl remembered.

"Well, ol' Tom, he gets a lot of information through his work. I mean, you can't imagine the number of newspapers that come through his post office. Not to mention official notices, court orders, warrants for folks' arrest ... things like that.

"I mean, Tom's a veritable library of information" he chuckled.

"See, that's your problem. Well, at least one of 'em. Even if you travel through Illinois, you've still got the fugitive slave act to deal with. Ol' Tom even tells me that there's a law that's about to be passed that'd prevent any out of state black man from stayin' in Illinois for more than ten days. Ten days! If he stays longer, then he can be arrested and jailed.

"And, if someone, like you" he whispered, "helped him, then 'wham!', you might be arrested as well, for aidin' and abettin'" he added, startling his horse by having unintentionally whipped the reins for emphasis.

Daryl thought about all the planning, all the rehearsals they'd done in anticipation of every possible contingency that could be thrown their way. But these revelations from George made his head ache. No plan stood out as the best. Each potential route only presented its own unique problems.

"Like I said, I can't speak for the people I'll be introducin' you to, but they'll most likely send you to Detroit. Their 'Underground Railroad' generally travels northeast from here".

Daryl just nodded as he contemplated how their sojourn would turn out.

Exhaustion set in, and he was quite relieved to see George's small farm house finally come into view.

* * *

"NOW, you two just relax and make yourselves at home" George's wife, Angel, said with a smile. "It's so nice to have visitors. George told me a little about you, but I have so many questions!" as she began placing plate after plate of vegetables, fried chicken, dumplings and hush puppies on the table.

Save perhaps Helen Donovan, there wasn't a kinder, gentler woman than Angel. She was like a mother to their employees, regardless of age, always inquiring about their health, clothes, and offering her assistance at every turn.

Someone's pants needed sewing? Angel mended them.

A child's toy was broken? Angel fixed it.

Sore tooth? Angel cured it, even if it needed pulling.

"Tabari, where are you from? I mean, before you came to America?" she asked, her eyes softly pleading for him to tell the story. She waited with infinite patience until he finally swallowed the bite of chicken he was chewing.

"Somewhere's in Africa" he answered, swirling half a biscuit in the thick salty gravy.

"Where in Africa?"

He set the biscuit down as he contemplated the answer.

"I's really don't know" he honestly replied. "I lived in a village. With my family". He sensed this short answer wasn't going to satisfy Angel's curiosity.

"Misses, I lived with about forty or so of my relatives. In a beautiful land with all kinda' fruit, maize, trees ... and a small river". That memory made him smile. "My, my. I do miss 'da cool water 'dat flowed in 'dat river" he reminisced as he daydreamed.

"And now" she continued. "Now you want your freedom!"

Tabari's thoughts instantly snapped to the present.

"Oh, yes 'em! Yes 'em! 'Dat's what I want most of all" he nearly shouted, the hot food having rejuvenated him from the day's long ordeal.

"'Ta Canada! 'Ta Canada! 'Dat's where Mister Daryl and I are headin'" as he looked to Daryl, pleading for confirmation.

"Ah, Tabari" George interjected. "Mister Daryl and I had a long conversation about this, while we were riding here" as he looked to make sure Daryl approved of continuing his explanation. Daryl nodded, and George returned his attention to Tabari.

"We ... well the misses and I ... have friends who we think can help. They're good friends. Good Christian folk. And they've helped others, just like you. Helped them get to freedom".

Tabari listened intently, struggling to keep from sobbing with excitement.

"Yes" Angel added. "They've helped a lot of people in your predicament. And I ... that is we" as she looked to her husband, "believe they'll be willing to help you, too".

"Daryl, what are your thoughts about the best way to travel?" George asked.

Daryl looked at Tabari as he answered, wanting him to understand the reasoning behind his decision.

"You made some excellent points, George. Travelling on to Minneapolis, and then possibly Winnipeg, places us at risk, at least so far as we use the Mississippi River. We'd be bordering Missouri much of the way, and we've already had problems with the law" as he looked intently at Tabari, who nodded his head in obvious agreement.

"And it's a lot farther, too. Maybe four hundred miles or so. To Winnipeg, that is.

"On the other hand, if we go to Detroit, well, Canada's right across the river. And, the states we have to pass through, are all free states".

"Free states!" Tabari whispered, obviously excited at this proposition.

"Mind you" as he addressed Tabari, directly. "Any way we go has its own problems. Like George said, where we're at right now, Illinois, is a free state. But, there's still plenty of people who want to hang on to slavery. That's just a fact. And, the fugitive slave act still applies here".

The fugitive slave act. Tabari was well educated with the devastating injuries that wretched law could extract. The Jeffersons, Tom and Melba, the Pastor and Reverend. Yes, he knew it all too well.

"Damn!" Tabari exclaimed. 'Dat goddamned slave act!" he whispered. "Oh! I's sorry Misses. Pleeze excuse me".

Angel just smiled.

"I think the answer's obvious" Daryl stated.

"I say northeast. To Detroit, then Canada. Of course, if that's what your 'conductor' friends think would be the best route. And, of course, assuming they're willing to help" he sheepishly added, a bit embarrassed that he'd announced his decision without having even met these 'conductors, let alone confirmed their desire to risk so much to obtain Tabari's freedom.

Angel, who hadn't been privy to all discussions about the best route to take, offered some additional thoughts.

"Why does he have to go all the way to Canada? Why can't we find safe refuge, in say, Ohio? That'd save hundreds of miles in travel and, best as I can recall, Ohio's always been a free state".

George nodded.

Daryl let out a deep sigh, somewhat exhausted by this continuing analysis but committed to explore all options and arrive at the best solution.

"All that's true" he began. "But something else has to be considered. Something we haven't discussed.

"The South's been spoutin' on for years about its commitment to slavery. We all know it. There's constant talk of them seceding from the Union" he found himself whispering, the topic seemingly too dangerous to speak about out loud.

Tabari nodded in agreement. Most of the slaves on the Winters' plantation had heard the rumors. Most dismissed them as just wishful thinking on the part of their enslaved comrades, hoping beyond hope that such a revolt would free them from captivity.

"And if they did" he paused. "I truly believe, *when* they do, then there's gonna' be a terrible civil war" as he looked to George and Angel to gauge their thoughts on the likelihood of his prediction.

They looked worrisome at each other, then nodded in agreement.

"And where does that leave Tabari? Maybe enlisted with the Northern army?" he asked. "Maybe running again, away from an advancing Southern army? No, I say. This man's suffered enough" as he placed his hand on top of Tabari's.

"There needs to be an end to his suffering. A place where there's no more fear that someone's about to knock on his door in the middle of the night, and drag him off to another plantation owner. No, it's got to stop. Canada must be the final destination".

Angel and George looked at Tabari, nearly shaking from this stark revelation. Then they looked into each other's eyes, acknowledging the truth of the prophecy laid out by Daryl.

"We understand" Angel stated.

"Tabari, tomorrow morning we'll have a talk with the people we feel can help you. You and 'Mister' Daryl".

"Yes 'em" he replied. "Thank you's so much".

28

COLLETTE WOKE UP IN BED, Trent having carried her from the parlor sofa where she'd fallen fast asleep after her intoxicated discussion with Caroline the night before.

"Oh, my!" she thought to herself as she placed her hand on her temple, feeling her heartbeat pound, the result of a regretful hangover. Sadie knocked on her door.

"Misses, how 'ya feelin' this fine morning'?" she asked, placing two carafes on the table and throwing back the window drapes, bright sunlight gushing in and causing Collette's eyes to burn.

"Oh, not too good I'm afraid". She was reluctant to tell Sadie the truth, not wanting to humble herself at the mercy of one of the servants.

"Oh, I's understands" Sadie responded. "Da Colonel 'axed' me to bring both tea and coffee for 'ya, 'jus in case 'ya might want somethin' stronger on a cause of your celebratin' so much wid' Miss Caroline las' night".

Collette fought hard to quell the headache and regain her garbled senses.

"Yes. I believe some coffee would do me good" she moaned.

"I'm embarrassed to say, but I may have gotten a little tipsy last night" she admitted, knowing Sadie wouldn't be fooled with any pretense of denial.

"Now, now Misses. Nothin' to fret about. You's had an awful time of recent, why wid' 'dat 'gata attack an' all. Lordie knows most womens would never have survived such a thing!

"And how nice it was for 'da 'Senata' and Misses Caroline 'ta come all 'da way here from N'awlins to spend time wid' you. I'd say you deserves a little celebratin', I do".

Collette took a sip of the piping hot coffee, the caffeine instantly improving her grogginess.

"Well, thank you Sadie. And, yes, I have been through a lot. And it *has* been wonderful to see Caroline and the Senator. Very much so" as she took another sip.

"See? You's soundin' better already. Miss Caroline and 'da 'Senata' is down in 'da kitchen, preparin' for breakfast".

"Oh, fine. Tell them I'll be down soon".

"I's already laid out yer' clothes for this morning, Misses. I'll let 'em know you'll be down soon 'ta joins 'em".

* * *

COLLETTE watched Amana as she prepared a feast for a breakfast.

She'd seen Amana before, of course, dressed for dinner in Collette's favorite gown, but never closely examined her physical features. No reason to. But after hearing Collette's sensational revelations about Trent's possible infidelity, she now scrutinized Amana's appearance and every movement.

"My, she is quite beautiful" she thought as she looked toward Trent who was heavily engaged in conversation with Jeb.

Then, she returned her gaze to Amana, then back to Trent, trying to detect any evidence that might confirm Collette's suspicions. Trent never diverted his eyes away from her husband, both men intently discussing matters of business, or politics, or both.

"Some more tea, ma'am?" Amana asked, catching Caroline by surprise.

"Why, yes. Thank you, Amana". As she poured, Collette scrutinized the profile of her face, her tone but feminine arms, the curvature of her breasts, and the tightness of her waist.

"Well, if Trent's interests were purely physical, the case is closed" she mused to herself. Amana was undeniably attractive.

She then turned her attention to her own husband, to see if he registered any lustful gaze toward Amana.

"What am I thinking?" she rebuked herself. "Collette's jealous concerns are now seeping into my mind?" she asked herself, incredulously.

Their conversation last night was all so surreal, obviously accentuated by too much alcohol. Were Collette's suspicions based in reality, or merely the result of momentary inebriation?

She suddenly felt like she was unwittingly playing the role of Collette's private detective, charged with the task of uncovering a diabolical plot between a husband and his mistress. A slave mistress at that.

"Enough!" she shouted to herself. "I'm not going to get caught up in uncovering some sort of sexual conspiracy" she defiantly stated. "Collette, if your husband's having an illicit affair with Amana, you're going to have to work it out for yourself" she demanded.

As she finished this thought, her eyes slowly looked up to see Jeb staring at Amana's backside as she bent over to pick up a towel she'd dropped on the floor. Jeb had a slight smile, a lecherous smile of sorts, which instantly vanished when he realized his wife was watching.

She stared in disbelief, then refocused her attention and saw Trent and Jeb fully engaged in conversation, Jeb being apparently oblivious to Amana's presence.

She shook her head in disbelief.

"Did I just imagine all that?" she asked herself, suddenly unsure if she'd seen what she just thought she'd witnessed.

She rapidly shook her head side to side, unintentionally causing her lips to flap, making a most comical noise.

This sudden spectacle caused Trent and Jeb to immediately stop their conversation and stare at Caroline in bewilderment.

"My dear, are you alright?" Jeb asked, a smile of amusement on his face. He'd never before seen such an un-ladylike convulsion.

"Huh?" she stammered, unaware of her uncontrolled spasm.

"Why, good morning ya'all!" Collette greeted them as she gracefully walked into the kitchen. Trent and Jeb immediately stood, Southern gentlemen always.

"Good morning, my dear" Trent said, as he pulled out a chair for his wife. "My, my, you look radiant this morning".

Collette knew that she'd pretty much passed out last night, and wanted to put that issue behind her.

"Well, I must admit, I'm doing much better now. I fear I had a little too much to drink last night. I don't know what got over me" she blushed, then looked at Caroline for some sympathy.

"Oh, nonsense" Trent replied. "Everyone's entitled to a little celebration from time to time" he calmed her. "And I can't think of a better cause for merriment! Our dear friends have been here to share in the speediness of your recovery and, for that, I for one am most appreciative".

"Here, here!" Jeb offered a toast, and raised his coffee cup for all to see.

Caroline rose, walked over to Collette, and gave her a soft hug.

All were seated, and Amana and Sadie continued serving the most delicious and decadent breakfast.

* * *

"I'M going to miss you so" Caroline gushed, as she and Jeb watched one of the servants place their luggage into their carriage.

Collette was nearly in tears.

"Oh, my. I'm so thankful that you and Jeb were able to come by and have such a nice visit. I'm going to miss you terribly".

"Good Lord, it was the least we could do. When we read in the newspaper about your … well, your 'accident' … Jeb and I both insisted we absolutely needed to come as fast as possible.

"And there's just no reason why you and Trent can't come to visit us in N'awlins. You simply must make the time for it. Even if Jeb's away on business, you and Trent come". She leaned in closer.

"And if Trent can't make it, then by all means make the trip yourself. It'd be wonderful to see you again" she whispered, with a hint of flirtatiousness.

Collette paused, reflecting on the intimacy they'd shared, alone, at Caroline's home. She instantly felt a slight arousal, but that was quickly replaced by a hot flash, the result of guilt welling up inside. She then remembered another concern.

"Caroline, I don't think I could make the trip without Trent. The last time, those vulgar thugs we encountered made me fear for my life! I'm afraid I'd be too … afraid … to travel without Trent".

Caroline had forgotten about that frightful ordeal.

"Oh, I forgot about that! I completely understand. We can figure it out. We'll make it happen one way or another.

"But, Collette, remember. Jeb and I are travelling the same roads back to N'awlins. We've never had a problem. The chances of that happening again are one in a thousand. Just think upon it. I truly want to see you again.

Collette extended her arms and Caroline joined her in a warm hug, kissing her on each cheek.

"Are you ready, my dear?" Jeb asked from inside the carriage.

Caroline stepped back, looking one last time at her dear friend as she blew her a kiss.

"Yes, my beloved" she replied, as a slave servant assisted her inside. A moment later, they began their trip back home.

29

THE DOCTOR HAD RETURNED TO NEW ORLEANS after having bid the Colonel 'adieu', promising not to fleece him in replacing the furniture the Doctor lost in the fire.

He sat in his usual chair at the Mad Dog Saloon, swatting away the repeated advances of the red-haired saloon gal who'd been celebrating with Seth and Randy on the night that he'd been called upon to provide urgent medical treatment for Mrs. Winters' as a result of the 'gata attack.

"Shit" he fumed, as he pondered how he was going to survive without the continued financial backing of his 'cash cow', Colonel Winters, now that his new house was nearly finished.

"Well, I still got the furniture to purchase" he chuckled, enjoying a slight diversion from his current financial worries.

The pecuniary contrast was traumatic. Before the Colonel, the Doctor's existence was hand to mouth. He had no real patients, and those he did have, rarely paid him money. They compensated him with butchered hogs, chickens, and some god-awful corn mash whiskey from time to time.

Certainly not worthy of a physician of the Doctor's caliber. At least that's how he viewed it.

Life within the Colonel's circle was relatively fabulous. He'd stayed in a palatial mansion, dined with the rich and powerful, drank the most exquisite liquors, and got paid handsomely to boot.

He felt some remorse for having blamed his house fire on Tabari, but not much. He could easily brush that injustice onto Mr. Tolivar. It was Tolivar's idea. He just went along for the ride.

But now the Colonel had essentially handed him his hat. Unless some miracle happened, there'd be no more Trent, no more gala gatherings, no more money.

"Shit!"

As he took another sip of whiskey, he began slumping in his chair, becoming more and more depressed on the prospects of earning a real living.

"Hey Doc! Hey Doc! It's us!" Randy and Seth greeted him. The Doctor looked up but was unable to force even the slightest smile.

"Boy, you don't look so good" Seth observed, seeing the Doctor's face contorted and his bloodshot eyes staring at his shot glass.

"What's the matter, Doc?" Randy asked, a genuine sense of concern over their friend.

"Well, shit. I'm just havin' a bad day, that's all".

The saloon gal was miffed when her prospective 'client' rejected her advancements and pushed her off his lap. But her face lit up when she saw her two best customers had entered the bar.

"Hey Shirley, how 'bout gettin' another round for the three of us?" Seth requested, as gentleman-like as he could muster.

"Jus' the 'three' of you?" she coyly asked, obviously hoping for a free one.

"Of course!" Randy half shouted. "Make it four!"

The saddle bums had been regular customers for some time. Before they'd met the Doctor, they'd spent many a day and night at the bar, mostly nursing their beers to make their small coinage last as long as possible.

But since their 'business venture', a la Doctor Jeramiah Wesley, they had some real cash in the form of their fifty dollar 're-wards', paid by the Colonel for their help in capturing Tabari.

But alas, all good things must come to an end, and that end was coming fast. Shirley had seen to that.

"Here 'ya are, fellas" as she set the shot glasses on the table.

"A toast!" she offered. "To the finest gentlemen this here N'awlins has ta' offer!"

Randy and Seth, and even the Doctor, looked with amazement at how she could slug the whole thing down without feeling even a tinge of burn.

She did slightly shake her head, though. She slammed the shot glass down on the table, then looked up, surprised to see them all staring at her.

"What?" she asked defensively.

The three looked at each other, then broke out laughing.

"Shirley! Any woman who can drink like that has my full respect. Will you marry me?" Randy teased, as he put his arm around her neck and pulled her closer.

"Marry you? Why, I believe I'm *still* married. To two men! Never did get a divorce" she laughed. The men couldn't tell if she was joking or serious.

"What's got you lookin' so down, Doc?" she asked. "You look like you've lost your best friend".

The Doctor briefly reflected on the Colonel.

"It's sorta' like that" he replied. "I kinda' did lose a ... friend".

"Doc, this appears to be serious" Seth observed, never having seen the Doctor look this depressed.

"Who'd ya' lose? Someone we know?"

The Doctor continued with his almost stuporous stare, wanting to somehow perversely enjoy his pity party alone, yet feeling the need to share his tale of woe with another human.

"It's the Colonel. Colonel Winters" he offered.

"The Colonel? Trent Winters?" Seth and Randy asked, almost in unison.

"That's right my friends. Colonel Trent Winters. The same one whose wife's life I just saved. The same one whose slave's leg I had to amputate. The same one who … ah … I could go on and on. I should wear a sign around my neck. 'No good deed goes unpunished'" he wallowed out loud in self-absorption.

"Damn!" Seth and Randy looked at each other with great big smiles.

"We're workin' for him right now!" Seth announced.

"Yea!" Randy added.

The Doctor's glazed eyes cleared momentarily.

"What? Whadda' ya' mean you're workin' for him? The Colonel?"

"Yea, that's right. Me an' Seth have been searchin' for that runaway slave. Tabari. He done escaped again. Can you believe that?"

"Well I'll be damned" the Doctor mumbled, incredulous that these two simpletons would be hired by the Colonel as slave capturers.

"How did he … when did the Colonel …?"

"It wasn't the Colonel. It was that Mr. Tolivar man. He's the one that told us that the slave escaped again" Randy explained.

"Well, the Colonel don't really know we're involved" Seth continued.

"Turns out, he sold the slave to a man named McKenzie. I guess the Colonel had put up with about as much as he could with that nigger. Decided he was too much trouble. So he sold him. It's McKenzie who owns him now. But before he could have his men pick him up, he escaped. Again!"

"Well, I'll be damned" the Doctor muttered.

"Yea. Turns out Mr. McKenzie was mad when he found out Tabari was gone. Real mad. He threatened to sue the Colonel to get his money back"

"But why on earth would the Colonel get involved with re-capturin' Tabari? He's got all the money in the world. Why wouldn't he just give that McKenzie his money back?" the Doctor pondered out loud. Then he answered his own question.

"It's not that he's afraid of bein' sued" the Doctor barked.

"He's going after Tabari because he's a gentleman and respected businessman" the Doctor explained, remembering first-hand the Colonel's reputation for honesty and integrity.

"He sold the slave and represented, as a man of his word, that he'd deliver the merchandise. That's why he wants to recapture Tabari. McKenzie would have drove all the way out to the plantation to pick up his property. Hell, yea. I can imagine he was pretty mad.

"I know the Colonel. He made a contract. A promise. And he's one to stick by his promises".

Seth and Randy listened. And learned. They hadn't the means to connect too many dots, mostly grasping only things that were obvious. No matter. They now had a job, and one that paid quite well.

Seth, perhaps the smarter of the two, but certainly not by much, looked at Shirley, balancing herself with one hand on a chair, the other on her hip, impatient that all this talk of business was impeding her prospects of getting another free shot of whiskey.

He slipped one hand into his pants pocket, a reminder that he'd spent nearly all of his 're-ward' money at this Saloon and, in particular, on entertaining this middle-aged call girl. By necessity, it was time to resume 'gainful' employment, even if the business venture involved capturing runaway slaves.

"Well, we don't know about all that, but Tolivar found us here, and told us that if we captured Tabari again, we could expect another big reward. Just like last time" Seth continued.

"Yea" Randy added. "'Cept this time, we ain't gonna' scare that damn hotel clerk, or break no expensive vase" Seth nodded in agreement.

"Say, Doc. You want a piece of this action?" Randy whispered as he looked to Seth to make sure it was alright to include the Doctor in their 'business venture'.

"I mean, I don't know exactly what you'd do, but if we need your help, maybe you can join us? Maybe get back in the Colonel's good graces?"

The Doctor's spirits lifted considerably. A few minutes ago, he was wallowing in self-pity, pondering life as a penniless physician, living off critters and varmints as payment for medical services rendered.

Now, suddenly, a slight sliver of a silver lining appeared. Hell, if he was able to take advantage of these two cowpokes before, he could most conceivably do it again. He smiled.

"Gentlemen, another round. On me!"

"Now we're talkin!'" Shirley shouted.

30

"HMM ..." THE DOCTOR MURMERED as he slowly walked up and down the aisles of the finest furniture store New Orleans had to offer.

He stopped to admire a credenza made of solid oak with what looked like lions' feet at the base of each leg.

"A fine piece of furniture indeed" the middle-aged salesman pointed out, dressed in a tailored three piece suit accessorized with a silk handkerchief. A set of round spectacles rested on the tip of his nose.

"I can see you're a man of exquisite taste" he continued, much practiced at flattering a potential customer who had money to spend.

"Well, it *is* a nice credenza" the Doctor responded. "Not exactly what I'm looking for" he said condescendingly, although he had no idea what to look for since the furniture in his burned house was nearly non-existent.

He continued to gaze around the show floor, enjoying the attention being showered upon him, and rightfully so, according to his perspective.

"You see, my house burned to the ground about a month ago, and I'm lookin for some replacement furniture. Some very nice furniture" he chuckled to himself, remembering his veiled promise not to fleece Colonel Winters.

"Ah, you must be the physician who lost his house. Am I right? Am I right?" he enthusiastically smiled, so excited to have pieced this together.

The Doctor was surprised the salesman would know.

"Well, yes. Yes I am" he responded, while the clerk vigorously shook his hand.

"Word travels fast in N'awlins" the salesman stated.

"Why then, you must know the Colonel? Colonel Winters" the man asked.

The Doctor eyed him suspiciously. It was one thing to connect the house fire to him. Hell, he'd told the clerk as much. But how did he know the Colonel was involved?

"Colonel Winters, why he's one of my best customers. One of my *very* best. He told me that you, well, the owner of the house, might be stoppin' by to purchase some furniture to, you know, replace what was lost in the fire. Well, I'll be!" he excitedly announced.

And he had reason to be excited. The Colonel's and Collette's purchases elevated him to be among the more 'well-to-do' furniture salesmen in all of New Orleans.

He'd taken over the business from his papa, who'd labored long and hard for years, scraping up just enough money to keep the doors open.

But he'd read about the success stories of other New Orleans' business owners who'd taken the risk to exclusively sell high end merchandise, and cater only to an upper class of clientele. He'd leveraged all he had, took in expensive inventory on a consignment basis, shared commissions and, slowly but surely, attracted the wealthier customers that he coveted.

Being relatively assured that the physician's purchases would be paid by the Colonel, the Doctor was now a very valued patron.

"My, my! That must have been just terrible!" he exclaimed.

The Doctor looked puzzled.

"The fire, I mean. Losing all your possessions. Why, I must think that a man of your stature would have had a house full of 'expen' … I mean … exquisite furniture" he smiled.

"Well, that's true" the Doctor lied, as he tugged at his vest hem and squared his shoulders, doing his best to appear as dignified and professional as possible.

"The fire *was* terrible" he concurred. "And, you're correct, I did lose an awful lot. Some of the furniture was imported from Atlanta … I mean … Athens" he stuttered, temporarily flummoxed as he sought to exaggerate the value of his 'imported' fixtures.

The clerk wasn't fooled, but wouldn't challenge the Doctor's honesty, or lack thereof. He'd learned many years ago that 'the customer was always right'. Whatever he could do to entice a sale, he'd be happy to oblige.

"I just hope that quack doesn't try and fleece me" the clerk remembered the Colonel saying. "I don't believe he had much furniture in his home, certainly nothing expensive. But I can't prove it. Besides, the doctor has been of some help to me and the Misses.

"If he shows up … well … hell … *when* he shows, let him buy what he wants. It just sticks in my craw" he bemoaned, the clerk offering a sympathetic smile but with no intention of trying to persuade the Colonel otherwise. A sale is a sale. The more the merrier.

"Yes sir, Colonel. I understand" he replied rather sheepishly, avoiding direct eye contact.

He returned his attention to the doctor.

"Yes, sir. The Colonel was very concerned about you and your loss. Said you were to spare no expense in replacing things" he lied.

"Did he now?" the Doctor smiled to himself.

"Mister?"

"Atkinson. Jeremiah Atkinson. At your service" the clerk introduced himself.

"Well, I'll be. 'Jeremiah' you say? I'm Dr. Wesley. 'Jeremiah Wesley'".

"Can't go wrong with that name!" Mr. Atkinson proclaimed. "So glad to meet you. Please, follow me, Doctor Wesley. I have some very nice pieces that I'm sure you'll be pleased with" as he took the Doctor's arm and strolled to one of the more expensive display areas.

31

NGEL AND GEORGE HAD PROMISED Tabari that they'd have a talk with the people they believed could help, as 'conductors', to get him to Canada.

True to their word, the next morning George appeared on the porch step of Samuel (Sam) Carter, a man he'd known for many years, a devout Christian and abolitionist.

Like George, Sam owned a small wheat farm, which he mostly tended himself, except in the rare season when he needed workers to bring in the much appreciated extra harvest. Sam and his wife had long attended the local church, although she'd passed away several years ago, never having children.

Her death caused him great grief. She'd died suddenly from cholera, the source unknown but most likely from drinking contaminated water while returning home after having visited her sister in the nearby village of Benton. It'd been a hot humid day, and her thirst simply overcame her better judgment as she repeatedly cupped her hands and drank water from a small stagnant pond along the roadside.

But during the last few years before her death, both she and Sam had worked together with the Underground Railroad, such as it was in the Clear Creek - McClure area in the mid-1840s. A loose knit group of abolitionists would gather in secret and formulate plans to aid the escape of a runaway slave, once they'd learned of the need.

It wasn't as dangerous as in, say, the neighboring state of Missouri, where such assistance could land them in jail for violating the fugitive slave act. This was Illinois, a free state. But, as mentioned, the 'Act' still applied, albeit in a watered down version.

"Why, George! If it isn't my good ol' friend, George Sheldon! How the heck are you?" as Sam opened the front door, the rusty hinges' squeaking going unnoticed.

George extended his hand, which Sam ignored and, instead, stepped forward with a great big bear hug.

"Come in, come in" Sam ordered, as his delighted smile welcomed the visitor. "It's been awhile".

"Yes. Yes it has!" George responded as he stepped into the living room. He noticed the many knickknacks Sam displayed in certain places, reminders of the love he still felt for his wife.

Sam noticed George's observations.

"Yes, I still miss her. Dearly" he said softly. "Every day".

George lowered his eyes to the floor, knowing he'd otherwise tear up if he looked directly at his friend.

"How 'bout some coffee?" Sam asked, obviously trying to ease the tension.

"Naw. But thanks, anyway". Sam waited for George to announce the reason for his visit.

"Sam, Angel and I have a visitor. Well, two actually. There's 'Daryl'. He owns a lumber business in Baton Rouge".

Sam nodded.

"And then there's Tabari. Tabari's with Daryl" he said, realizing his beating around the bush was confusing his friend. Several seconds passed, then he looked up at Sam.

"Tabari's like … Luke" he blurted out, having to ask even himself what the hell that meant, other than the obvious, that Tabari was a black man.

"Jesus!" George chastised himself. He realized his hesitation was because he was about to ask a man, his friend, to risk his livelihood, perhaps his own freedom, to help a complete stranger.

Sam sensed George's unease. They'd known each other a long time. Intuitively, he detected George's visit required a bit of secrecy, of something difficult to speak of.

"I'm thinkin' … Tabari is a … runaway?" Sam surmised. "Is that right? Is that why you're here?"

"Well … yea" George answered as he slapped his hands on his thighs, feeling like he'd just been caught with his hand in the cookie jar.

Sam laughed. "George, it's alright. Really, it's alright. I understand. Most folks never encounter this their whole lives. It's not somethin' that happens even ever so often. It's not like you answer the door every day and there's a black man standin' there, just standin' there, and askin' for help! Askin' for you to help him find a way to freedom" he laughed again at the absurdity.

"Now, tell me all that's happened. I don't know that I can help, but I'll have a much better idea if I know all the facts".

And with that, George started from the beginning. For the next fifteen minutes or so, he explained everything he knew about Tabari, Daryl, and their travels so far, including their run in with the Missouri Sheriff.

"That's it, Sam. That's where I'm at. Or I should say, that's where they're at".

Sam took it all in, hardly interrupting, as George had indeed told the whole story, including the reasoning behind the northeast travel route they were considering. To Detroit, then Canada.

"Hmm ... I see" Sam thought out loud as he ran his fingers through his thick hair.

"It makes sense. That's the route I'd be considerin' also. It makes sense. Goin' up the Mississippi, through Missouri, is dangerous. Too dangerous, given the fact that the law is already lookin' for these two, like you said.

"My, my. Tabari dove overboard to save that little girl's life? That's just amazin'. And ironic, too! That the Sheriff would be set to arrest him the next morning. On accounta' he didn't have his 'papers' with him! He saves a child's life, and then faces arrest!"

The irony wasn't lost on George.

"Well, that's why I'm here, Sam. So, what da' ya' think? Is there anything you can do to help them?"

Sam was resting his face in both hands as he pondered the question.

"Sure. I mean, of course!" he replied, wanting to cover up his initial unassured response with a more confident reply.

"Tell me what you need" George asked.

"Well, first off, I'll need to meet with Daryl and Tabari. Obviously. Otherwise, I'd be putting the cart in front of the horse, meaning I need to hear from them before I speak with the 'conductors'. That's the first step.

"Then, I'll arrange a meeting with the people who can help. Get their input.

"How are they right now? I mean, are they safe staying at your place?"

"Yea. As you can imagine, Angel's takin' good care of them. Probably puttin' a few extra pounds on each of em', what with all the 'vittles' she serves". They both laughed.

"Alright then" Sam continued. "How 'bout tomorrow morning? Bring them both by tomorrow so we can all chat. Later in the afternoon, I'll ride out to speak with those involved, and get a meeting started".

"That'd be just wonderful" George said. "Just wonderful. And Sam, I can't thank you enough".

"Nonsense. But, come to think of it, it'd be nice if Angel could fix up some of her 'vittles' for me, when she gets the chance" he half joked, as he remembered her fine cooking skills.

"Done!" George exclaimed with another laugh. As he began to leave, he glanced again at the many knickknacks Sam displayed about the room, loving reminders of his deceased wife.

"Thank you again, my friend. We'll see you tomorrow morning".

32

CAROLINE AND THE SENATOR had left Collette and Trent, and were heading back home to New Orleans.

"My, I must say, Collette looked fantastic" Caroline told her husband as their carriage gently rocked back and forth on the dirt road.

"Agreed" Jeb replied. "Hmm ..."

"What?"

"I was just thinking of the absurdity of it all. I mean, a 'gata attack for Christ's sake! Of all the horrible things this world has to offer, one minute you're sitting down peacefully reading a book, and then 'whack'!" clapping his hands together for added effect.

"Oh, goodness. Please don't relive that terrible experience" Caroline softly pleaded. The ludicrousness of it all gripped her as well. Her best friend nearly lost her life, being either eaten or drowned, by an alligator.

"They have such a marvelous place" Caroline reflected. "But I must say, I'm glad we live where we do. You don't see 'gatas just walking down the street and grabbing people".

Jeb chuckled.

"Well, I can't argue with that" he added.

"My dear, I'm off to Baton Rouge in a couple of days. I've told you about the uphill battle that's taking place with the 'Compromise bill'. I'll probably be gone for several weeks".

Caroline let out a deep sigh. She'd been thoroughly versed by Jeb. The 'Compromise Act of 1850' included the fugitive slave act, again requiring law enforcement of the free states to assist in the return of escaped slaves. It also increased penalties against persons who refused to cooperate.

"The 'bloodhound act'" she moaned, citing the slang term that referenced the dogs used to track down the victims.

"Jeb, I know we live in a slave state, and your constituents expect you to keep it that way. But isn't there anything you can do … anything … to stop this abominable practice?" she pleaded, knowing the answer before asking.

Jeb glared at her sternly. They'd had this conversation on many an occasion. She knew his response.

"Look, Caroline. It's just the way things are for now. My, God, I truly fear that civil war will break out sooner than later. I pray it isn't so, but I believe in my heart that's what's going to happen. A civil war for God's sake!

"What's the alternative for us? Resign? Resign as a United States Senator?

"Then what? You and I move to a free state? I join a law firm, or open my own practice? I can tell for a fact, our income would drop substantially. Our lifestyle would change completely.

"And how would that help change society? How impactful could I be as a private attorney? I'd be whistlin' in the wind, that's all. Get my name in the newspaper maybe once in a while. I can see it now:

Jeb Harrison, local attorney, representing a fugitive slave, fights case in court'.

"That's all she wrote. What an impact" he loudly mocked.

"Don't you see? This is where the battle has to be fought. In the legislature. This is where the power is. Sure, it's a slow process. A *very* slow process. But trying to make change through the courts, one case at a time, is like riding in a carriage. Slow.

"But working through the legislative process is like riding on a train. Much faster" he reasoned.

"Jeb, you're right. You're always right. It's just so … frustrating. That's all.

"You're doing the right thing. I know that. I just find this whole matter, well, like I said. An abomination".

Jeb smiled. He knew his wife understood. He too was frustrated.

"I'll be gone for maybe three weeks. And I promise you, I'll look into any reasonable avenue available to curtail the 'Acts' enforcement".

He thought hard.

"You know, I'm pretty good at introducing competing bills when necessary. A sort of 'check and balance' to offset any harm that might be cause by the enactment of certain laws".

He thought harder.

"For instance, if law enforcement is compelled to assist in the round up of fugitive slaves, then that distracts from their other obligations which they're duty bound to uphold. Mrs. Smith's concern about her recent burglary won't be investigated because the Sheriff's out lookin' for runaway slaves.

"Mr. Jones' cattle thief can't be caught because the Deputy is chasin' the bloodhounds that are trackin' down the black fugitive. The list goes on and on.

"You see, my dear? The people of Louisiana who vote for me expect me to enforce the fugitive slave act. Plain and simple. Slavery's been a part of the South for too long. The economy's bound to it. That's an undeniable fact.

"But, it's also my duty to inform them of their rights. Make them fully aware of how the law could adversely affect them. They'd expect no less of me.

"That's the advantage my position carries. Again, it's a slow process, but that's how change is made. One *slow* step at a time.

"Tell you what. As soon as I get to the Capitol, I'll bring it up with Roxanne. I know she'll be excited. She can start outlining some of the arguments I can make on the Senate floor.

"Damn! Did I just say Roxanne's name?" Jeb silently anguished. "What the …?"

"Roxanne?" Caroline asked, her question slightly laced with a hint of suggestiveness. She remembered Roxanne.

She'd met her twice while visiting her husband at the Capitol. Beautiful woman. Tall and slender, with gorgeous red hair and sparkling green eyes that seemed to flash when she blinked. Ah, yes. Caroline remembered Roxanne.

Particularly how the other Senators swooned in her presence, like little schoolboys mesmerized by the prettiest girl in class.

And she noticed how her own husband's demeanor changed when in her company. His posture straightened, his conversation more engaged. An obvious sign of his desire to impress her.

Jeb gathered himself to respond.

"Yes. You remember Roxanne?" he replied, the tone of her voice had obviously conveyed her full recollection.

"She's my legislative 'assistant'. She's done a marvelous job. She's been quite a help" he added.

He was about to tell her all about 'R.A Flowers', and how she'd drafted the 'Act to provide for the payment of the members, officers and contingent expenses of the General Assembly', and thus convince

Caroline of Roxanne's usefulness. But he immediately dismissed the idea. Better to keep quiet.

"She's that good, eh?" Caroline coyly asked, a slight tone of accusation in her question.

Jeb remembered Trent having asked the exact same question when they were talking on the veranda and he was privately reminiscing about the first dalliance he'd had with Roxanne.

"My God!" he stammered to himself. "It's like she can see right through me". He strained to remain composed and not let her veiled innuendo give his secret away.

"I'm simply saying that she's been very helpful, that's all" he replied with a dismissive tone. It was time for a diversionary tact.

"Why, you sound almost jealous" he calmly shot back.

Caroline immediately became defensive.

"Jealous? Why should I be jealous?" she asked.

She knew why. For the first time, she wondered if Roxanne could be the reason Jeb no longer found her physically attractive. "Could that be it? Could Roxanne have stolen Jeb from me?" she asked herself.

"Oh, stop! Just stop it" she ordered herself.

They rode some distance without speaking a word. Then Caroline broke the silence.

"I'll miss you" she softly confided. "You think you'll be gone a full three weeks?"

Jeb felt the tension dissipate immediately.

"Most likely. Like I said, the 'Compromise bill' is consuming everyone's time right now. And that's on top of all the other matters that are pressing. We'll see".

"I'll make sure everything you'll need is packed and ready to go" she promised.

They hardly spoke the rest of the way home.

33

THE DOCTOR STOOD ON THE threshold of his brand new house, hand on each hip, feeling like a conquering hero as he watched several buck wagons arrive, each fully loaded with precious cargo, courtesy of Jeremiah Atkinson, the furniture store owner.

True to his word, Mr. Atkinson did indeed have a vast supply of some of the most exquisite pieces, even a seventeenth century vase from Athens, Greece. The Doctor felt as giddy as a child on Christmas Day.

"Careful, careful!" he barked at his employees, while looking at the Doctor to gauge his excitement.

"Yes, yes. Bring it right in" the Doctor commanded, as one by one each worker carried one of the valuable items to the front door.

Mr. Atkinson inhaled deeply as he shook the Doctor's hand, at the same time wiping his own sweaty forehead with his handkerchief.

"Ah, there's nothing better than the smell of fresh wood!" he proclaimed, the bitter sweet aroma saturating the entire house.

The Doctor also inhaled. Not just the smell of the freshly cut wood, but the fragrance of satisfaction that only a member of the 'landed gentry' can truly appreciate.

The Doctor didn't have many 'feelings'. He certainly had sensitivities that all human beings suffer from, particularly selfish ones. In that regard, he was overly sensitive.

But he was generally immune from normal feelings of guilt, shame, or any similar human emotions. He'd convinced himself that he'd 'earned' the house. The fact that it was twice the size of his old one was irrelevant. If it were three times the size, he could rationalize that also.

And so it was with everything in his life. The furniture was no different.

What price tag could be placed on Mrs. Winters' life? He'd practically saved her! If it weren't for him, the Colonel and Mr. Tolivar would probably have botched her care, and caused her leg to become infected and then amputated. Or worse.

The same with the Colonel's house servant, Amana. She might well have died if it weren't for him and his medical know-how. Expertise that could only come from years' of experience.

It was so natural for the Doctor to convince himself of his own self-worth, and that society in general owed him a living. At that, he truly was an expert.

"Oh, no, no. That piece is to go along this wall. Right here, next to the credenza" he instructed the worker.

Mr. Atkinson smiled, delighted that the Doctor's purchases were three times the money he'd normally make in an entire month.

He remembered the Colonel's warning: "I just hope that quack doesn't try and fleece me". Oh, well. It wasn't for the salesman to make that determination. That was between him and the Doctor.

Besides, the Colonel also told him the Doctor would be coming by to buy some furniture. The Colonel somehow felt responsible for the fire. That's what he recalled.

Anyway, Colonel Winters had plenty of money. It was because of him and Mrs. Winters that the salesman's business was booming. That, and the referrals they made to other wealthy persons.

"Ah, what a beautiful day" he smiled to himself.

"Doctor! No, no. Let my men handle that" he warned as he'd watched the Doctor struggle to place a chair into another spot.

"Yes, yes. That's much appreciated" he responded. "Gettin' too old, I guess" he smiled as he reached for his handkerchief.

"Nonsense!" Mr. Atkinson reassured him. "Those hands are for healing the sick, not manual labor".

"You're right" the Doctor agreed. "It's just that I'm so used to doin' the work of regular men. Strong men! In my youth, I was quite a tough guy" he lied.

"Well, you certainly don't need to be that way now". He slowly looked about the room, then scurried to help his men tote a large wooden bed frame up the stairs to the second floor.

"Knock, knock" a man's voice bellowed from the front porch.

The Doctor looked up.

"Well, well. My good friends, Seth and Randy! Come in, come in. Please come in and have a look see at my humble abode".

"Humble abode?" Randy replied. "Damn! I ain't seen such a fine a place since … never!" they both laughed.

"Well, it'll keep the rain off my head" the Doctor chuckled back.

"My, oh my" Seth said as he exaggerated a deep breath. "Jus' smell that fresh wood".

"And look at all this fancy furniture. Doc, you're sure doin' good for yourself!" Randy added.

"Well, life has been good, Randy. Gotta' say though, I've earned it. Never got anything the easy way".

He opened his arms as if to lasso and display all of his worldly possessions at once.

"It's no different with all of this. Hard work, gentlemen. This is what happens when you develop a plan. You plan your work and you work your plan, as the saying goes. Yes, this is what happens when hard work pays off".

The two bumpkins were momentarily mesmerized. The Doctor was a genius. And a wealthy one at that.

"Gosh, Doc. We'll remember that" he said respectfully as he looked to Seth to confirm he understood and agreed.

"Yea, Doc. We'll remember it".

"Damn, our news doesn't seem so important now" Randy mumbled as he stared at the floor.

"No, it don't" Seth concurred.

"What news, fellas?"

Randy looked once more around the room, then looked the Doctor directly in the eyes.

"Tabari" he said. "That slave done left the state!"

"Tabari! What? How do you know?"

"Mr. Tolivar. Me an' Seth been searchin' all of N'awlins for him. Not a sign a' hide nor hair. Then we run into Tolivar at the Sheriff's office. The Colonel's been askin' for him to help capture the slave. So, Deputy Harley's been searchin' too.

"Nothin'".

"Yea" Seth continued. "The Colonel sent Tolivar north, along the river. A long ways".

"That's right" Randy interrupted. "He got as far as Jackson. Mississippi!"

"Probably two hundred miles" Seth calculated.

"The Sheriff there told Tolivar that some lawmen up in Cape Girardeau … that's Missouri … spotted a runaway that looked just like Tabari. He was travelin' with some fancy dressed business man of sorts".

"Yea. As I heard it, the man was supposed ta' bring Tabari to the Sheriff's office there, in Cape Girardeau. But they never showed. So they been tryin' to track him down. Enlistin' all kinda' folks along the river. The Colonel's been payin' a lot to get him captured" Randy asserted.

"Yea. A lot" Seth confirmed.

"So, that our bad news. That niggers gone. At least as far as our bein' able to catch him. Hell, I'm too old to ride two hundred miles!

"So, ya' see Doc? We was hopin' ta' give ya' some good news. Let 'ya get in on some of the 're-ward' money. But, as you can see, that ain't gonna' happen. Not now, anyways".

"Ah, he don't care. Just look at him" Seth said to Randy. "He's got this brand new house" again taking in an exaggerated breath to smell the fresh wood.

"He's got all this expensive furniture. Hell, he don't care" as he looked upon the Doctor with the utmost respect and admiration.

The Doctor sat stymied as he stared blankly at the wall.

Before he'd met the Colonel, he basically lived hand to mouth. Sure, he now had a brand new house and some truly nice furniture, all bought and paid for. But without any foreseeable prospect on the horizon for earning some money, he might soon find himself selling off his new furniture just to make ends meet.

Making some reward money from the Colonel was his last and only hope. Now, that dream was dashed. He'd have to find some real patients. Ones that actually paid with cash.

"Well Doc, we'll be seein' ya' around" Randy said as the two walked out the door, arms over each other's shoulders as they enjoyed their friend's prosperity.

The Doctor sat slumped in his new chair.

"Ah, shit!"

Mr. Atkinson walked down the staircase as he was preparing to leave.

"Yes. This is … magnificent! Your humble abode now reflects your true stature. A man of education and distinction. I'm happy for you".

The Doctor appreciated his heart felt words. A new house full of the finest furniture money can buy, and the adulation of his community. Yes, he'd finally made the big time.

"Doctor, I've got to return to my store. My men will see to it that everything's brought inside, and placed exactly where you want. If you change your mind about any particular location, then just tell them. They're happy to do whatever's needed to please our customers.

"Sir, I will bid you adieu for now" as he turned and headed for the door.

"Oh, and don't you worry none. I'll be sendin' your bill right away to the Colonel for payment".

The Doctor slumped farther into his new chair.

"Ah, shit!"

34

"I CAN'T BELIEVE MY EYES! Caroline shouted as she opened the door.

"Collette! Collette! It's you!"

She held out her arms. Collette stepped forward for a warm hug, but fumbled as the luggage she held in each hand barricaded the embrace. Both laughed as she dropped her bags, then each hugged like long lost friends.

"Oh my, I'm just so ... excited to see you! I was sure you'd never visit again, after you told me how frightened you'd be to make the trip". She looked out the door.

"Trent must have brought you. Is he here?"

"Ma'am" Hank softly addressed her, as she stepped aside to allow him in, followed by Cooter and Billy Bob.

She looked at Collette for explanation.

"These are my, well, I guess 'entourage'" she giggled.

"Trent was insistent. He knew how much I wanted to see you, and how afraid I was, after my last visit. So, he sent these three brave, strong men to escort me".

Caroline approvingly sized up their muscular attributes.

"I'm assuming then, no one gave you any trouble" she coyly asked, causing each man to blush.

"No trouble at all. Actually, it was quite an enjoyable trip.

"I'm so happy to see you" she gushed, as the two embraced once again.

"Ma'am" Hank addressed Collette. "We've brought in all of yer' luggage. Is there anythin' else we can do?"

"My goodness, no. You've all been so helpful. I'll see to it that the Colonel rewards you with some extra pay this month. Thank ya'all very much".

"Yes, ma'am" Hank replied, all three smiling while tipping their hats. "We'll be back next Saturday, then. Hope you enjoy yer' visit here".

"Oh, I shall. And thank you again".

They turned to each other and giggled once more.

"Is Jeb home?"

"No, unfortunately. He's business in Baton Rouge. He'll be gone for likely three weeks.

"My, my, you look just wonderful" Caroline gushed. She leaned in to whisper. "I didn't notice any limp" she said.

Collette momentarily forgot about the 'gata bite.

"Oh, that" she replied. "It's all behind me. He may be a quack of a doctor, but he did do an excellent job. There's no scaring and, you're right, I'm not limping at all".

"And how's Amana doing?" Caroline asked, before she remembered how distraught Collette had been about Trent's possible infidelity.

Collette paused as she fought back the jealous feelings and maintained her composure.

"Amana's fine. She has a bit of a limp. The 'gata broke her ankle, if you recall. As to any scaring, I don't know. I suppose Dr. Wesley did the best he could".

Caroline took her hands in hers. "I'm so sorry. I didn't mean to upset you".

"Forget it. I mostly have. I'm just looking forward to enjoying some time together" she lovingly smiled.

"Oh, and we shall! I'll have Malika cook up some of her world famous alligator jambalaya!" "Did I just say that?" Caroline scalded herself. "My God, woman! What were you thinking?"

Collette saw Caroline's look of regret.

"I'm so sorry" Caroline rebuked herself again. "Just forget I said anything about having 'gata jambalaya. Disgusting!"

"It's alright. You know what? Maybe I'll just eat some 'gata meat. Sort of get some revenge!" she laughed, surprising Caroline and causing her to laugh uncontrollably.

"That would be ... "How do the French say it? 'Apropros'". They both giggled.

"I remember last time I was here, and ... Malika?"

"Yes".

"Malika prepared it. And it was wonderful. I'm looking forward to it".

* * *

AFTER Caroline helped Collette unpack, the two strolled along the streets of the French Quarters, stopping in a few quaint shops, not looking for anything in particular.

"This looks lovely" Collette observed, as she held a thin scarf up for further inspection.

"Hmm ... I'm not sure" Caroline responded. "Maybe it's just the heat. Anything that adds an additional layer to my clothing just doesn't seem appealing. At least right now".

"I understand" Collette replied, still pondering whether she liked the item enough to make a purchase.

Caroline slowly moved along the countertop, lightly running her fingers over some items, feeling the softness of the fabrics while leisurely enjoying the company of her dear friend.

"Oh, I'm sorry" she apologized as she accidently bumped into a person standing behind her. She spun around to see it wasn't a person at all, but a mannequin.

Caroline couldn't take her eyes off the figure. It was the spitting image of Roxanne, her husband's political confidant. The same bright red hair, same green eyes, same voluptuous figure. She found herself suddenly gripped with jealousy.

Collette watched her friend appear mesmerized by the figurine.

"What is it, my dear?" as her gaze bounced between Caroline and the mannequin.

"It's ... just uncanny" Caroline pondered out loud. "She's ..."

"What?"

"She looks exactly like Roxanne!"

"Who?"

"Roxanne. Jeb's girl". "Damn! How could I refer to her like that?" she scolded herself.

"I mean, his legislative assistant. The mannequin looks exactly like Roxanne!"

Collette methodically examined the model. It wasn't the amateurish, non-descript figurine one generally observed in a store. Someone had paid particular attention to detail in creating this near-human creature.

"I must say, she's beautiful" Collette offered, not knowing that Caroline was beginning to harbor some jealousy over her husband's associate.

"The red hair. Normally, I'd think it's too bold. But on her, it's quite attractive" Collette pointed out the obvious.

"And those eyes! What a contrast with her red hair" she innocently observed, unaware of Caroline's uneasiness.

"And her figure! What a beautiful ..." she stopped in mid-sentence, seeing Caroline's face recoil as she stared at the 'woman'.

"Caroline? Caroline?"

She snapped out of her jealous imaginings, then looked about to make sure no one was listening in.

"I've just got to tell someone" she blurted, as she took Collette's arm and began walking to the door. She spied an outside café and led her to a patio table.

Collette anxiously stared at her friend, wondering what was making her so keenly upset.

"Remember I told you that Jeb wasn't interested in any intimacy?" she whispered. "I mean, physical intimacy. With me?"

Collette remembered. She and Caroline had both shared their intimate secrets.

She remembered the horseback ride where they sat under the shade of an old oak tree while enjoying some 'fruit juice'.

"Jeb's never home" Collette remembered her saying. "And when he is, he just doesn't have an interest in sex. When it comes to physical intimacy, he's just not interested".

"Yes, of course I remember" she answered.

"When Jeb and I were riding back home, from your place, we had a bit of a spat. He mentioned the name of his assistant, 'Roxanne', and said he'd be speaking with her about some arguments he'd be preparing in the Legislature".

She thought better about divulging the type of 'arguments' she was referring to, knowing that any legislation that challenged the fugitive slave act might be unsettling to the wife of a plantation owner.

Collette looked confused as she watched Caroline stare off into the distance.

"Caroline, go on".

She came out of her trance and looked Collette directly in the eyes.

"It was the *way* he looked. When he mentioned her name" she began to explain in earnest. "Almost … lecherous!" she announced, surprising herself to have used that description.

"Lecherous?" Collette asked.

"Well, perhaps it was more like … no, Collette. It was lecherous. There was that certain twinkle in his eyes when he said her name.

"I've seen her. And you're right. She is beautiful. But you only saw the mannequin. She's every bit as beautiful. But real.

"Oh, Collette. Am I going crazy? I have no proof, just an intuitive sense about it. Could that be the reason Jeb has no interest? Am I just imagining all this?" she pleaded.

"Mannequin … Roxanne. What is she talking about?" Collette wondered silently.

"Caroline, you need to get a hold of yourself. I mean, there may be more to this but, so far, what you've told me doesn't add up to anything like you're suggesting. Is there more?"

Caroline sat in quiet desperation. She so wanted her husband's physical affection, and berated herself for not being more attractive to him. How could she care so much for him, and not have the affection returned? What had she done wrong? What could, should, she do differently?

She felt a failure as both a woman and a wife. She began to sob.

Collette gave an angry stare to the middle aged couple seated near them, instructing them to divert their eyes away from her grieving friend.

"Caroline. Come with me. Let's go back to your house where we can speak in private" as she stood and gently placed her hand on Caroline's, encouraging her to leave. "I'll make us both a long, tall drink".

35

TRENT WAS ESPECIALLY HELPFUL in seeing to it that Collette would have safe travel to visit her friend, Caroline, in New Orleans.

Her last trip could've been disastrous, if it hadn't been for his overseer, Mr. Tolivar, in bravely warding off what was essentially a small lynch mob who'd just killed a slave.

Hank, Cooter and Billy Bob were all ordered to escort her, fully armed with shotguns and pistols.

For the remainder of the week, he had the run of the mansion to himself. And Amana.

"I'll come to your room tonight" he whispered, as he left the dining room while she cleared the table.

Her body stiffened and blood pressure rose. "Damn" she shouted to herself.

This wouldn't be like the last time. She'd feel no passion, no arousal. There'd be no panting. This time, she was a slave. No more than a soldier marching to orders. She could have no enjoyment, knowing that this act would bring her ever more precariously close to suffering the wrath of the Colonel's wife.

"Oh, pleeze Lord, pleeze Lordie. Don't put me through 'dis" she prayed almost out loud as she paced back in forth in her room, dreading his arrival.

He didn't even knock. She heard the door creak, and saw the soft light from the hallway illuminate the room. The door closed, and the room became dark again, the moon's light not cooperating.

Startled by the flash as the match flared, she watched as Trent lit a candle on her dresser, making the room glow and their bodies slightly visible.

He motioned with his hand, inviting her to come closer. She froze, remaining motionless. If he was to take her, it'd be against her will.

Trent was confused. Although they didn't speak during or after their prior 'meeting', he knew that she'd thoroughly enjoyed herself. It lasted nearly an hour, and her many moans, heavy breathing, and occasional screams were evidence enough to attest to his masculine prowess.

No matter. Collette was away, he needed intimacy, and his banal urges couldn't be suppressed any longer. Besides, he was her master, and she was his property. He'd certainly prefer a willing concubine, but he remembered the sailor's old axiom that 'any port in a storm will do'.

"Amana, come here" he ordered, above a whisper but loud enough that he needn't repeat himself.

She remained still for a moment, her body beginning to tremble as she stared at the floor, tears beginning to stream down her cheeks.

"Yes 'em". She cautiously walked toward him as he sat down on the edge of the bed.

"Sit next to me" as he patted the mattress. "I don't know why you're suddenly finding me ... repulsive" he whispered, cupping his hand under her chin and turning her to face him.

"It wasn't that way last time" he reminded her, studying her expression to confirm the truth.

"I's ... I's jus' afraid. I's afraid of the misses" she declared in all honesty.

Trent fully knew this to be true. And for good reason. But, again, no matter.

"Listen to me, my dear. Mrs. Winters knows that you saved her life from that 'gata. She'll never forget that. She's told you so. And she knows that you were bit too, and broke your ankle. She'll never allow any harm to come to you" he knowingly lied.

"Now, just relax. I'll not allow any harm to come to you, either" he softly stated, as he placed his hand on her chest, applying enough pressure to force her to lie on her back.

This 'meeting' didn't last long. Amana just laid there. She didn't resist, but she didn't offer any encouragement either.

That is, until the last few seconds, when she felt Trent's climax. That sensation caused her to uncontrollably orgasm herself, albeit involuntarily.

It ended like the first time. He quietly stood, turned and walked out of the room. She silently sobbed until, emotionally exhausted, she fell asleep.

36

A S PROMISED, GEORGE BROUGHT Tabari and Daryl to Sam's place to get acquainted and make plans for Tabari's journey to freedom. There wasn't much for them to add, as George had thoroughly informed Sam of their predicament.

Sam later met with three of his 'conductor' friends and, after much deliberation, all agreed that the safest and quickest route was to Detroit. The main concern was finding a permanent place for Tabari to live, once he crossed the river into Windsor, Canada, a small village of about three hundred people.

Scores of slaves had used the Detroit River to escape from slave catchers, and Tabari was now to be included in that number.

* * *

AND so, they began.

Obviously, they couldn't travel by foot.

"Sam, please take this" Daryl pleaded as he tried to pay his new friend for the rental of a horse and buck wagon.

"No, no. Listen, now. You and Tabari are going to need money, probably much more than you know" he winked. "'Ol Daisy there, she's a good horse, but she's getting' old" as he looked toward his faithful mare. "She may not even make the whole trip" he reflected, as a look of sadness swept across his face.

"This is how I can help. I'm too old and tired to travel with you. I don't know the way and, hell, even if I did, I'd surely slow you two down. Let me contribute this way. Of course, I expect you'll make it just fine. And you'll pass this way on yer' way back. Please. Do this for me".

Daryl was much appreciative, and his smile said all that was needed. Transportation was crucial, and he was grateful that he could now check that item off his list.

"Remember" Sam cautioned him again. "You'll never get anything in writing. No directions, no names, no addresses. All instructions are done 'word of mouth'. The people I'm sending you to know this, and they'll remind you again.

"Your first stop's gonna' be Indianapolis. Now, know this! Indiana's a free state. But, I fear we're gonna' be in a civil war soon" he whispered, looking around to make sure no one could hear. He had a quirky look of embarrassment on his face, quickly realizing that no one was within at least a mile of them. But the mere thought of a civil war was frightening.

Daryl focused intently on every word.

"So, ya' see, there's no safety, no matter what state yer' in. But stay away from the southeast portion of that state, especially near the Ohio River. There's a lot a' Southerners that've moved there, and they don't take too kindly to black folks" he cautioned, looking at Tabari to confirm he understood.

"Now, you've no cause to go that route. But this Underground Railroad don't necessarily go from point A to point B".

"Tell me about it!" Daryl exclaimed as he looked to Tabari. "Our whole plan was to travel up the Mississippi River to Minneapolis. And look where we're at now" he almost cursed. He consciously calmed himself when he realized his voice sounded frightened.

"No, we understand completely" Daryl continued. "We've told you about all the unexpected things we've encountered. Tabari diving overboard in the middle of the night to save that little girl. Her father drowning. My wallet stolen, along with Tabari's bill of sale. The Sheriff's after us. Oh boy, do we understand".

Sam chuckled out loud. Not at Daryl and Tabari, but at the caustic circumstances where the predictable seems to always become the unpredictable. Tabari and Daryl chuckled nervously, as well.

They watched Sam's face, deep in thought.

"Immigrate" he mumbled out loud.

"What?"

Sam paused, then shared his thoughts.

"Immigrate. Tom. You've met Tom? The postmaster?"

"Oh yea" Daryl answered.

"Well, he told me that Indiana just passed a new law. Actually, it's an amendment to their constitution. Black folk can't immigrate into Indiana. They can't permanently move there, from another state, that is. If they've already been livin' there, then they can register and get the right to work there.

"Which don't really effect Tabari, except, you lost his papers. Is that right? His bill of sale?"

"That's right. It was stolen along with my wallet while we were on the steamboat" Daryl answered. Tabari nodded.

"Hmm … then we've got to fix that" Sam stated.

"You're absolutely right!" Daryl acknowledged. "I guess I've been so preoccupied with figuring out where we're at, how we got here, and what to do next. I completely forgot about it. The bill of sale".

"There's a lot on your plate" Sam stated the obvious.

"Yes, we absolutely must attend to that" Sam continued. "I get the newspaper, but not as much as good 'ol Tom. But I tell you, they're full of page after page of notices about runaway slaves. Lengthy descriptions of what they look like, who their owners are and, unfortunately, how much of a reward there is for the person who captures 'em. Or gives information leadin' to their capture.

Tabari imagined himself being described in one of the newspaper notices:

"Thirty years old. Speaks English. Callused hands. Scars on back ..."

"Yes, we'll prepare a very legal paper that attests to your ownership of Tabari. We'll do that right away. 'Forthwith' as the attorneys would say!"

They all chuckled.

* * *

THEY used the same information they'd included on the first bill of sale. Tabari was 'Lazarus', and Daryl had purchased him from one 'Sam Thomas', a made-up slave trader, for the sum of two thousand dollars on August 29, 1852 in New Orleans.

"Looks good to me" Daryl told Sam as he folded the paper and carefully slid it inside his vest pocket, making double sure it was securely enclosed. Didn't want to lose this one.

They shook hands, and Tabari and Daryl began the next leg of their journey, Tabari gently coaxing 'Daisy' to start forward, the reins firmly in his hands. Sam waved goodbye, and said a silent prayer:

"Dear Lord, watch over these men as they begin their dangerous journey. Keep 'em safe from harm, and guide them to loving people whose purpose in life is to help those less fortunate than themselves. Amen".

Indianapolis was nearly three hundred miles away, nearly two weeks travel according to Daryl's calculation.

They had plenty of hay for 'ol Daisy, and enough food and water, thanks to Angel and her generous supply of home cooked 'vittles'.

They'd reached Indianapolis without any hiccups, other than sore backs and their respective bruised buttocks.

The pair stopped their buck wagon on a dirt street with a modest looking hotel on each side, and waited patiently.

"Mister Daryl? Why we jus' sittin' here?"

"I want to see whether any blacks go into the hotel. I don't want to register for a room and have the clerk question me about you. If they don't accept blacks, then we're gonna' draw suspicion. We don't need that".

"Yes 'em".

They waited. And waited. No luck. Only white folk entered and exited. But there were quite a few blacks who strolled down the street and in and out of various store fronts, obviously free men and women.

Finally. A white man entered one of the hotels, followed by a black woman and her two small girls.

"This is it" announced Daryl. "Come on now, let's go".

They entered the hotel lobby, such as it was, and stood near the registration desk, waiting for the white man and his companions to rent their room.

A heated discussion ensued, the clerk vigorously shaking his head, an obvious disagreement about something, but neither Daryl nor Tabari could hear what the problem was.

Suddenly, the white man violently slapped the negroe woman across her face, nearly causing her to stumble. Her two girls screamed hysterically, horrified to witness this vicious act against their mother.

Tabari instantly became incensed, his hands balled into fists as he lost all control and was about to pounce on this bully.

Daryl immediately threw his arms around his friend, pinning his body to prevent an attack.

"No, Tabari! No!" Daryl loudly whispered, as he struggled to restrain him. Tabari twisted his body back and forth in an attempt to free himself. Then suddenly, he relaxed his muscles, realizing that Daryl was intervening only to protect him.

"Don't!" Daryl ordered, as he slowly released his grip.

Tabari understood. Creating a fight with this man would surely bring in law enforcement, and cause their journey to freedom to come to a crashing halt. His anger remained, but his heated look of attack washed away as he watched the woman kneel down and bring her daughters into her arms.

A minute or two later, the situation resolved itself, and it was now Daryl's turn to address the hotel clerk.

"I ... I ..." he stuttered.

"Yes, that was awkward" the clerk responded. "I think the darkie gave her, ah, 'boss' some back talk. Somethin' about her young'uns and stayin' in the same room. I dunno'.

"How can I help you, Mister?" he asked as he examined Tabari, dressed as a gentleman in his fine business attire.

"Yes. Me and my man here would like a room for the night".

"Certainly, sir" he responded as he reached for a reservation paper and asked Daryl to sign. Not a hint of a problem. Great relief for them both, as Daryl looked sideways to catch a glimpse of his friend's smile.

It was a smile that grew from a feeling that he'd never experienced before. The feeling of a joyous release. From being a prisoner one's whole life, and now, suddenly, the delirious sensation of becoming a free man, never again to be ordered what to do, nor how and when to do it. Never again to be beaten, whipped or sold. Never!

He wasn't free yet. They had many more miles to travel. But the belief that it would happen was becoming more and more real.

Daryl saw Tabari's eyes well up with tears.

"What do the British say? Stiff upper lip!" he gently chided his friend as they exited the lobby and headed for their room, not wanting to cause attention by revealing tears in public, even if those tears were ones of joy.

* * *

THEY stood at the small dock, looking across the river, waiting to board one of the two steamboats that ferried livestock and passengers.

Daryl smiled as he watched Tabari anxiously gaze to the other side, the river quite wide but seeming almost swimmable were one brave enough to try. He thought Tabari might just do so. He kept nervously looking back to see if any slave capturers were about to pounce and destroy his dream at the last second.

"It's alright, my friend" Daryl offered to reassure him. "You're almost there!"

"I jus' can't believe it!" Tabari beamed with excitement. "Mister Daryl, I almost 'bout ta' pee my pants!"

Daryl burst out laughing. "No, no!" he cried. "Remember what happened last time you thought that?"

Tabari instantly remembered having to use the steamboat's men's room in the middle of the night, and diving overboard to save little Lisa's life.

"Oh, yes. Yes, sir. I remembers" he laughed.

"Tabari. This is where I say goodbye. I've got my own family to return to and, as you know, it's a long trip". He held out his hand.

Tabari looked at it, then stepped forward and threw his arms around his good friend.

"Mister Daryl ... I's don't know what to say. You's saved my life!" he cried softly, tears streaking down his cheeks.

He remembered all the white folk who'd helped him. Tom and Melba, Frank and Freda Jefferson, the Reverend Baxter and Pastor Jessie, Max and Helen Donovan. He remembered them all.

Daryl began sobbing too. "Now, now. Stop. You're making us both slobber" he teased, wiping his runny nose.

"Take this" he said, as he held Tabari's hand. "It's two hundred dollars. We all chipped in before we started this trip. It's not a lot, but it'll help you get started".

Tabari was speechless. He started to speak, but Daryl held a finger to his lips.

"Shh!"

* * *

THE steamboat was half way across. Tabari looked back toward the Detroit shore. His good friend was gone. But he looked forward and saw the Canadian shoreline coming closer and closer.

"Freedom! Thank you, Bwana! Freedom at last" as tears of joy streamed down his cheeks.

37

COLLETTE AND CAROLINE RETURNED home, both feeling emotionally drained. Collette made two stiff 'fruit juices', and they sat together on the couch, a warm breeze coming from the open windows, providing some relief from the oppressive heat.

They each took a long sip, then collectively sighed.

Caroline spoke first.

"I'm exhausted. These horrible feelings of jealousy are giving me a terrible headache".

Collette knew the feeling, all too well.

"Caroline, we two are quite a pair" she reflected. "Here we are. We both have husbands who love us dearly, but there's always this intolerable jealousy. I don't think I can stand it".

They each took another sip.

Caroline was quite deep in thought, and Collette wanted to know.

"Caroline?"

The drink was calming her considerably.

"I remember seeing a child, oh, about five or six years old" Caroline reflected, almost speaking in a soliloquy. "No one I knew, but I watched her running out of a store front, just playing, chasing another child. But it was the look on her face that caught my attention".

"What look?"

"A look of utter happiness" she continued.

"Collette, it was like there was a 'bubble', an 'aura', around the little girl's face. A bubble of happiness. It was like a magnetic field, and none of her thoughts could escape outside the bubble. All of her thoughts were happy ones. No other thoughts, other than 'happy' thoughts, existed inside her bubble. I swear to you, I could actually see it!"

Collette looked puzzled, but interested. She took another sip.

"Here's what I'm saying. It's like the pastor said last Sunday. 'We're all created in God's image'. What does that mean?" she asked out loud, not at anyone in particular.

"All God does is create. That's all He does! Don't you see? Everything there is, is part of a creation. The plant seed grows roots, then a stem, then leaves ... or whatever plants do. We're born to grow.

"But our minds are also a part of God's 'creation'. Our minds' aren't stagnant. We don't just have only one thought. One thought that never ends.

Our minds' 'think'. And continue to think. All day and, well, even when we're sleeping. God, do they think! Think, think, think. That's all we do!

"The point is, we create each and every one of our thoughts. No one's selecting our thoughts for us. *What* we choose to think, is entirely up to us.

"That's what it means to say 'we're created in God's image'. He gave us the gift to think. To think creatively. No thoughts are restricted".

Another sip for each.

"For better or worse, God gives all of us the gift to create any thought we want. There's no exclusion. Only inclusion.

"Want to create horrible thoughts of jealousy? 'Your wish is My command', He says.

"Want to create beautiful thoughts of love and happiness? 'Your wish is My command', He says.

"What does all this talk have to do with a little girl's 'bubble'?" Collette asked herself.

"And the 'bubble' that the little girl created, is just that. Her 'creation'" Caroline continued to explain.

"Don't you see?

"That little girl 'created' thoughts of happiness. Only happiness. Nothing else. And those thoughts create who she is. At least for that moment.

"The pastor told me this. The little girl showed it to me".

"But how can I 'create' loving thoughts when I'm faced with realities that I have no control over?" Collette asked.

"I didn't create an affair between Trent and Amana. But I'm convinced, well, at least right now, that one occurred. I'm not creating my thoughts of jealousy. Amana and Trent forced them on me!" Collette reasoned.

"Did someone force the little girl to think only happy thoughts?" Caroline replied.

"Maybe. I don't know. I wasn't there" Collette answered defensively.

"And what about that 'gata? Did I 'create' horrible feelings and thoughts of dying? Or the real pain I felt? Or did the 'gata create them for me?"

More sips.

"The pastor spoke about this also" Caroline replied.

"No one suffered more than Jesus did at the cross. He was being tortured. Crucified. And despite all the pain, *during* all the pain, he repeatedly forgave the Roman soldiers who were killing him. He didn't react to the horrible acts. He created his own thoughts instead".

251

A moment of silence, then Collette responded.

"I'm not Jesus" she muttered.

"Well, I'm certainly not, either". They both giggled.

"I know one thing. I'm tired of torturing myself with these thoughts of jealousy".

"Amen!"

Collette reflected on her many 'ugly' thoughts. So many. So burdensome, including the loss of her young son, her miscarriage, and her lack of desire to be physically intimate with her husband.

"Let's resolve to at least try. What can it hurt?" Caroline asked.

"What does 'trying' mean?" Collette asked.

"It's simple. When those ugly thoughts pop up, see them for what they are. They're just 'thoughts'. Don't judge them, just acknowledge that they exist.

"Then, remember that you can instantly create your own thoughts. We don't have to be glued to ugly thoughts. Simply focus on the thoughts you'd like to enjoy. Focus on thoughts that make you feel good.

"And when those ugly thoughts come back, do the same thing.

"I say we at least give it a try. What've we got to lose? I suspect, the more we try, the better we'll get at it. Wouldn't that be wonderful?"

Collette raised her glass to toast.

"To the 'bubble'!"

"To the 'bubble'!" they both laughed.

38

COLLETTE RETURNED FROM CAROLINE'S feeling much refreshed. Trent met her at the front door.

"My, my! You look … refreshed!" he gushed. "I'm so glad you're home".

"Me too!" she replied, patting some dust off her dress and untying her bonnet.

"And did you have a good time?" he asked.

She paused to gather her thoughts. "Why, yes. I truly had a marvelous time. Caroline is such a dear friend. We shopped, ate wonderful meals. Oh, their cook, Malika, is fantastic. She makes a 'gata jambalaya that's to die for!"

Trent was taken aback. "Did she just say she'd eaten 'gata meat?" he wondered.

She could see the surprised look on his face.

"Yes, that's right. I thought maybe I'd get some revenge on that monster" she giggled.

Trent was thrilled by her attitude. And quite surprised that she'd put aside any fear of the horrible incident and was getting on with life as normal.

She remembered her talk with Caroline, particularly concerning the 'bubble', when she asked: "How's Amana?"

Trent nearly choked. But there was no suspicious tone to her question. No hint of accusation.

"Amana? Amana's fine, I suppose".

"Good".

Sadie had stepped into the doorway to greet her.

"Oh, Sadie. Would you see to it that my things are unpacked? And give my clothes to Amana for washing. I've been gone a whole week and Mrs. Harrison and I just didn't find time for washing".

"Wonderful!" Trent thought.

"Well, now. You must tell me everything you did. Did you buy anything?" he asked.

"No, not really. Oh, I did find something for you, though. But for now, it'll remain a secret. I'll give it to you tonight, after dinner" she teased.

"I can hardly wait" he said excitedly.

"And how did you get along without me?" she asked.

"Terribly! I find it difficult to work when you're gone. I kept wondering if you're alright. If you encountered any problems on the trip home".

"No need to worry. With escorts like Hank, Billy Bob and Cooter, the ride was as safe as safe can be. And, oh, I hope you don't mind, but I told them you'd give them a little extra pay for their help".

"Of course, my dear".

* * *

"WHAT a delightful dinner. Sadie's as good a cook as Malika" Collette announced.

"The Harrison's cook?" Trent recalled.

"Yes. She's not a 'servant'. Oh, you know that. She's a paid employee. A wonderful woman".

Trent stared at his wife, admiring her physical features but, more than that, her feminine voice and the genuine compliments she so freely gave to others.

* * *

THEY retired for the evening, Trent trying hard not to fall asleep before he finished the chapter he was reading. The light from the candle was lulling him toward slumber despite his best efforts.

"Trent? Do you believe in 'bubbles'?" she giggled to herself.

"Dear, remember the secret I told you I'd give you after dinner?" she whispered seductively.

He heard her voice but was absorbed in his novel.

"Yes, my dear".

"Well, I want you to have it. Now" she cooed.

He set the book on his leg and turned to her.

She scooted closer, her body now touching his. She slid her leg on top of his, and then her hand under his pajama top and onto his stomach.

She breathed into his ear and whispered. "Why don't you blow out the candle?"

39

"**W**ELL, I'LL BE DAMNED!" Max hollered as Daryl handed him a letter.

"Helen! Helen, come quick" he shouted, as he motioned for Daryl to have a chair at the dining table.

"It's a letter from Tabari!"

"Oh, my Lord!" Helen exclaimed. "A letter from Tabari!"

"Open it" Daryl pleaded.

It'd been nearly six months since Daryl and Tabari parted company. Nobody expected to hear from him, ever again.

"Read it! Read it!" Helen pleaded with her husband.

"Give me a second" Max reacted, his hands shaking slightly as he opened the envelope and retrieved the letter.

"It begins:

Dear Mister Daryl".

"I wanted to write and send my sincere thanks to you and everyone who helped me get to Canada and freedom. Mr. Pickerel is writing this for me. He is my employer here at the post office. My job is mostly to deliver mail, but I do many others things also. I get paid money to work, and I rent a nice room from him and his wife. They are very good to me. Please tell everyone who helped me that I want to thank each of them. I am free at last and very happy.

With my warmest regards,

Tabari"

"Well, I'll be!" Max said as he handed the letter to Helen.

Daryl was speechless, wiping his own tears away.

The three looked lovingly at each other, then Helen motioned for all to draw near. They embraced, words unnecessary.

Other Books by *Dickie Erman*:

Antebellum Struggles:	Book One in the Series
Slaves of Fools:	Book Three in the Series
A Spy's Eyes: Rachael's Story:	Book Four in the Series

Dear Readers:

You've given me such a wonderful response to the First Book ("**Antebellum Struggles**") in this series, and I hope you've enjoyed Book Two ("**Keeper of Slaves**") at least as much. Your encouragement has inspired me to write the Third Book ("**Slaves of Fools**"), and the Fourth Book (**A Spy's Eyes: Rachael's Story**). Thank you sooo much!

And again, I'd be very appreciative if you'd be so kind to take a moment and write a review of "Keeper of Slaves" on Amazon.

Made in the USA
Coppell, TX
07 May 2021

55227611R00150